ALSO BY GLENN BECK

Dreamers and Deceivers: True Stories of the Heroes
and Villains Who Made America

Conform: Exposing the Truth About Common Core and Public Education

Miracles and Massacres: True and Untold Stories of the Making of America

Agenda 21

Control: Exposing the Truth About Guns

Cowards: What Politicians, Radicals, and the Media Refuse to Say

Being George Washington

Snow Angel

The Original Argument

The 7

Broke: The Plan to Restore Our Trust, Truth and Treasure

The Overton Window

Idiots Unplugged: Truth for Those Who Care to Listen (audiobook)

The Christmas Sweater: A Picture Book

Arguing with Idiots: How to Stop Small Minds and Big Government

Glenn Beck's Common Sense: The Case Against an Out-of-
Control Government, Inspired by Thomas Paine

America's March to Socialism: Why We're One Step
Closer to Giant Missile Parades (audiobook)

The Christmas Sweater

An Inconvenient Book: Real Solutions to the World's Biggest Problems

The Real America: Early Writings from the Heart and Heartland

AGENDA 21:

INTO THE SHADOWS

GLENN BECK

WITH HARRIET PARKE

THRESHOLD EDITIONS • MERCURY RADIO ARTS

New York   London   Toronto   Sydney   New Delhi

Threshold Editions/ Mercury Radio Arts
A Division of Simon & Schuster, Inc.
1230 Avenue of the Americas
New York, NY 10020

First Threshold Editions/Mercury Radio Arts hardcover edition January 2015

THRESHOLD EDITIONS and colophon are trademarks of Simon & Schuster, Inc.

GLENN BECK is a trademark of Mercury Radio Arts, Inc.

For information about special discounts for bulk purchases, please contact Simon & Schuster Special Sales at 1-866-506-1949 or business@simonandschuster.com.

The Simon & Schuster Speakers Bureau can bring authors to your live event. For more information or to book an event, contact the Simon & Schuster Speakers Bureau at 1-866-248-3049 or visit our website at www.simonspeakers.com.

Jacket design by Jae Song
Photograph of Ferris wheel © Razvan Bucur/Shutterstock
Photograph of roller coaster © Marcio Jose Bastos Silva/Shutterstock

Manufactured in the United States of America

10 9 8 7 6 5 4 3 2 1

ISBN 978-1-4767-4682-1
ISBN 978-1-4767-4685-2 (ebook)

To all those who are running—from their past, from their fears, or from their demons. Step out of the shadows and into the light. The journey may be scary, and it certainly will not be easy, but I know for a fact that it's worth it.

AGENDA 21:

INTO THE SHADOWS

CHAPTER ONE

EMMELINE

Day 1

We didn't look back. We moved quickly toward the sound of running water somewhere ahead of us. Behind us we heard shouts and gunshots; flames licked the black night sky. The damp, slippery ground was uneven under our feet.

Elsa began to cry, a piercing sound that cut through the silence of the forest. My heart raced. Would the Enforcers or the Gatekeepers hear her?

David stopped and handed Elsa to me. She curled into my arm and I let her suck on my finger. David took the boy's hand—it looked so small and fragile. The boy, clutching his bundle of clothing tightly, worked hard to keep up with David.

The unfamiliar sounds of the woods were ominous: rustlings in the grass, branches creaking, and our own rapid breathing—raspy and harsh. I heard the strange hooting of a bird. *What kind of bird makes that noise?* No time for questions. We had to travel as far and as fast as we could.

Back in the Compound someone rang the bell that signaled a half hour till dawn. Fools! The place was on fire and still they rang bells. Soon the Citizens would stand together and say the pledge: *I pledge allegiance to the Earth and to the animals of the Earth . . .* making the circle sign on their foreheads, their thumb and forefinger touching.

Dawn was our enemy. It would steal our blanket of darkness. But I soon realized that sunrise doesn't come to the woods like it does in the Compounds. It creeps in, wrapped in soft gray. The leafy branches overhead kept us shaded from the early light. We took advantage and kept scurrying downhill, slipping on the damp leaves, tripping over roots and rocks.

David and the boy were a few steps ahead of me. David looked back at me, then pointed ahead. I saw the silvery reflection of a wide stream through the trees. We walked faster. David began to run, pulling the boy by the arm as he went.

David tripped and fell, his full weight smashing against a rock, our bundle of supplies rolling ahead of him. Clutching Elsa, I ran to him. Blood seeped through the sleeve of his uniform. He groaned, sat up slowly, and cradled his right arm with his left. The boy ran ahead and retrieved our bundle. I knelt beside David and brushed some dirt from his face.

"I'm okay," he whispered. But I could tell from his voice and the look on his face that he was in pain. He struggled to stand up, and then gingerly tested his right arm.

"It's not broken," he said. "Let's keep moving."

He started walking and we followed, each of us more careful with our steps, until we finally reached the bank above the water. I had never seen water like that before. I had only seen it in our ration bottles—confined, measured, limited. This water danced and twirled over the stones, rippling, turning, moving with purpose. Mother had told me about lakes and rivers; I had even seen her map that revealed vast blue oceans. But this was the first time I had seen so much water with my own eyes. Overwhelmed, I stood and stared, realizing all at once that I wasn't prepared for what the real world looked like. I wasn't prepared for how *big* it was.

David slid down the bank and stepped into the stream, moving from stone to stone along the edge, then into deeper water, pushing forward to the other side. The boy rushed to catch up with him. With every step, David looked back at me, beckoning me forward. He dipped his injured arm into the water, letting it flow over his sleeve, washing away some of the blood. Halfway across, the water was up to his knees. The boy held onto David's uniform with one hand and, with the other, held our bundle high over his head. He was wet to his waist.

Could I follow? What if I fell and dropped Elsa? The boy looked back at me and motioned with his head, urging me to come. David stopped and called my name. *"Emmeline."* His voice was pleading; he risked being heard. They had faith in me; they needed me. I slid down the hill, sitting, and the wetness of the earth seeped through my clothes. At the bottom, I stepped into the stream and gasped at how cold it was. But I didn't stop. Step by step, clutching Elsa tightly, I walked forward. The current pushed against my feet, my legs. I was so focused on not falling or dropping Elsa that my temples throbbed and I could feel my pulse in my ears like a drumbeat.

David and the boy waited for me on the other side and together we scrambled up the steep bank, grabbing at whatever strong plants or branches we could use to pull ourselves up with using our free hands.

Finally, we were all together at the edge of the forest. We looked below at the stream that separated us from the Compound, then turned and walked into the dimness, surrounded by the tallest trees I had ever seen. Most were straight with thick brown trunks and leafy branches reaching up. But one had green needles instead of leaves and the branches sloped down so low that they brushed the ground. David pushed the branches aside and motioned for us to crawl into the space underneath them. It smelled sweet and clean in that small, cramped space. I took a deep breath, filling my lungs with the fragrance. A few ferns grew in the dark soil, graceful in the dimpled light. I had seen ferns growing along the bicycle path in the Compound but I'd never seen a tree like this.

"We'll rest here," David whispered. "When it's dark, we'll move on." He nodded his head toward the boy. "Who is he? Why did you bring him along?"

I glanced at the boy, worried about how he'd react to David, but his face was flat, expressionless. "I'll explain later," I said. "Let me see your arm."

He rolled up his wet sleeve. The skin was ripped from his elbow to his wrist in a long, shallow gash with uneven edges. Dark red blood, thick and sticky, oozed from it. "It looks deeper than it is," I told him. "We just need to keep pressure on it. You'll be okay."

He quickly rolled his sleeve back down, twisting it so it was tight against his arm. "It's time to sleep."

The ground under the tree was covered with fallen needles but it was surprisingly soft. The sun had fully risen; warmth was wrapping around us, soft and moist.

In spite of his wet clothes, the boy curled up, using a roll of diapers as a pillow, and was asleep almost instantly. David sat propped against the tree trunk. I leaned against him, my head on his chest. I could hear his heartbeat, strong and steady. Elsa, pink and warm, was safe in my arms.

"The boy," I whispered, "was awake one night at the Village. He was near tears. Said his belly hurt. Seems that he wanted to use the washing-up area but couldn't. Said it was against the rules."

"The rules? For the washing-up area?"

"Yes. The children could only go when the Caretakers said they could. No other time."

"That's ridiculous." David whispered.

"Right. So I gave him permission to break a rule. I let him go. After that, he told me he always wanted me to be with him. He said I was important because I could break the rules. I told him *he* was important because I broke the rule for *him*. He trusted me. I couldn't break his trust. I had to bring him."

"I understand." But David didn't look like he understood. He sounded worried because we were now responsible for two children. Little did David know that I wished I could have saved more of them from their cold world. All of them.

We didn't talk anymore. We needed to sleep.

I put my free hand into our bundle and tried to guess how many diapers and bottles we had. I knew there weren't enough of either to last for very many days.

We spent our first day of freedom huddled under that tree, listening for the sound of footsteps in the forest and waiting for darkness so we could move on. But move on to where? Was any place safe?

I thought back to the old photograph that Mother had kept hidden in her mat. I treasured that picture of her holding me, both of us smiling into the camera. Behind us in that photo was a sturdy home, a loving place. A safe place. Every fiber in me longed to return to that home, to a new beginning free from punishment and rules and Gatekeepers and Enforcers.

I had the first pangs of hunger, but worse, I felt the sharp chill of fear. What if we couldn't find a safe place to call home? Would we die out here alone in this forest?

I laid my head close against David's chest to better hear and feel his strong, steady heartbeat.

Finally, I fell asleep.

CHAPTER TWO

JOHN AND JOAN

Day 1

John and Joan had woken in the middle of the night to the sounds of shouting and gunfire. John rushed to the door of their Living Space and flung it open. Flames, gyrating red and orange, came from the direction of the Children's Village. He stood with his hand on his chest, staring. Joan stood behind him, her hands over her mouth. Then, in an instant, she pushed past him.

"Stop!" John grabbed her arm, his fingers digging into her skin like clamps.

She pulled her arm free and whirled around to face him. "There's a fire! The children need me."

"No! It's too dangerous! Give me a minute. Let me think, for God's sake, Joan!"

He closed the door, and quickly put on his Transport uniform pants and then pulled the shirt over his head. "I'll go," he said. "Get dressed and wait here. Don't go outside. Let me find out what's going on."

Joan's hands shook. She tried to change her clothes but struggled to get her arms into the sleeves and fumbled fastening her headscarf.

"Promise me you'll wait here."

She nodded reluctantly. He kissed her forehead and left, slamming the door behind him.

There was no Gatekeeper to stop him. There should have been a Gatekeeper. There was *always* a Gatekeeper.

John made his way along the perimeter of the bike path, crouching low, moving toward the flames, his eyes scanning for any movement. Instinctively, he picked up a rock and held it so tightly that his fingers cramped.

He passed by the gate where their son, David, should have been stationed. He wasn't there. The door to Emmeline and David's living space stood open. He ran to it and looked in. Empty. Emmeline must be at the Children's Village, but where was David? John felt his pulse race, his hands damp with sweat.

Moving forward up the path, he saw that the fire was at the Social Update Stage, and not at the Village itself. He breathed a quick sigh of relief. A few yards ahead of him was an armed man, apparently stationed to guard the bicycle path. Not wishing to startle the guard, John called out to him. "Hey, what's going on?"

"Who goes there?" the guard shouted, pointing his pistol in John's direction. John couldn't make out the man's features but he was leaning forward with two hands on the dull gray gun.

"John. Transport." He moved one step closer.

"Return to your Living Space immediately." He kept the gun leveled at John's head.

"I'm here to help. Do you need help?" He took two more tentative steps closer.

"Stop! Transport isn't authorized . . ." Intense shouting erupted from around the corner and the guard stopped and turned his head to look. John crouched to his knees and then lunged, springing to his full height, arm raised. The rock in his hand struck the side of the guard's face with brutal force. He crumpled to the ground in the shadows at the side of the path, motionless. John looked around, but saw no one.

No witnesses. He stooped, grabbed the pistol from the guard's hand, and, staying on the dark fringes of the path, made his way back to Joan.

* * *

Joan jumped up from her mat and rushed to meet John at the door. He wrapped his arms around her, felt the warmth of her against his chest and the firmness of her back under his hands. He leaned against her for a long silent moment before turning to shut the door. She gasped when she saw the moonlight glistening off the gun tucked into his waistband.

"John!" She stepped away from him and sank to the sleeping mat. "A gun? They could kill you for that!"

"I don't care. It's more dangerous not to have one on a night like this."

"Is it that bad?" she asked. "It's the Village, isn't it?"

He sat beside her, clicked on the gun's safety lock, and laid it on the mat.

"It's that bad. But the Children's Village is fine," he said, knowing that the Village and the young lives it housed was the most important thing to her. "It's the Social Update Stage."

Joan breathed a sigh of relief. "Why? How?"

He rubbed his forehead with his right hand and laid his left hand on her knee. "I don't know. But David wasn't at his post. Their Living Space somehow . . ."

"David wasn't at his post?" Her voice was sharp, slicing through the air in the dark room, and the words hung like cold daggers above their heads.

"No. And their space is empty. But our Gatekeeper wasn't at our gate either. So I don't know. I don't know what's going on."

"Where could David be? What about Emmeline and Elsa?"

John walked to a window slit and looked out. Their Gatekeeper had returned to his post and was pacing nervously back and forth, talking to a guard. They were both waving their arms, shaking their heads.

"I don't know. Emmeline and Elsa should be at the Village." He turned back to her. "But I have no way of knowing for certain. Emmeline must have heard the rumors about the relocations."

She nodded. "I think everybody heard them."

"You know how she feels about Elsa."

Joan nodded.

They heard people running on the bike path past their Compound and then more gunshots.

John took a deep breath and looked his wife straight in the eyes. "I'm afraid that Emmeline could be involved in all of this."

Joan gasped. "How?"

"She would have been frantic hearing about the relocation."

"I was going to try to stop it. After all, I'm the manager at the Village. She should have talked to me."

John shook his head wearily. "I know you would try to do what you could, but the rumor was spreading fast and ringing true. The relocation was going to happen. And soon. Emmeline would have been desperate. She wouldn't have had time to talk to you."

"Well, then, maybe David knew she was upset and went to the Village to calm her down."

"He wouldn't leave his post and he wouldn't be allowed in the Village."

"Well, then, maybe . . ."

"No more maybes, Joan. We know three things for certain. There's a fire, David's not at his post, and outside there's chaos and gunfire." John rubbed his temples with his fingers in small, tight circles, then put his hands on his knees and sighed. "She probably told David they had to leave and take Elsa with them."

"Leave? There's no way to leave the Compound. You know that."

John stood and paced back and forth in their small space, then went back to the window slit. The Gatekeeper and the guard were still talking, still agitated.

He stopped pacing and faced Joan.

"The fence is not perfect."

Joan frowned but said nothing. She sat with her hands in her lap, waiting.

"There's a way to get through. A way to get to the other side."

"The other side . . ." Joan's voice trailed away as though the enormity of what he was saying was too dangerous to comprehend. She looked at him with skepticism. "That's impossible! How would David even know how to do that?"

John stared at the floor. He knew Joan would be upset but it was time to tell her everything. She needed to know the truth. "Because I made a hole in the fence and told him about it. He probably told Emmeline."

"John!" Joan stood up and faced him, her face tense with deep frown lines. "You did what? You made a *hole* in the fence? What were you thinking?"

"I know. It was dangerous. I just needed to know that every once in a while I could be on the other side, free." He shrugged. "But I was fooling myself. It was false freedom."

"And nobody saw this hole? What if somebody discovered it and knew you made it? They would have taken you away. Then how good would your *false* freedom be?" She clenched her hands into fists.

"Nobody can see it. It's hidden."

"Hidden? They see everything, know everything." Joan paced in a tight circle. "How could it possibly be hidden?"

"It's behind a broken down bus-box that's parked by the fence." Large wooden bus-boxes were used to transport people, when necessary, and to move food from the farm commune to be processed into nourishment cubes for the Citizens. Bulky and heavy, they were pulled by men assigned to Transport Teams, harnessed like workhorses.

"I suppose a bus-box would be big enough to conceal a break in the fence. But you never told me about it?"

"I wanted you to be completely guiltless, completely unaware, in the event it was discovered and linked to me. I'm sorry. I should have told you."

"Yes, you should have. But you shouldn't have done it in the first place."

"It was something I had to do. I needed it for me. But we can't debate this right now, we're losing time. We've got to figure out if they're really gone. If they are, we've got to follow them through that hole before the chaos dies down. They need us."

"You've lost your mind! How would we ever survive out there? It's called the Human Free Zone for a reason."

"For starters, we've got a gun. But beyond that, you're going to have to trust me. I know it's asking a lot. But this is our son, his wife, and our grandchild that we're talking about here. They're out there somewhere. I think a little blind faith is justified. Besides, what's the alternative—to sit here in this cement box of a home saluting the Republic while we never see our family again? Is that what you want? To stay here and do nothing?"

Joan knew that *if* John was right and David had taken his young family to the other side, she would never see them again. She also knew that if she and her husband were taken into custody by the Authorities, they would be held out as examples or, worse, used as bait to lure David and Emmeline back to the Compound.

That is, *if* John was right.

"I don't know what I want," she answered, her lips barely moving.

They sat side by side and the tiny Living Space settled around them like a shroud, airless and tight. Joan pushed her clenched fists against her forehead so tightly that her knuckles turned white. John picked up the gun, turned it over in his hand, and felt the smooth gray metal, cold against his fingertips.

The door to their space opened and, without notice, the Gatekeeper rushed in. John quickly pushed the gun under the mat. The Gatekeeper grabbed Joan by the arm, pulling her toward the door.

"Hurry, Citizen, hurry. You're needed at the Village immediately."

"Yes, yes," Joan said, "I'll come. But my husband must come too, for protection. I need him."

"I don't care if he comes or not. I was told to get you quickly." He pulled her through the doorway. John grabbed the gun from under the mat and followed behind them, pushing the weapon deep into the waistband of his orange Transport Team pants and pulling his shirt down to cover it.

They ran toward the fire and noise. Joan saw the dark shape of a guard lying motionless beside the path. "Look," she called out to the Gatekeeper. "Over there, someone is lying there. He's not moving."

"Not my problem," the Gatekeeper said. "My orders are to get you to the Village. Keep moving."

They passed by the burning Social Update Stage where Citizens, under the watchful eyes of guards, were beating at the flames with bed linens. Water was limited in the Compound; there was none available to put out fires. The air was heavy with the smell of smoke. They kept hurrying toward the Village.

Once there, the Gatekeeper turned them over to an Enforcer. "I'm going inside with you while you inventory the children," the Enforcer said, pointing his pistol at Joan. "If any are missing, inform me at once. And you," he said, pointing at John, "stay in my sight at all times."

Joan rushed inside past the cramped supply cupboard. The fire cast enough light through the windows for her to see the two Caretakers huddled in the corner. The Enforcer stayed so close to Joan that she could smell the cold carbon of his gun.

"What are you doing, sitting in here?" Joan screamed at the Caretakers. "Have you checked the children?" The stale odor of alcohol wafted from them and out into the hallway. "Hand me a torch."

As her eyes adjusted to the darkness, Joan recognized one of the Caretakers. Lizzie. Lazy, nasty Lizzie. She was the one who had told Emmeline about the mass killings that occurred before Citizens were loaded onto trains and moved into Compounds—killings that counted Emmeline's grandmother and aunt among the victims. Emmeline had been devastated after hearing the story. Joan couldn't remember the name of the other Caretaker. They both looked dazed—probably a combination of the alcohol and the confusion from the fire outside. The Caretakers felt for their torches. Gone. Their torches were gone.

Dusk to dawn, Caretakers always had their torches. Always. They couldn't function without them. Joan knew then, with absolute certainty, that Emmeline and David had escaped. They'd taken the lights, grabbed Elsa, and fled. There was no one else with access to the precious torches and no one else but Emmeline with access to the drunken Caretakers. There could be no other explanation. John was right. There was no more *if*. Her doubts were replaced with grim determination.

"I can't inventory without light," she said to the Enforcer. "Let me get a torch from my office. Please." She knew there was no torch there, but she wanted to delay any inventory of the children and confuse the Enforcer if she could. She rushed down the corridor and into her office. Flinging open closet doors, pulling open desk drawers, she searched with frantic hands. The Enforcer stood close, watching her.

"Help me, John. Do something." John stood in the doorway and watched the corridor, hoping no other Enforcer entered. He heard the urgency in her plea and immediately understood what she was doing. "Put down your gun and help us search," he said to the Enforcer.

"No. Never," the Enforcer said, keeping his eyes on Joan. "Do you think I'm a fool?"

John reached for his gun. The movement of his arm seemed like slow motion. He pulled the weapon out, raising it in his hand, pointing it, curling his finger on the trigger, each motion deliberate. It felt like the whole process lasted an eternity, yet it happened in the space of one short breath.

A shot rang out.

The Enforcer collapsed to the floor. The bullet had hit him directly in the center of his head. No one seemed to notice the sound of one more gunshot. John, who, before that day had never hurt another human being, had now struck a guard with a rock and shot an Enforcer—all in one night. He felt like a stranger in his own skin. A cold shiver ran down his spine, sharp as a bony finger.

Joan leaned against the wall, her mouth open.

John bent over the Enforcer and began unfastening his jacket, slipping the sleeves off his limp arms.

"What are you doing?" Joan asked.

"I'm getting us out of here. No one will stop us if they think I'm an Enforcer." He began putting the Enforcer's uniform on over his own clothes, then picked up the Enforcer's gun. "Go confirm that Elsa is gone from her crib. Then gather some supplies. Grab whatever you can carry. Hurry." He tucked both guns into his waistband. His fate was sealed. He was now a Citizen with not just one gun, but two.

Joan nodded and ran down the corridor to the nursery. Feeling her way in the dim room past crying babies she reached Elsa's crib. It was empty. It had been empty long enough that the mattress was cool to the touch. She went back into the hallway, running, glancing into the rooms as she went. In the flickering light from the fire, she glimpsed an empty cot in the boys' sleeping space, an empty chair where the next day's clothes should be laid out. In other cots, boys sat upright, frightened, holding their thin blankets tightly against their chins. She paused in the doorway and whispered, "It's okay," but she couldn't stop to say anything else.

She ran back to the supply cupboard. The two Caregivers were still huddled in the corner like frightened, cornered animals. "Get up! Do you hear me? Get up! Go tend to the children. Now!" They stood, unsteady, staring at her.

"I said *go*. I'll report you if you don't." She pointed to the corridor and the two of them left the closet quickly. With rapid frantic movements she randomly pulled things off the shelves, filling a flimsy trash bucket. She put as much as she could into it before returning to the office.

"Elsa?" John asked, the Enforcer's black uniform now completely covering his orange Transport one.

"Gone. And one other child, too. A boy. They're gone."

"Oh my God. Oh my God." John pushed his hands through his thick dark hair, trying to think. "Is there another exit from the Village?"

"Just this door at the back of my office." She pointed to it.

"What does it lead to?"

"A metal shed behind the Village but inside the fence. There's broken equipment in it. It's locked."

"Do you have the key?"

"Yes." She rummaged through a desk door. "Why?"

"We've got to get rid of him. Get him out of sight. Otherwise, they'll know his uniform was stolen. That would blow my cover. In all this chaos it will take them some time to realize he's missing."

Together they dragged the heavy body out of her office and into the windowless shed. Dark shapes of broken equipment littered the floor and were piled against the walls. The Enforcer became just another broken shape.

"Now listen. Do what I say. Pretend I'm arresting you. Don't say a word." He put the key to the shed in his pocket.

They left the Village together through the main entrance. Joan was in front carrying the small, shiny metal bucket by its thin handle. John, in the Enforcer's uniform, was behind her, holding the gun in full view. No one stopped them. No one would ever question the actions of an Enforcer.

He urged her forward, forcefully, with one hand on her shoulder, his face grim.

Another Enforcer, seeing John with his prisoner, made the circle sign in approval. "Looks like she was stealing. Look at all the things she has in that bucket."

A clipboard and nourishment bottle were clearly visible above the edge.

"Taking advantage of the situation, was she?"

John said nothing but simply nodded.

"What are your orders? Hope they're tough on her."

"Stick to the perimeter. Take her to Recycle."

"Good. Recy is where she belongs. Any problem with the children? I hope they are all right."

"Caretakers are with them."

"Praise be to the Republic."

John nodded. "Praise be to the Republic." The other Enforcer gave the circle sign and walked back toward the Village. John felt the weight of possible discovery lift slightly. He pushed Joan forward again.

She sobbed as she walked, great heaving sobs, sucking in air to keep from collapsing upon herself. An observer might think it was because an Enforcer had captured her but in truth she cried because her world was crumbling around her. She mourned for all that had already been lost, that which could be lost in the future, and fear of the unknown.

"Keep moving, Citizen," John said loudly. Then he whispered: "See that bus-box straight ahead? Walk behind it."

A few steps later Joan saw why he said the hole was hidden. The bus-box, useless and unrepaired for so long, was covered with wild ivy. The wooden wheels had rotted flat against the ground. Behind it was a hole cut into the bottom of the thick wire fence.

The doorway to freedom.

CHAPTER THREE

DAVID

Day 1

Emmy looked peaceful as she slept. Her face reminded David of a painting he had seen long ago in a book—before the books were all taken away. Her skin was so smooth, her lips so full and soft. Her arm curved around Elsa and her hand cupped Elsa's foot. David noticed the way the sunlight slipped in between the branches and danced on her hair. Hair soft as silk that curled at the ends and lay in the hollow between her cheek and shoulder. Yellow sunbeams, golden hair. He had loved her from a distance for a long time. He had ached deep inside knowing bad things were happening to her. First, both her father and her original Authority-assigned partner had died in a suspicious accident. Then her newborn was taken away. Then her mother was taken away for being non-productive. The Authorities had paired her with an immature brat who eventually deserted her. Now she was all alone in the world.

All the while, he was at a distance, watching, knowing she was alone. But he had no power to change anything. As a mere dusk-to-dawn Gatekeeper, he could only monitor people, make rounds, nothing more. His job was to report Citizens for whatever they might do against the rules. But he had never reported anyone for anything. It wasn't in his nature.

He had felt helpless and thought he had no chance to ever be near Emmy. Gatekeepers could not socialize with Citizens. That was a rule. But she'd begun to wake up before dawn and sit in her doorway looking at the stars. When he saw her there the first time his heart had raced so quickly that he got dizzy. She had been so beautiful in the moonlight. He wanted to bring her everything she desired and spread his gifts out at her feet with a grand flourish. But what could he bring to her? He had nothing. None of the Citizens did. Finally, he risked picking flowers. The Authorities said flowers were protected, but he didn't care. He had pushed his fingers through the fence and picked the flowers growing outside the Compound. He had picked them *for her*!

He had become a Citizen who broke the rules.

He had given her his hard-boiled egg snack and watched her lips on the whiteness of the egg. When she smiled at him his heart had pounded in his ears.

And then the unbelievable happened.

The Authorities paired him with Emmy. He knew his mother had somehow manipulated the system to arrange it. She must have said the right thing to the right person. Next, his mother had hired Emmy as a night-shift Caretaker at the Children's Village so that she could be near her daughter.

What his mother had accomplished was amazing, almost magical. David wondered if other mothers would risk everything for their children. Then he looked at Emmy holding her daughter. And he knew the answer.

Emmy had been so happy about the job at the Village. She'd never held Elsa, not even when she was a newborn, but now she could nurture her, care for her, love her. Emmy's face had been joyful, radiant even, as she'd told him how it felt to have the little girl in her arms after her first shift.

But things changed. Emmy told him things weren't going well at the Village. She said her coworkers were lazy and the children weren't thriving. Removing a child from the Village was forbidden, but Emmy had run to him last night with Elsa in her arms, explaining that the children were going to be relocated to another Compound. She said that Elsa would be gone from her forever. Her eyes were filled with fear but her voice was firm, unwavering. When she told him they were leaving, David knew he couldn't stop her. She said if he didn't come with her, she'd go on her own. No negotiations. If he wanted to be with her and Elsa then he'd have to escape right along with them. And he wanted nothing more than to be with her. In the end, there was really nothing to think about.

Now, under the low branches of a pine tree, David felt like he'd been caught in a tornado, twirled about, and set back down, dizzy and disoriented. It was all a blur: they were running, carrying Elsa, and a bundle of things Emmy had grabbed, including the treasures Emmy's mother had kept hidden from the Authorities for so many years. Then they'd set fire to the Social Update Stage using the forbidden matches from the bundle. Sounds of gunfire had mixed with screams. Finally, they'd escaped from the Compound through the hidden hole in the fence his father had created.

David shifted his weight, and tried to find a comfortable position. He wondered if his mother and father were safe. Maybe they got away, too, using that same hole. He found comfort in the thought, unlikely as it was.

Once the Authorities figured out which Citizens had disappeared, they would do everything to find them and punish them. That's just how they worked. Always punish, never reward—unless you were a snitch. Snitches thrived.

David tried desperately to sleep, but it wouldn't come. He had too much adrenaline, too much uncertainty, too much fear, too many thoughts racing through his mind. His arm throbbed like a beating drum.

How stupid he felt for running and falling like that. What if he had been carrying Elsa? His arm hurt terribly but he didn't want Emmy to know. She didn't need anything else to worry about. Even worse, it was his right arm, his strong arm; the arm he'd need to protect them all.

Elsa was curled up like a little pink ball on Emmy's lap. Mother and child. The defender and the defenseless.

Small birds hopped freely from branch to branch in the pine tree. A fly struggled in a spider web near the sleeping boy.

David looked closely at him for the first time. He was a cute little fellow with spiky hair and a splash of freckles across the bridge of his nose and the roundest part of his cheeks. He wondered what his name was, how old he was. He struck David as a pretty spunky kid and smart, too, the way he went after their bundle when it was rolling down the hill. He saw something that needed to be done and he did it. *Maybe he's like Emmy,* he thought. She saw something that needed to be done and she did it. She'd saved Elsa from the relocation of the Children's Village. Desperation overruled danger. Love eclipsed fear.

David tried to remember the stuff he'd learned at Boy Scouts, in the before-time. Their motto had been "Always be prepared," but he didn't feel that way now. What's safe to eat and drink? How to find shelter? He didn't realize back then how important survival skills could be. Their very lives depended on him now. Responsibility settled as heavily on his shoulders as the branches of the tree pushed against him.

Emmy was the bravest, most loving person he'd ever known. She was more than his partner. She was his wife. She was his *life*. He would do anything necessary to protect her.

Anything.

CHAPTER FOUR

JOHN AND JOAN

Day 1

Hidden from view by the bus-box, John pushed the small metal bucket of supplies through the hole in the fence. It made a harsh, scraping sound against the concrete base and the handle caught on the cut metal wire. John pulled the handle loose and shoved the bucket through. It tipped over, and a nourishment bottle rolled out onto the ground.

Joan watched, glancing frequently over her shoulder at the fire and chaos behind her.

"I'm going through. Follow me. Hurry." John pushed his head and shoulders through the opening, his face mere inches above the cement base, the hard concrete smell filling his nose. His sleeve caught on a sharp piece of wire; he pulled it free, tearing the sturdy fabric of the Enforcer's uniform. Once on the other side, he picked up the nourishment bottle and shoved it back into the bucket.

Joan followed, using her elbows to propel herself forward, inch by painful inch. Once she was through, John helped her stand, and tried to steady her. He put his hands on both sides of her face, tilted her head up, looked into her eyes, and whispered, "Trust me." He held her close a few seconds more, then took her arm, and started down the same slippery hillside that Emmeline and David had scrambled down just a few hours earlier.

They moved quickly and were soon at the edge of the stream. "David would follow this downstream. He knows that would be the smart thing to do. He'd know that it will likely lead him to a river or lake." John looked over his shoulder as he talked. No one was following them yet. But they would be. "We'll go upstream."

"Upstream? Why wouldn't we go in the same direction as David? Don't we want to find him?"

"We want to *protect* David. I want to throw off whoever comes to find them. Better they follow us than David and Emmeline."

"I don't understand. Throw who off?"

Exasperated, John answered sharply. "For God's sake, Joan! You aren't thinking clearly."

"How can I think clearly? David's gone. Emmeline's gone. Two children are missing. You keep saying 'God' even though that word is banned." Joan answered. "What if someone heard you?"

He set the bucket of supplies on the ground and gripped her shoulders firmly. "Look at me. Think. We're on the other side of the fence. We're already guilty of breaking every law they have." He relaxed his grip slightly but his face was firm, his forehead furrowed. "And so are David and Emmeline. Look around you. Who is going to hear me say the word 'God'? No one but God Himself."

Joan looked at the dark wilderness surrounding them, her face pale. John lowered his voice. "Do you see anyone?" She shook her head.

"Right. No one is near us now. But soon enough, trust me, Earth Protectors will be deployed to find all of us: the children, Emmeline, David, you, me. As soon as they figure out who is missing, they will hunt us down and recycle us. All of us. We have to do all we can to protect those children, protect our son, even if it means dying for them. Do you understand?"

"Yes," she whispered. "Yes, I understand. There's no turning back.

I'm ready to do whatever we need to do." She stood and squared her shoulders.

"Good."

"What's your plan?"

"Time to focus," John's tone was suddenly decisive, businesslike. "We'll be sloppy. Leave a trail. Drop things. Break off branches. Make it easy for them to track us. Let's go."

"It's still pretty dark and hard to see. How soon till dawn?"

"Moon's bright enough. And dawn's not far off."

He started along the edge of the stream and Joan followed. He stopped abruptly. "Give me the bucket." She handed it over and he rummaged through it until he felt the clipboard. Ripping off a piece of paper, he crumpled it and tossed it where it could easily be seen.

They walked on a little farther. The paper, lifted by a small breeze, rolled into a stand of high weeds, partially hidden.

"And if they do follow us, what can we do?"

"We have two guns. We can protect ourselves. Emmeline and David most likely can't." He broke off a small branch overhanging the stream. It dangled there, useless as a broken crutch.

They walked slowly through the darkness.

Dawn came. They walked faster.

When the sun was directly overhead, they sat briefly in the woods beside the stream.

"It's not going to take them very long to figure out we're missing," Joan said.

He thought for a moment. "I don't know about that. They didn't have any control of the situation, from what I saw. Things broke down pretty quickly. But, yes, eventually they'll know we're gone. It's inevitable. I just think it might take some time."

John stared at the water, watching it ripple, bits and pieces of leaves and twigs floating past them. "Strange, isn't it," he said after a moment. "They had total control over us for so long. And we let them."

"You're right. But why talk about that now?" Joan said. She looked around at the wilderness surrounding them, the trees that towered over them, and the deep shadows of the forest. "What difference does it make?"

"None, I guess. Time to get moving again."

"How far do you plan on us going?" Joan asked. She stood and brushed leaves off her uniform.

John thought for a moment. "We've already walked maybe eight to ten miles. The further upstream we go, the farther downstream David can go. We'll keep dropping clues." He took the shed key from his pocket and pushed it deep into the underbelly of a rotten log. Then he took her hand, and squeezed it briefly, his large hand wrapped around her smaller one.

"Then what?"

"Pray that Earth Protectors will follow us. Pray that Emmeline and David have time to find a safe hiding place downstream. Pray."

A fish splashed in the stream, a silvery image that disappeared under the water. John broke off another branch, dropped another small bit of paper. They walked on.

"And if the Earth Protectors do follow us, then what?" Joan asked.

"Then we'll do what we have to do." John's voice was firm. "Whatever it takes, by whatever means necessary."

They walked until dusk without stopping. After sharing one of the nourishment bottles from the bucket, Joan fell asleep on a mossy patch of ground. John stayed awake listening to the sound of the stream alongside them, the scurrying of animals in the underbrush, and Joan's rhythmic breathing. In the distance, animals howled long, mournful crescendos that cut through the night like knives. Pinpoint lights appeared, white against the dark sky. The full moon looked swollen, as though it could burst and pour its soul out onto the Earth.

This was no longer a false freedom. It was now a real but fragile one. John lay on his back staring at the tree branches above him and the faraway heavens beyond.

CHAPTER FIVE

EMMELINE

Day 1

Elsa's soft whimpers woke me. How long had I slept? It was still daylight, not yet time to move on. David was awake and looked flushed, his face and forehead red and damp with sweat. Using his left hand, David pulled a bottle from the diaper bundle and handed it to me. Elsa quit crying and sucked on it eagerly, her eyes fixed intently on my face. The boy woke up and whispered something to David.

"Okay. Bring your clothes." David, cradling his arm, let the boy push aside the low branches of our hiding place. Together they went behind some tall, thick-trunked trees. There was no washing-up area here and no nourishment cubes. The only supplies we had were a few bottles and diapers. What were we going to do? What was I thinking? David was already injured; what if he got worse? What if they found us? What if? What if?

A tear slid down my face but I quickly brushed it away. I had to be strong for Elsa. She took the bottle out of her mouth and squirmed, pushing herself into a sitting position.

"Hello, little teapot," I said and she smiled, little bubbles of milk shining silvery on her tongue. I kissed her forehead.

David and the boy came out of the shadows of the forest carrying something rough and brown in their hands.

"Tell her," David whispered to the boy. "What I taught you. Our nature lesson."

"It's moss," the boy spoke quietly but proudly in my ear. "For her diaper."

David nodded. "Sphagnum moss. I'll show you how to use it."

I pulled a clean diaper out of our bag of supplies and David laid a handful of moss on it. I unfastened Elsa's wet diaper and laid her on this strange-looking grass. She squealed with pleasure and kicked her pink legs, her small perfect feet, in the air.

"How did you know about this?"

"I was a Boy Scout, once upon a time. Help me with my arm."

I tried to prop Elsa beside the boy on the soft carpet under the tree, but she leaned away from him. She didn't want to be propped. She wanted to sit alone.

David rolled up his sleeve. The skin along the gash was red, angry-looking, and so swollen that it looked shiny and tight. Some yellow fluid seeped along the edge.

"Lay moss on it," he whispered, "and tie my shirt around my arm."

His skin felt hot. I tried my best to get the moss to stay in place while I wrapped his shirt around and around his arm, tying it tightly in place with the sleeves. He moved his arm a little, testing it, and the shirt stayed in place without slipping.

Tired of sitting in a cramped position, I slipped through the low branches and walked behind a cluster of trees. There, alone in all this greenness, I knew what Father meant when he talked about the smell of growing things and how much he missed his farm. I could smell the moist dirt and the small flowers growing nearby. They were flat, round, and yellow with dark green leaves. I took a deep breath, pulling that sweet smell into me. On an impulse, I picked off one of the green leaves and chewed on it. A little bitter, but still, it tasted good.

A bird, brown with a red breast, landed on a branch near me, balancing on two spindly yellow legs. I moved slightly and the bird flew away. A single tail feather drifted down. I picked it up and studied it. I saw how the strands of the feather fit together, and felt the firmness of the thin central spine. I ran my finger along the edge; the strands moved together as I moved my finger, and returned to their original shape when I took my finger away. Amazing! I picked a few flowers, some of the green leaves, and took them, along with the feather, back to our hiding place under the pine tree.

The boy examined the feather eagerly, just as I had, smelling it and touching it. He did the same with the flowers, pushing his nose deep into the petals until the tip of his pert little nose was caked in yellow flower dust. He smiled and hugged me.

We sat quietly, waiting for dusk so we could move on. Flies buzzed about and butterflies flitted here and there in the sun. The boy reached an arm out through the branches, trying to catch one, but it looped away from him. He sat back down beside me with a frown.

"I wanted that," he said.

"Why?"

"So I could sit on it and fly away."

"Fly away to where?"

"I don't know. Someplace safe." His voice had a soft, pensive tone.

I pictured him like the Little Prince from my mother's stories, flying to different lands, searching. The Little Prince didn't have a name. And we didn't know the name of this boy.

"You don't need a butterfly. We'll keep you safe. My name is Emmeline. This is David and this is Elsa." I bounced Elsa up and down and she giggled. "What's your name?"

"My name is Micah, but mostly the Caretakers just called me 'stupid.'"

They called *this* child stupid? No wonder the children didn't thrive. "Did you say Michael? Is your name Michael?"

He smiled, a crooked, lopsided little grin, and I noticed a dimple on his right cheek just like mine. "Micah. Not Michael."

"Shh," David whispered, his head cocked to the side. Then I heard what he heard. It was the deep gravelly voices of men, two of them, it seemed. Their voices carried all the way to the pine tree.

"They must have crossed the stream," the first voice said. "No telling where they are. Let's report back. There will be hell to pay."

"For sure," said voice number two. "But for who? Hell for them escaping or hell for us if we don't catch them?"

There was a pause.

"Do you think they're all together? His parents and his partner and the two kids?"

"No way of knowing. Think we'll be in trouble for not finding any of them?"

"Hell, they can't blame us." It was the first voice again. "We're not trained for the Human Free Zone. That's the Earth Protectors' job. This isn't in my job description."

"Just saying they can't blame us doesn't mean they won't. You know that. Bet they've already requisitioned Earth Protectors from the agency."

David stared at me, eyes wide and mouth open. I wanted to reach out and touch his face, but I was frozen, couldn't move.

"They'll find them all soon enough."

"At least one of them is hurt—given the blood we saw back there on a rock."

"That'll slow them down. We'll report that. Maybe hell is already being paid." One of them laughed.

David turned white, his lips pinched together in a thin, straight line. He didn't look at me.

"Authorities will use them as examples. Punish them. Let everyone see . . ."

"Recycling is too good for them. Too easy, too fast. They need to suffer first."

They were walking away from us, their voices fading away. But I could still hear their shoes on the leaves, a faint crunching sound. We sat motionless for what seemed like an eternity. A tiny black ant walked up my arm. I made no effort to brush it away. Finally, the only sounds were those of running water, the wilderness around us, and our own pounding hearts and shallow breathing.

"My parents! They got out. They must be searching for us. Do you think they'll find us?" David looked at me as though he expected me to know the answer.

"I hope so. I hope they're safe. I hope we find each other."

Hope. Such a tiny word with such outsized meaning.

I shuddered thinking of the fire, the chaos, and the gunshots. I held Elsa closer to me; Micah moved closer to David. David wrapped his arm around Micah's shoulders, tilting the frail child close to his own strong chest, and bent his head down, his dark hair near the blondness of Micah's. The brief moment of joy with the flowers and the feather had been crushed under the sounds of those footsteps, those voices.

I knew those men were our enemies, but they, like everyone else in the Republic, were nothing more than servants. Rule followers. They were cruel, but they didn't know any better.

But I did. I had a choice and I made it. I knew then and there that, no matter what happened, I would never go back.

Never.

CHAPTER SIX

JOHN AND JOAN

Day 2

John finally drifted off propped up against a tree, his two layers of clothing isolating him from the roughness of the bark. He had one gun in his hand, the other one firmly tucked into his waistband.

Joan woke him at dawn with a gentle shake, and then sat beside him. He put his arm around her and pulled her close. She fit so well in the curve of his arm, her shoulder tucked against his chest. His neck felt stiff and sore. They sat silently, watching the sun rise slowly over the treetops. Some birds, brown, blue, and red, flitted from branch to branch. Others hopped along the ground, dipping their heads for insects among the leaves. Large dappled birds, their wings wide with graceful, smooth outlines ending in a fringe of feathers at the tips, circled overhead, calling out in lonely, mournful whistles.

"What do we do now?" Joan asked.

"First we get some water from the stream," John answered. "Then we decide whether to keep moving or wait. If the Earth Protectors are following us, maybe we could ambush them. That would be ideal."

John stood and stretched. His back ached. "I'll be right back. I want to check out this area, see if anybody has been here." He slipped deeper into the woods. How strange he felt to be walking in a forbidden area, walking where the Authorities ruled that human beings had no right to be.

The leaves, brown and paper-thin, crunched under his feet, stuck to his shoes. Could anybody hear him? He stepped carefully around fallen logs, brushed hanging cobwebs from his face, and constantly scanned his surroundings. There was no sign that anyone had ever been here.

Even in the deep shade of the woods, he was beginning to get hot from his two layers of clothing. He slipped off the Enforcer's uniform and laid the two guns on the ground. *Should have left one with Joan*, he thought. He went through the pockets of the Enforcer's clothing and found a silver-colored whistle tied to a strong strip of leather and six bullets, along with bits of lint. After laying everything on the ground, he took off his bright orange Transport uniform. The smell of leather harness straps still clung to the stained fabric.

The beginning of a high-pitched scream echoed around him then stopped abruptly. Joan! Stripped down to his underwear, he grabbed all of his clothes and ran shoeless to her. The stones and twigs on the forest floor were sharp against his feet. The clothes in his arms dangled down and slapped against his thighs. He gripped the guns, one in each hand, both cocked and ready.

He found her standing white-faced, her back against a tree. Dropping everything but the guns, he ran to her.

"What happened?" he asked.

She pointed, wordlessly, toward a pile of leaves near a log. He couldn't see anything.

"What?" he said. "I don't see anything."

"A snake. There was a snake. I think it went in there." She was still pointing, her finger shaking. "I started to scream but then was afraid someone would hear me."

"What color was it?"

"Black. Black and long."

Relieved, he put the safety lock on the guns, picked up the Enforcer's uniform, and started dressing. "A black snake? Don't you remember from the farm? Black snakes are harmless. They eat rodents." He reached down and tucked one gun back into his pocket. "I'm surprised you've forgotten."

"A black snake. Of course. I should have remembered. I just feel so disoriented and afraid. I'm sorry. I hate feeling like that." She took a deep breath. "It's so different out here. I'm going to have to get used to it."

John looked around at the trees and the stream. No fences. "Well, I admit it's different than how we've lived for the past eighteen years. But you're the strongest, smartest woman I know." He pulled her close to him, put his finger under her chin, tilted her face up, and kissed her. "We're in this together. We need to stay strong. Both of us."

She smiled in agreement. "Yes, you're right. The last thing you need is me falling apart. It won't happen again."

John quickly rolled the rest of the clothes together, and scrambled to the stream with Joan at his side. The water was ice cold against his hand. Minnows swirled near the surface of the water and the branches of a nearby willow tree hung low, dipping their long fingers into the stream.

Their bottles filled quickly. John overturned some rocks. They looked naked among all the other moss-covered ones around them. A good tracker would notice the difference. He broke off some fern fronds, knowing they would shrivel and turn brown, and placed them far from the original plants. Joan started doing the same.

He smiled, watching her, then sobered. If the unthinkable happened to David, Emmeline, and the children, his wife would be the only living person on earth who cared about him. The enormity of that struck him like a bolt of lightning. And if anything happened to Joan . . . no, that was unthinkable.

Before they started off, he handed her one of the guns. He showed her how to lock and unlock the safety, how to cock it, how to hold it and point it. She returned the demonstration, clicking the safety on and off, pulling the hammer back and releasing it, until he was satisfied. The metallic sounds were alien in these verdant surroundings. They tucked the guns into their clothing, the metal cold against their skin. John turned over some more small rocks, placing them moss side down, shiny side up, then they sat and considered their options.

Would Earth Protectors follow the deliberate clues on the trail?

Should they continue walking upstream, leading whoever came for them even farther in the wrong direction? Or had they gone far enough?

They sat, thinking, discussing, never letting go of each other's hands.

Either way, they were in this together.

CHAPTER SEVEN

EARTH PROTECTION AGENTS

Day 3

The local Authority stood with his hands on his hips, his feet in a wide stance, looking at the six people in front of him. The tallest of the group was Steven, a man with broad shoulders, a thick neck, and a permanent scowl on his face. Steven had never met this particular local Authority.

Steven had once been the highly celebrated leader of the EPA, the Earth Protection Agency, put into that post because of the large number of shadow people he had captured after the relocations. Of course, he was younger then. That was what, eighteen years ago? Once the Authorities were convinced that all the shadow people had been captured and destroyed they rewarded Steven with a permanent position as chief sentry for the Central Authority's mansion. Steven felt that he, more than anyone else, deserved all the privileges that came along with the job, things like the spa, the gym, and the chef-prepared meals. In return, he was responsible for protecting the mansion and its elite occupants.

The mansion he and his underlings guarded, away from the eyes of the common Citizens in the Compounds, represented great wealth and privilege. Built of white marble, it stood on a vast area of neatly manicured lawns, gardens full of fresh vegetables, and a barn full of livestock. An ornate, massive fence surrounded it. Dogs and guards patrolled the perimeter. The Citizens who worked there were never allowed to leave, for fear that they might tell others about the luxury the Authorities lived in. But it wasn't very difficult to keep them there—Citizens fortunate enough to be assigned to the mansion never tried to return to their gray, sparse Compounds.

Upon getting the job, Steven had demanded that two of his previous team members, Adam and Nigel, be assigned to assist him at the mansion. Adam and Nigel were men he had worked with, and he trusted them. They were with him today, along with three others he didn't know. All were wearing newly issued camouflage uniforms.

The group was gathered behind the shell of the recently burned Social Update Stage in the center of the Compound. Bits of blackened wood lay at their feet. The charred smell of smoke was oppressive.

"This is a crisis. Listen carefully," the local Authority said.

They all nodded except Steven. His face remained firm, unreadable.

"Central Authority dispatched you here." He paused and crossed his arms against his chest before he continued. "Three days ago a number of Citizens breached the perimeter fence and left the Compound."

The team remained motionless, without reaction. But Steven felt his jaw tighten with anger. Couldn't these fools even control their own Citizens? Their heads should roll for their incompetence. Why should *he* have to give up the luxury he'd earned to clean up their mistakes?

He knew where he stood in the chain of command, but he resented it.

At the top of the bureaucratic pyramid was the ultimate Central Authority. Steven had never met the Central Authority, the big guy in a black uniform trimmed with gold. Although Steven was given the responsibility of guarding his mansion, he had never even gotten a simple "hello" from the man.

Under the Central Authority were the handpicked local Authorities, like this clown standing in front of them, barking orders. They oversaw multiple Compounds, running around as crony mouthpieces of the big guy. Anytime they showed up at a Compound, they had access to the special supplies in the Authorities' storage building. Things Citizens weren't allowed to have, like alcohol and fresh food.

Power breeds privilege.

And under the Authorities were the Enforcers—men in black uniforms who could order that a Citizen be recycled if they thought he was not productive, not obedient. That was the ultimate power. Steven had seen some of them when he entered the Compound earlier. They were strutting around as though they were important and questioning terrified Citizens.

It was a bloated, blighted system.

Steven, and the Earth Protection Agency as a whole, dangled outside the chain of command, a sidebar away from the linear structure. The only time he had any meaningful power was when he was sent into the Human Free Zone to capture those who had slipped away. He had done that eighteen years ago and now, because of the incompetence above him, he had to do it again.

Steven stood with his feet close together, arms at his side—the standard posture whenever one was standing in front of any Authority. Rules were rules. He didn't have to like them, but he did have to obey them.

The rest of the assembled group consisted of three muscular men, each over six feet tall, plus two smaller men, the shortest of whom looked as though he was barely five and a half feet. All were in camouflage uniforms, with the blue-and-green Earth logo on the right upper side of their shirts. Most stood stiff and straight, their eyes focused on some nondescript point in the distance rather than on the Authority himself—just as the rules dictated. But Steven stared directly into the man's eyes, daring the Authority to challenge him on this one small rule.

The Authority pointed at the six men gathered in front of him. "You are assigned to find those Citizens and bring them back to me. There will be no discussions with anybody outside of this group." He began pacing back and forth in front of the men, speaking in rapid, short bursts.

Pace, pace, pace. The Authority's black boots dulled with soot. He approached one of the tall men, who had carrot-colored hair, and pointed at him. "Your name and experience?"

"Adam, sir. Earth Protection experience."

He went to the next man, pointed, and asked the same question.

"Nigel, sir. Earth Protection experience." Nigel's hair, even his eyelashes, were white as icicles.

"And you?"

"Winston, sir. Maintenance experience. Earth Protection training completed."

"And you?" He was now in front of one of the two smaller men.

"Guy, sir. Recycle experience. Earth Protection training complete." His left eyelid twitched as he spoke.

The Authority pointed at Steven.

"Steven. My name is Steven."

The Authority stared at him with hard eyes but made no comment. He moved down to the smallest in the line.

"Your name?"

"Julia, sir . . ."

Steven did a double take. On second glance she was obviously a woman, though she wasn't wearing a headscarf. Her dark hair was pushed into a mottled green beret that slanted across her forehead. The men had nothing on their heads.

"Well, well, well, Central must have a new policy allowing women to share the responsibility for protecting our way of life. What's your experience?"

"Energy board walking, sir. And now I am orienting to Earth Protection."

Steven felt the blood rush to his face. The last thing he wanted in his squad was an orientee, and a woman at that. She would be a distraction at best, and a liability at worst.

"Who is in charge of this team?"

Steven stepped forward. "I am, sir. I am captain of this team." Couldn't that fool see that his logo was larger than the others? Larger logo meant team leader. What good were symbols if they were ignored? Was he blind as well as incompetent?

"Well, then, Steven, you and your team are going to the other side of the fence."

The local Authority kicked up puffs of gray ashes as he paced back and forth in front of them.

"Into the Human Free Zone." He paused. He seemed to enjoy the theatrics his power afforded him. "Your sole duty will be to capture the traitors."

"How many are out there?" Steven asked, wondering why he had to pose the question in the first place. Surely the Authority should have thought to tell them. What a stupid man.

"Six. Two men, two women, a young boy, and a baby." He hesitated, then added, "We have not determined if they all escaped at the same time or not."

The incompetence on display was beyond belief.

"Sir, if I may?" one of the men asked. "What are we to do if they resist? What results do you expect?" Steven stiffened, hearing that stupid question. He would decide what they would do, he alone, and he would make that decision based on circumstances. Who dared to ask that question? He looked at the group. Guy, one of the new members, fidgeted and looked flushed and nervous. Steven vowed to keep an eye on him.

"Are you not strong enough to overcome them? Have you not been properly trained?" The Authority's voice was louder, demanding. He took a step closer to Guy. "But since you asked, bring them back alive, if possible, so that all true Citizens can witness their punishment. All will know the consequences of disobedience."

He took a step back and looked into the face of each person, one by one, studying them for long seconds. None but Steven returned his stare. "If you have no other options, kill the adults, bring their bodies back, and we will let them rot in full display of all. Their stench will overwhelm the stink of burned wood. But do not kill the children.

"We need the children to be the productive Citizens of tomorrow. Praise be to the Republic!" His voice took on a deep vibrating tone.

"Praise be to the Republic." The six responded in robotic unison, their right hands raised to their foreheads in the mandatory circle sign.

"I will issue you one gun." He slipped a pistol out of his pocket and handed it to Steven. "The gun will be Steven's responsibility. The Gatekeeper will escort you to the Recycle Center; your backpacks are located beside it. Dismissed." He clicked his heels together; another puff of soot rose and coated his black boots with one more layer of the remnants of the Social Update Stage.

CHAPTER EIGHT

After retrieving their backpacks piled outside of the Re-Cy building, they all recited *I pledge allegiance to the Earth and to the sacred rights of the Earth and to the Animals of the Earth*, and made the circle sign. Each member of the squad slipped the straps of the canvas bags onto their shoulders. The Gatekeeper then led them into the Recycle Center, past the large ovens, the buckets, and mops. Two Re-Cy workers kept their heads down, eyes on the filthy gray cement floor, as the group passed by. The room smelled of charred remnants; the buckets full of ashes. The Gatekeeper unlocked the back exit door with a large key hanging from a chain around his neck.

"They got a gun," the Gatekeeper mumbled before he opened the door.

"What? What did you say?" Steven asked.

"Heard that a guard got knocked out and someone took his gun."

"Who did that?" Steven demanded.

"The people who escaped." He looked sideways at Steven. "Didn't they tell you?"

"No, they didn't."

"And they got away. Imagine that. And nobody told you?"

"No." Steven said, his voice cold and hard as steel. Was it purely incompetence on the Enforcer's part to not make him aware that there was a missing gun? Or was it something else?

The heavy metal door creaked open on rusty hinges; the team stepped through and the door slammed shut behind them. The harsh metallic click of the key in the lock signaled the total separation of the team from the Compound on the other side of the fence.

The terrain ahead of them was relatively flat. There were some scrubby trees in the area but the ground directly around the Re-Cy building was barren, blackened. Nothing could grow in the heat that radiated from its walls. Steven headed toward some meager shade; the team followed.

"Check your backpacks. Take inventory."

Obeying his command, they all squatted on the ground and emptied their packs. Each had the same contents: several nourishment cubes, refillable water bottles, a switchblade, a small box of matches, a change of clothing rolled tight and tied with a piece of thin rope, a waterproof hooded jacket, a torch fastened to a headband, and a small bottle of sanitizing solution. There was also a polished wood nightstick with a canvas wrist strap, spray bottles filled with foul-smelling ammonia, and a small ax with an expertly sharpened edge.

Steven's backpack held extra items, such as ammunition and handcuffs. He also had a device the others did not have and weren't aware of: a heat and motion sensor that could be adjusted to detect unusual warmth or motion from fifty yards away. This device was issued only to Earth Protection team leaders and was designed to vibrate when it picked up a heat signature or detected motion anywhere within a fifty-yard radius. A blinking red light was activated when the device was turned on. That light would stop blinking and become a steady red beam when anyone was detected. Turning his back on the rest of the team, Steven slipped the small device into his pants pockets, knowing he would be able to feel any vibration through his clothing.

"Fewer supplies than in the past," Nigel said, as he examined his pack. "I wonder why."

"They have their reasons. It's not for us to question," Adam said. Guy's eyelid twitched, but both he and Winston remained silent.

Julia studied the items carefully. She unrolled the clothing, noting that it was far too large for her. The headband on the torch was also too large; she adjusted it by tying a small knot in the strap, but it still slipped down over her forehead. Frustrated, she pulled it off and tightened it with another knot. The men had already repacked their supplies and watched as she struggled with the torch.

"Here, let me help," said Winston. He started to stand up, but Steven held him back just by raising his hand.

"Let her do it. She has to learn."

Winston frowned but made no further effort to help Julia. Steven's power was limited to commanding the Earth Protectors, but he had a reputation of never hesitating to use that power to its fullest extent when necessary—a reputation solidified over many successful missions capturing those who had slipped away.

Steven remembered the early days of the missions. Nourishment was provided to the teams; the shadow people who had slipped away had to forage and were weak. Extra clothing was provided for the teams; the shadow people eventually had nothing but rags on their thin bodies. Guns were provided to the teams; the shadow people had nothing but rocks and sticks for protection.

When the Authorities were convinced that no shadow people still survived, the teams had been recalled and disbanded. Members were returned to their original Compounds and examined by Enforcers. Those who seemed fit were assigned tasks. Those who had physical injuries or stress disorders received no treatment and were never seen again. Why waste valuable resources on less-than-valuable Citizens?

A small boot camp of a few young trainees was established as a precautionary reserve. Winston and Guy had been in that boot camp.

Julia finally got her headband adjusted. She had the same items as the men; there was nothing in her pack that was specifically made for a woman. Though the Authorities had drafted her, they clearly had made no special accommodations for her. They made no special accommodations for anyone but themselves.

"Are you ready?" Steven stood, casting a shadow over her. She rapidly repacked her items and slung the sack over her shoulders. The straps were too narrow for how heavy it was and they dug into her skin.

He watched her without comment, then told her to put the pack on the ground and empty it again. She looked puzzled, but quickly obeyed.

"Now, show me each item one by one and explain its use."

"Change of clothing." She held up the rolled bundle. "Knife." She started to put it in the pack.

"Open and close it."

She fumbled with the button on the side, her long fingers shaking. Finally, it snapped open; she closed it.

"Again. Faster."

She pushed the button with more assurance, and opened and closed the knife.

She had to demonstrate wrapping the strap of the nightstick on her wrist, how to swing the ax, open and close the water bottle, and squeeze a tiny drop of the sanitizing solution into her palm. Nigel smirked when she appeared unsure of herself. Adam, paying no attention to this exercise, pulled out his own knife and used the tip of the blade to carefully clean under his fingernails. Guy put his hand over his eyelid to quiet the tic. Winston watched, frowning, his fists clenched.

Julia stared at the spray bottle in her hand. It was the last item to be repacked.

"What is it? How do you use it?" Steven asked.

Julia was silent.

"Well?" Steven walked in a circle around her. "Since you obviously don't know, I'll tell you. It's ammonia spray. Use it if you are being attacked by anything. Animal, human, anything. Spray it directly into their eyes."

"Even animals, sir?" she asked.

"Yes, even animals."

Steven knew from past experience that the Authorities would label leaders who lost team members on a mission as inadequate. Steven knew he was more important than animals and more competent than the Authorities who gave him orders. After all, his team had captured more shadow people than any other. And now he was being called back into action with a female orientee. It wasn't right. Just looking at her, he knew she didn't have the physical capability to be a warrior. He certainly wasn't about to lower his standards just because she was a woman.

"All right. Everyone ready?" They stood, backpacks on, waiting for instructions.

"Here's the plan. They're three days ahead of us, so we have to travel quickly. They'll head for water. That's what they always do. Once they find water, they never leave it. We'll check for tracks and follow them. By now they'll be tired and their shoes will be falling apart. We should close on them in no time."

They walked single file, Steven leading, Julia last, Winston in front of her, glancing frequently over his shoulder, making sure she was able to keep up. In single file, the five men and one woman walked deeper into the Human Free Zone until they came to the stream.

At the bottom of the hill, Steven walked a little way downstream, then reversed and walked upstream. When he stopped, the team stopped behind him, still in single file.

"What's he doing?" Julia whispered to Winston.

He turned his head and talked over his shoulder. "Looking for clues. Tracks. To see which way they went."

"Oh. I would think anybody running away would head downstream. Follow a stream; it will turn into a river. Just makes sense."

Steven turned and glared at Julia.

Winston whispered to her, "Don't talk anymore. I don't think he likes his team talking."

They stood in silence until Steven finally called out: "This way." He had spotted a piece of paper in the grass and some broken twigs on trees. He began to walk and his team followed, tracking people they didn't know, people who had several days' lead on them, people they were determined to destroy. A confident smile formed on Steven's lips as the group began their long march upstream.

CHAPTER NINE

EMMELINE

Days 2–4

We had more days of hiding, crouching behind shrubs, rocks, and trees. More days of putting fresh moss on David's arm and in Elsa's diaper. But she was irritable and crying frequently, a shrill sound that threatened our security. Micah was adjusting well to sleeping by day and walking at night, and David and I were used to working the dusk-to-dawn shift in the Compound anyway, so it wasn't a problem for us.

The real problem was our cheap, thin-soled shoes issued by the Authorities. Who knew shoes could be so important? The Authorities knew. Their shoes were sturdy, made to last. Citizens were issued flimsy shoes that wore out quickly and were only replaced after a long waiting period. Citizens had no power. You could tell who was important in the Republic just by looking at their feet.

We were about to embark on the fourth night of walking on thin soles. Before escaping, I had taken our shoes for granted. I thought other things were more necessary to bring along, but I quickly realized they weren't. I thought diapers were a priority, but I'd given up on diapers for Elsa and instead just dressed her in a little sleeping gown. Even when I rinsed the cloths in the stream, they never dried. I kept the diapers we hadn't used in case we needed fabric for something. Bandages, maybe—I still worried about David's arm.

Now we faced another night of using the blanket of darkness to put more distance between us and our pursuers. I knew they were out there, somewhere. Getting ever closer. Walking much faster than us with their sturdy shoes and well-nourished bellies.

They were the hunters. We were the hunted.

The stream meandered across the terrain as though it couldn't decide which way to head. The ground along the edge was relatively flat; banks of earth rose up on each side. David and I took turns carrying our bundle and Elsa. Both got heavier and heavier as the night wore on. David pulled moss off rocks and we chewed on that. *Lichen*, he called it. Seems many green things in this world are edible. I trusted David to know what was safe and what wasn't. But no matter how much moss we ate, we were still starving. Hunger gnawed at our bellies. Hunger filled our thoughts, made our mouths water.

As the night wore on, our pace got slower, our steps shorter. I shifted Elsa from one arm to another and held her at arm's length when she peed. It splashed at my feet and made my arm wet when I tucked her back against me. Memories of the washing-up area in the Compound flashed through my mind but I pushed them away. What good was a washing-up area if you couldn't even raise your own child? What good was a nourishment cube if you couldn't move from one place to another without being tracked? What good was anything without freedom?

Still, hunger was a worrisome thing, always lurking in our thoughts.

I was startled out of my thoughts by the sound of Micah crying. Small sobs poured from him.

"Stop," I whispered to David up ahead. He turned and walked back to us. Micah had sat down; his face was buried in his hands and his shoulders slumped. How small, how sad and helpless he looked. I reached out to him, stroked the back of his neck.

"What's wrong?" I asked.

"Nothing."

"But you're crying."

"No, I'm not. We're not allowed to cry. It's a rule." He started to make the Pledge to the Earth sign, his forefinger and thumb held against his forehead in a circle, but I took his hand and held it firmly in mine.

"I say you can break the rules. And it's okay to cry. But you must tell me why." Elsa, wide awake and sitting on my knee, reached a little pink hand toward Micah as if she knew something was wrong and wanted to help.

Micah looked up at me with his dirty tear-streaked face, his spiky hair now flat against his head. "I'm sorry," he said.

"Sorry for what?" David was standing over us, looking down, anxious to move on.

"I broke my shoes. I didn't mean to." He started to cry again. "And now you will have to send me back."

"We would never send you back! You're part of us now," I told him.

He stared at me unblinkingly, his lower lip quivering. "Promise?"

"I promise. And you can call us Mommy and Daddy now. That's what kids call the man and woman who take care of them."

"I know that. Kids at the village told me. Kids know more than the Caretakers think." He wiped his nose with the back of his hand. Back at the Village, the night we escaped, he said the other children were whispering about the relocation, wondering if it was true. Yes, the children knew more than the adults realized.

"Good. I'm glad you know what a Mommy and Daddy are."

"I can really call you Mommy and Daddy?" He asked, between sobs.

"Yes, really."

David bent and slipped the shoes from Micah's feet. Both of them had holes worn through at the heels and near the big toes; holes big enough for David to put his fingers through. In the dim light of the moon, I looked at the bottom of Micah's feet. The skin was red and raw.

"My feet hurt when I walk. I can't do it." He was almost wailing now.

David led us to the edge of the stream and told us to sit. "Put your feet in the water," he said. "Rest awhile."

I slipped off my shoes; they were almost worn through, too. Slowly Micah and I dipped our feet, toes first, ever so slowly, into the cold dark water. How good it felt once we got used to the cold! Flowing over our feet and ankles, the moving water seemingly transferred its energy to us. I held Elsa in front of me and let her soft pink feet touch the water. She pulled her knees up at first, then straightened her legs so her feet, too, were in the water. Those tender pink feet, not yet callused from constant walking and working.

David was busy gathering something from beside the water. Micah kicked his feet; the water splashed me. He laughed when I looked surprised. He was having fun, as a child should. As every child should. Then I splashed him and we both laughed. I put my arm around his shoulders, his small warm body close to me. I truly felt like his mother at that moment.

David was back with us, carrying some green things. "Cattail leaves," he said. "And moss. We'll line our shoes with these. It will help for a while."

It did, and, following the stream, heading toward the shadows of the unknown, we walked on.

CHAPTER TEN

EARTH PROTECTION AGENTS

Day 3

Steven kept the team walking past dusk, until total darkness settled around them, heavy as wool blankets, making them stumble over rocks and broken branches, slowing them down. He switched on his torch long enough to find a flat area with trees a few feet from the stream. One of the trees had a faded yellow notice nailed to it: *Private Property No Trespassing*. Steven ripped it off and tossed it to the ground. There was no such thing as private property anymore. The Republic owned everything. The Citizens owned nothing.

"Here," he said to the group, shining his torch on them. "This is where we bivouac." Their tired faces angered him. He didn't feel tired; why should they? He felt energized, as eager to find his prey as a hungry wild animal. "We'll keep sentry in groups of two. Nigel and Winston, take the first shift. Adam and Guy, second shift. Julia and me, last shift. When you feel you can't stay awake any longer, wake the next team. You cannot leave your post while on duty. If you have to relieve yourself after your shift, go as a team. Go only when the next team is awake and on guard." He deliberately paired seasoned members with new members, the experienced with the novice, and the strong with the weak. "Sleep facing away from each other. Sleep lightly, wake easily. Any questions?" He spat his words with a razor-sharp tone that did not invite any.

Nigel and Adam took their positions at the edge of the area, back to back, one looking upstream, the other downstream. The dark moving water was louder than the sounds of their breathing.

Winston and Guy sat propped against tree trunks, arms across their chests, hands under their arms for warmth. The night air was cool and smelled of musty wet leaves.

Julia stretched out on the ground.

"Get up," Steven commanded. "Sit like they do, against a tree." He pointed to Winston and Guy. "Their backs are protected. They're less exposed, less of a target. Got it?"

"Got it."

"Got it, what?"

"Got it, *sir.*"

She pulled her backpack close and leaned against a broad tree trunk. Steven leaned against the same tree, on the other side. He could smell her hair, the clean smell of sanitizing solution. It was a sweet, lemony, yellow smell. He took a deep breath, closed his eyes, and waited for sleep. It took a long time. The lemon smell kept him awake. It was a distraction. Steven hated distractions.

He reviewed the assignment he had been given. *Unbelievable,* he thought. A total of six people. Two men, two women, a boy and a baby. And nobody knew if they escaped all together or in separate groups. They might even have a gun. Fools. The Authorities must be angry, losing control of those children, those workers. The Authorities were the ones who should be punished, for allowing this to happen. He closed his eyes, trying to decide who was more likely to have a gun. Odds were in favor of it being one of the men. But still, he'd have to be cautious approaching anyone they encountered.

Julia's breathing had become slow and regular. It had a gentleness that made his face feel warm, his mouth dry. He tried to picture what she looked like, softly asleep and vulnerable. The rustle of leaves nearby startled him. An animal, pale white in the moonlight, passed by his outstretched legs, dragging its long scaly tail behind it. When he bent his knees and pulled his feet close to his body, the animal rolled over, motionless. Damn possum, one of the ugliest animals on earth. He'd sit motionless and listen to Julia breathe. Focus, he told himself. *Focus.*

Should he tell his team about the missing gun? No, why should he? The Authorities hadn't told him; only the lowly guard at Re-Cy had. Information was power, and withholding it was the same as withholding power. If they could do it, so could he.

Finally, the possum slunk away, dragging its prehensile tail through the leaves.

He heard Winston and Nigel waking Adam and Guy. He watched as their dark shadows walked past him, then back, settling against trees nearby. He wished they weren't so close. He wanted to be alone with Julia.

Finally, he dozed off into a light sleep. Light enough that he was still aware of the sounds around him, muffled noises that floated into his mind, his dreams. Winston coughing. Damn! That cough could be heard at a distance. He opened his eyes, giving up on the idea of sleeping for the moment. He heard Julia shifting her position, the sound of her legs moving on the ground.

The night dragged on and on, cloudy, with the stars blurred and indistinct. The moon slowly slid across the sky, slipped behind branches of the trees, then reappeared in open spaces.

Adam touched his shoulder. He must've slept more than he thought as it was already time to switch guards. Steven stood, his feet numb from sitting so long. Julia was awake quickly, pulling on her beret, picking up her backpack.

"Stay on guard," he said to Adam. Turning to Julia, he commanded, "We're going to relieve ourselves. In the woods. Come with me."

She hesitated, then followed him. She stood with her back to him until he was finished.

"Now you," he said.

"Turn your back," she said.

"Turn your back, what?"

"Turn your back, sir."

"That's better," he said as he slowly turned. "Remember that in the future."

* * *

They took their positions, back-to-back, one looking upstream, the other looking downstream. A bat swirled over their heads, then flew in circles over the stream. Another bat appeared, followed by another. Soon there was a black cloud of them, screeching, and hunting for food.

Steven shifted his weight and felt Julia's slim back against his, warm and firm. She leaned forward, moving away from him. But again, he shifted his weight against her back. "We're a team. We need to lean on each other for support."

"Yes, sir."

A few minutes passed. Steven slid his hand back, laying it on her leg. She didn't move. He began to rub his hand up and down her leg. Moving slowly, she reached into her backpack, groping past the items, until she found what she needed. Pulling the item out of her pack, she aimed it above and away from them and squeezed the nozzle several times, shooting large volumes of the mixture in the air.

The ammonia.

The smell was acrid. The bats flew away.

She pointed the bottle at Steven.

"You wouldn't dare," Steven said.

"Yes, I would. *Sir.*"

He took his hand off of her leg.

He would be patient, for now. But not forever.

CHAPTER ELEVEN

EMMELINE

Day 4

I thought as I walked. How many days and nights of this could we endure? Three nights of walking so far, but it felt like ten times that. We were so hungry. David said we could go ten days with absolutely no food, but that didn't mean much to my growling belly. I ate the bugs we caught: grasshoppers, beetles, and caterpillars, because I had no other choice. David told me the names of the bugs and I quickly learned where to find them. They lived under rocks, in deep grass, and on leaves. I became a hunter and a woman determined to feed her children. The insects crunched when I bit down and exploded into wet masses in my mouth. I forced myself to swallow even though nausea always passed over me in relentless waves.

Micah didn't complain, but he also didn't smile anymore. David's arm was more swollen and red than before; he cradled it in his other arm, so I carried Elsa and Micah carried our supplies. Our progress was slow. Our thin-soled shoes were padded every day with fresh moss and cattails, but they barely protected our swollen feet.

We occasionally found other small things to eat besides bugs. Some berries, if we were lucky, and a few hard apples that made our mouths pucker. We even ate the bitter leaves of cattails. I chewed whatever we found into a pulpy mass and fed it to Elsa with my fingertips. It was hard to find food in the dark, but at least we had the stream. It was larger now, wider and deeper. David said it would soon be a river. Whatever it was, we always had plenty of water, and I was thankful for that.

Today may be better. That's what David and I whispered to each other. That's what we said to Micah. He nodded, but still he didn't smile. We didn't smile, either. We just walked in the dark, placing one foot in front of the other, every sharp stone on the soles of our feet a painful reminder of what we were doing.

The harsh clanging of the bell for half hour till dawn rang out. My heart jumped. Confused, I looked around, but it was too dark to see more than a few feet in front of me. David looked frightened. Micah's face was twisted, ready to cry. We all stopped, frozen like statues mid-stride. Where had that bell sound come from? We had been walking away from the Compound for four nights. Had we become disoriented and walked in a circle? My mind swirled as panic overtook me.

David crouched down, and slowly moved forward toward a cluster of low shrubs. It wasn't a very secure place to hide, but it was all that was nearby. Micah imitated him, and crouching, he made himself small. I did the same, holding Elsa low, like an anchor. Behind the shrubs, we huddled close to each other, but we were still exposed. I smelled our odor, unwashed and sour.

The sun rose slowly as we waited, a golden globe that both warmed and exposed us. It was round and yellow as an egg yolk. We heard distant voices, male voices, giving what sounded like commands. David stretched his head above the shrubs, scanned the area, then fixed his gaze across the stream. He slid back down, his face near my ear.

"The farm commune," he whispered. "There, on the other side of the stream."

I raised myself up a little and allowed myself to breathe for the first time in what seemed like an eternity. There was a large flat area, and an expanse of brown earth with rows of plants. I saw a long straight line of tents with people coming out of them, stretching, bending, like they were performing some kind of morning ritual, their movements in unison. Men with guns on their shoulders watched the routine, then one of them blew a whistle. The people moved forward, their backs to us, and took their places at the ends of each row. The guards along the edge of the field moved forward alongside them.

The workers picked up baskets and began bending and picking things off the crops. They put what they picked into the baskets, dragging them as they moved forward. They worked slowly, no one any faster than any other except for one man, who was bigger than the rest. There was something vaguely familiar about him, though I couldn't see his face. Often he pulled ahead, but the pickers on either side of him made hand motions to slow him down, to make him pick at their rate.

David whispered, "The farm commune isn't that far from the Compound. Even though we've been walking for three nights, our path has been along the stream and it meanders. And we can't cover much distance in the dark. I don't think we're all that far from where we started."

My heart sank. All that painful walking! My bones shouted out to me as though angry at what I'd put them through.

David leaned close to my ear and whispered. "They're picking the food used to make the nourishment cubes."

Food! My mouth watered.

David pulled some clumps of grass and did his best to shake the dirt off them. He handed it to Micah and Micah chewed it eagerly, bits of green sticking to his teeth. David gave some to me; I chewed and swallowed, then chewed some more until it was pulpy and put it on the end of my finger. Elsa, still asleep, sucked my finger. Green drool ran down her chin.

David whispered again. "Quick, while their backs are to us—" He motioned with his head toward some bigger, thicker shrubs a short distance away. We scurried toward them quickly, like I've seen animals scurry through the woods.

We sat there, behind the shrubs, watching the farmworkers. At the far side of the field was a bus-box, filled one basket at a time by workers who'd reached the end of their row. Six men in the orange uniforms of the Transport Team stood in their harnesses, standing straight and stiff, just as Father had when he was on the Transport Team back in our Compound.

When the bus-box was full, they strained forward, their harness straps tight against their chests and shoulders, and moved the bus-box forward with a little puff of dust. I guessed they were taking the produce to the Nourishment Center, where it would be dehydrated and condensed into nourishment cubes. I remembered the brown taste of those cubes, gritty against my tongue. I hated them at the time but what I wouldn't give for one now. Another bus-box pulled up, waiting to be filled.

"The train. Do you see it?" David asked me.

I squinted and saw a row of old rusty train sections, connected, but motionless and useless. Faded letters on the sides of the cars read *P & LE RR*. Beneath the train were parallel tracks that had become overrun with small trees that had sprouted up in front of and behind the train. It was trapped by neglect.

"I see it."

"They used to transport the food, people, and lots of other things by train a long while ago. Then they switched to bus-boxes because trains need energy and that energy has to be drilled or dug out of the Earth. The Earth had to be protected," David whispered to Micah.

Clearly, the train and its tracks had been mismanaged by the Authorities and their policies. It was as useless as the bus-box with the broken wheel in our Compound that had never been fixed.

The bell rang and the workers stopped picking, stood, and repeated the ritual of bending, stretching, and moving their arms in circles, until the whistle blew again. On that signal, they bent and began picking. When they reached the end of their rows, they marched single file to new rows and resumed picking, heading back in our direction. We kept our heads down and stayed below the top of the shrubs.

Confined to a small area, we found no bugs to eat that morning. By noon, we'd consumed most of the grass around us, but we were still hungry and too close to being detected to sleep. David stroked Micah's thin back. How much weight had the child lost? David's face was gaunt, his cheeks sunken, and my hip bones felt sharp. Even though I had eaten little, I was almost always nauseous.

Yet, on the other side of the stream on that flat piece of land, food was growing. Food that would be dried, condensed, and molded into nourishment cubes. *Control the food, control the people.* I heard Mother's voice in my head.

David rummaged through our little bag of treasures that Mother had saved and pulled out *The Little Prince.* Micah leaned against him and pointed to the picture of a boy on the cover of the book. "How old is he?" Micah asked.

"Six years old," David answered.

"I'm eight years old. I'm older than him."

"Yes, you're quite a big boy," David said. He opened the book.

"What's that ugly thing?" Micah said, pointing to a picture on the first page.

"A boa constrictor," David said, his voice patient.

"What's a boa constrictor?"

"It's a big snake."

"Are there any here?" Micah looked around at the packed earth.

"No boa constrictors here. They live in the rain forests."

"What's a rain forest?"

"It's a place with lots of rain and lots of trees."

"Are there Compounds there?"

"Yes. The whole world has Compounds." David turned the page of the book. "Let's not talk about Compounds right now. Let's read."

I smiled watching them. Micah was so eager to learn. David was always patient, even when he didn't feel well. I remembered trying to ask Mother questions so I could learn. That was back in the Compounds, where everything, even questions and answers, were so tightly controlled. I remembered the first time I had seen Micah in the Children's Village classroom, standing with the other children reciting *I pledge allegiance to the Earth.* They were all so solemn, with their thumbs and forefingers making the circle sign on their foreheads. All except Micah. He was grinning and making the circle sign on his nose until the Caretaker sternly rebuked him. His grin had faded quickly.

I sat, holding Elsa, listening to David and Micah whispering, and almost felt safe. Safe enough to open our bundle and look at the other things Mother had saved. I held the recipe cards one by one to my nose, trying to catch the scent of pumpkin pie or vegetable soup. David had told me his memories of Thanksgiving before the relocations: eating a big meal with family and giving thanks for the good things in their lives. He said pumpkin pie smelled like Thanksgiving. If the recipe cards ever held any scents, they had faded long ago. Would I ever be able to give thanks like they did in the before-time? If I did, what would I be most thankful for?

Dear, sweet Jesus, I'd be thankful for freedom. Mother used to say "Dear sweet Jesus" when she was upset or afraid. I still didn't know what those words meant, but they seemed to fit.

The picture Mother had tucked into *The Little Prince,* the one I had drawn of the Little Prince looking up at a star, fell out of the book. Micah picked it up, holding it carefully by its edge.

"She drew that," David whispered, motioning to me.

"You did?" Micah asked, eyes wide.

I nodded.

"Can you teach me? Please?"

I smiled and stroked his cheek. "Yes. Someday." I tried to sound confident, but I wondered if that someday would ever really come. That truly would be something to be thankful for. Something as simple as a pencil and clean, blank sheet of paper to be filled with a child's imagination would be a blessing. I would let Micah draw whatever he wanted. No rules. *Draw what you want to draw.* That's what I would say to him. Every child could be an artist. Every child *is* an artist until a grown-up tells them they're not.

David read on.

I put the recipe cards back, pulled out the New Testament, and turned the fragile pages. Why had Mother saved this? *Save what you think you are going to lose.* I slid it carefully back into our bundle. Someday, when the running and hiding was over, I would read this. Someday.

We should have been sleeping but instead we sat huddled behind the shrubs, afraid to make any moves or noises.

I peeked over the leaves again. The workers had reached the end of another row. A guard blew a whistle and they did the bending and stretching again, then marched single file toward new rows. They now had their backs toward us again, and were farther away from the tight, straight line of tents that must have been their lodgings. The sun was high overhead. We were all sweating, David more than any of us. Maybe . . . A thought came to me.

I knew what I had to do. We needed food and clothes. We couldn't survive much longer without them. The tents would house supplies we could use. Maybe some morsel of food would be left on plants near the tents.

I whispered to David. I would run, cross the stream, sneak into a few tents, grab whatever I could. The guards were made complacent by their guns and never looked around. They simply moved forward with the workers. They did not worry like we did about what could be shifting in the shadows.

David gripped my arm and shook his head no. "Too dangerous," he said. His lips were thin, tight lines of disapproval.

I pulled my arm away. Was he not as hungry as I was? Couldn't he see the children's discomfort? Nothing could stop me; my mind was made up. I shook my head, then bent low in front of the shrubs and ran into the water, fighting the current, slipping, stumbling, but never stopping.

I heard splashing sounds behind me and turned. Micah was crossing the stream with me, his face determined, though the water reached his chest.

I stopped and waited for him to catch up. "Go back," I told him. "It's too dangerous."

"I can run fast," he said. "And two of us can get more than just you by yourself." His jaw was set firmly, the sprinkle of freckles across his nose darker than usual against his pale face. He was right. Going back was not an option for either of us.

I grabbed his hand tightly. Together we moved forward through the water.

The stream had widened greatly since the beginning of our journey. David told me it was now a river, shallow right now, but it would get deeper. The banks on each side had gotten higher and steeper the farther we traveled. The water was faster, too. It churned with a constant low roar, like an animal stalking its prey. The current was powerful, trying to push us sideways. Each step forward was a struggle, and my leg muscles ached and burned in spite of the cold water.

Finally on the other side, we rested. I heard myself breathe, great gasps, sucking in as much air as possible each time. Micah was breathing hard too, his little shoulders pulling up with each inhale; his lips pursed with each exhale.

From here, we could see the patch of shrubbery where I knew David and Elsa were hiding. Good, we couldn't see them; they were well concealed.

We had to search quickly for whatever we could find.

Drenched and shivering, Micah and I slowly pushed ourselves up onto our hands and knees, then crawled up the steep bank until we could see over the edge. I had mud under my fingernails. One thumbnail was broken off, the edge ragged. Blood spotted my cuticle.

The workers were not quite halfway to the end of their long rows; their backs still toward us. The tents were about ten yards from the edge of the bank. I nodded at Micah and he nodded in return. We were ready, both of us. Scampering, I ran behind one tent, he to the one next to it. The fabric was heavy, pegged into the ground at the corners. I tried lifting the edge but it wouldn't budge. Micah pulled on one his tent pegs, then pushed it back and forth, his thin arms straining. The peg made a squeaking sound as he worked it loose. He pulled it out of the ground; the muddy tip of it had been whittled into a sharp point. He lifted the edge of the tent and slipped inside. I managed to loosen a peg just as he had, my hands gripping the wood until my knuckles were white. I almost fell backward when it suddenly came out of the ground. I quickly slipped into the tent.

Inside, it was dark and smelled of dirt and sweat. I could make out a sleeping mat, and under it, a rubber mat to keep the dampness from seeping through. There was a basin full of cold water and, beside it, a bottle of sanitizing solution. Folded in the corner was an extra uniform and sleeping clothes.

I dumped the cold water out of the basin and loaded the clothes and sanitizing solution into it. I shoved the basin out of the tent and looked around. What else? What else could I take? The rubber mat! Surely that could be useful. I pushed the sleeping mat aside and rolled up the stretch of rubber. Finally, I threw the sharp wooden peg into the basin. When you have nothing, everything becomes a necessity.

I slipped back out with the rubber mat under my arm. Outside the other tent, Micah had piled a rolled-up blanket and another bottle of sanitizing solution. I crawled over to his tent and looked inside. He wasn't there. Where was he?

Frantic, I whispered his name, "Micah." No answer. I whispered again, a little louder. No answer. From between the tents, I could see the workers, backs still toward us, moving closer to the ends of their rows, closer to the bus-box. Soon they would turn and be facing us.

I slipped between the tents, and crawled toward the field. Micah was there, at the edge of a row of plants, picking something and quickly, ravenously, putting it in his mouth, his little jaw moving as fast as his fingers could pick. Even when I whispered his name a little louder, he didn't look up, didn't respond. Putting food in his mouth was all he cared about.

On my hands and knees, I moved close enough to touch his arm. He jumped, startled and looked around, dazed, as though he couldn't figure out where he was and what he was doing. Then he relaxed, smiled at me, and handed me something. It was about three inches long, narrow, and dark green, with bits of dirt on it. He motioned for me to put it in my mouth.

I bit down on it and it crunched, the taste exploding in my mouth. It was so good. I didn't mind the dirt. Even *that* tasted good. My throat was dry as I swallowed. I could see lots more of the same thing on the green vines around us, food the workers had missed.

I could see that the workers were just a little distance from the end of the rows where they would turn and face us. As quickly as I could, I pulled more and more of the green things from the plants and shoved them in the pockets of my uniform. Micah, seeing what I was doing, started stuffing his pockets, too. We would bring food to David and Elsa. My heart was beating hard, and fast, and my hands were shaking. Food. Oh, dear sweet Jesus, food.

Then the whistle blew and the workers straightened up. The routine of bending, stretching, moving their arms in circles began and ended. We had just a little time before they would turn and head in our direction.

Their picking resumed. I motioned to Micah; we needed to leave, go back across the river. As we scuttled backward toward the tents with our loot, I saw a female worker fall to the ground with a heavy thud and lie motionless. Her headscarf lay in the dirt beside her. Had she fainted? Died? I stared in horror, unable to blink.

A guard walked over to her and shook her roughly. She did not respond, but stayed motionless, facedown on the ground, her arms outstretched. The guard kicked the woman and shouted at her, but still she did not respond. The others appeared not to notice anything, but picked with their heads down, except for one of them, the bigger man I had noticed before. He took an awkward step over a row of plants, toward the woman on the ground. His one leg appeared to be dragging. A nearby guard pointed his gun at him and the big man retreated back to his place in his assigned row.

How could the rest of them ignore this? How could they just keep their heads down as if nothing was happening? They just kept bending and picking, bending and picking, like machines.

Two guards grabbed the woman by her arms and dragged her, limp and lifeless, to the bus-box. The Transport Team, six men in harnesses like horses, stood silent, staring straight ahead. With great effort, the guards threw her body into the bus-box, where it lay on top of the pile of food that had been picked.

Micah was watching, his eyes wide. "Can we help her?" he whispered. I put my hands over his eyes. A child should never have to see this kind of inhumanity. No one should.

I felt the need to run to her but knew we were helpless to do anything. There were guards with guns. A few guards with guns controlled the many without. Tears burned hot behind my eyelids and I fought the nausea gripping me.

"Not today, Micah," I whispered back.

As we struggled back to David and Elsa, our arms and pockets full of stolen treasures, I hoped that someday, somehow, I would be able to offer help to anyone who needed it. But today, I could help only those closest to my heart: David, Elsa, and Micah. For now, they were my entire world.

CHAPTER TWELVE

Holding our precious contraband tightly, Micah and I slid down the bank and began sloshing through the water. Our arms were too full; I couldn't hold his hand. The current was stiff, pushing us sideways against the large rocks that jutted out of the water. The rush of water was like an angry, constant roar. I feared Micah would slip and fall; to save him I'd have to drop everything into the cold water, but I *would* save him. I couldn't help hearing Mother's voice in my head: *You save what you think you're going to lose.* I couldn't lose this boy. He had faith in me.

One of the green things in my pocket floated out and tumbled end over end in the current. Something, a fish maybe, splashed through the surface and the green thing disappeared. We were more than halfway across. The water was becoming shallower and we could move a little more quickly.

Finally, we were out, at the top of the bank, back behind the shrubs. Elsa was lying on her back in the grass and rolled onto her side when she saw me. She pushed with her arms and sat up. Dropping what I carried, I scooped her up and held her tight. She gave a little coo, then squirmed to be put back down. David was flushed red, sweating and holding his arm.

"I tried watching as much as I could over the top of the shrub but after a while I had to lie down. Did anyone see you?" he asked.

"No, nobody saw us. But we can't stay here," I said. "They're soon going to know someone took their supplies."

Micah pulled a green thing out of his pocket and held it out to David with a proud little smile.

David raised his eyebrows. "A pea!" he said, stuffing it quickly into his mouth.

I spread out everything we had for David to look at and we emptied our pockets of the peas, making a little heap of them. David winced every time he had to stop cradling his arm to reach for a pea. I looked at what we had taken from the tents. I needed to make some sort of harness for him.

The rubber mat! Maybe I could make something out of that. I felt around in our bundle and pulled out the knife. How much of the mat would I need? I held it up against his forearm; the width was perfect. I cut through the mat, slicing off a wide piece. *Thank you, Mother, for this knife.* David watched, puzzled. Now, how could I fasten it? I needed straps of some sort. I had to work quickly so we could leave this area as soon as possible. David might be able to walk faster if his arm was supported.

"We saw a worker fall down and get kicked," Micah whispered to David. "She didn't move."

David looked at me and I nodded.

"That's why we have to get away," I said as I punched holes into the rubber. Grabbing a diaper, I ripped it into thin strips and threaded it through the holes. David now understood what I was doing and he helped me place his arm into the contraption. I tied the ends of the diaper behind his neck. He sighed with relief when I was done. "That feels better." He touched my cheek with his hand. It was hot on my skin.

"We have to get out of here soon."

"But it's daylight," David said.

"I know that. But you didn't see what we saw. We have to move on fast."

"We're safer moving at night. We should stay here till it's dark."

Micah picked up the leftover part of the rubber mat and ran his hand along it, studying it intently.

"I'm telling you, David, we have to get away from here. They're going to see things are missing from their tents."

"They won't be back in them till dusk. We can wait till then."

"We're not waiting till dusk. You didn't see the workers ignoring one of their own when she fell down. Nobody helped her get up. The guards kicked her. Kicked her! The workers didn't even look up when she was carried away and tossed lifeless into the bus-box. Nobody is going to help us here. If they treated her like that, imagine what they would do to us."

"But my shoes," Micah said. "Can you fix them?" He pointed to the rubber mat. "That would be better than the moss and stuff. I can walk faster if you fix them with that." He pulled the pulpy mass of cattails and moss out of his shoes.

I nodded. "We'll fix your shoes. Then we move on."

I quickly traced the outline of his shoes on the rubber mat with the knife, cut through the outline, and slipped the pieces into his shoes, completely covering the worn-out holes. He put them on and smiled. He reached up and touched my cheek, just as David had done. He was learning from us. We were his protectors, his teachers. He was our future.

There was enough rubber left to repair my shoes and David's as well. What good luck that we had found that mat, and how smart of Micah to think of using it for our shoes. A warm feeling of pride and gratitude washed over me. I smiled at him and he flashed his crooked little grin back at me.

We tied everything up in our first bundle and made a second one, using the blanket Micah had taken. The workers were picking at some distance away from us. We'd travel until they turned back in our direction. Then we'd hide again, in whatever shadows we could find. Crouching, we started moving downstream, following the water as it flowed rapidly, in choppy little waves with whitecaps leaping and twisting.

The terrain was becoming rockier. Big boulders stuck out of the hillside. Some had cracks where trees had managed to grow, their roots splitting the rocks. I couldn't imagine how strong a tree needed to be to grow out of a rock and split it. Outside the Compound nature was a wonderful but curious thing. So far, the only animals we had seen were small: rabbits, squirrels, and a red fox that yipped as it ran. There were fish in the water, but we had no way to catch or cook them. Still, I was hungry enough to eat anything we caught raw. The peas were not enough. I rummaged in my pocket hoping that maybe there was one left, but it was as empty as my stomach.

The sun was low in the sky now. We had walked all last night and hadn't slept during the day because we had come so dangerously close to the farm commune. I could see that David and Micah were exhausted. I was, too, but fear and determination overruled fatigue. I urged them to keep moving.

Off to my right I saw something shining white in the distance. Even though it was far away, I could tell it was big. "Look," I said, pointing. "What it that?"

David squinted. "I have no idea."

"Let's check it out. Maybe we'll find something we can use. Maybe it's a place we can hide."

"Or maybe we'll find something that puts us in danger." David said.

"We're checking it out. Come on."

"Emmy, I can't. I'm too tired." His face was pale, but he had dark circles under his eyes.

I had to find out what that was. I just had to. Some instinct was driving me, and making me push my limits. Whatever that something was, it could not be ignored or denied. I knew one thing: I was not going to walk away without exploring that place. Of that I was certain. But just because I was determined to push myself, didn't mean I had the right to push David. He was sick and I had already insisted he stay awake for almost twenty-four hours. I had to somehow balance curiosity with compassion. And most important, while he was weak, I had to grow stronger. Surprisingly, I knew I could do that. I already had.

"All right. Stay here with the children. I'll go investigate while you rest."

"I'll go with her," Micah said. "I'll help her."

"No, Micah. Stay here with Daddy. He doesn't feel good and you can help by watching Elsa."

Without any further discussion, I climbed up the bank and, moving from tree to tree, slowly closed the distance to the object I'd seen. The sun was already noticeably lower in the sky.

As I got closer, I saw that the object was a huge house of shiny, smooth stone surrounded by a high fence made of tightly spaced metal spikes. Who could possibly need a house that big, surrounded by such a foreboding fence? And why was this area so flat? Except for the farm commune, we had seen only rolling hills covered with spiky weeds, shrubs, and rocks. But this place had a large level expanse covered with short grass.

The trees gave me cover. I got as close as I could until the trees ended. I crouched behind the last one and peered around it.

There was a massive front door with round white pillars on either side. The building didn't have narrow window slits like the Living Spaces back in the Compound. Instead, the windows were large and covered with something that sparkled and glistened in the sunlight. A crew of workers was busy washing them. Children ran on the lawn inside the fence and chased each other around a pond filled with large white birds with curved necks swimming lazily about. In the middle of the pond was a statue of some sort spraying arcs of water into the air. Rainbows formed in the sunlight.

These children were not corralled in any Children's Village. They weren't forced to practice walking on energy boards to teach them how to produce energy for the Authorities. They ran freely under the watchful eyes of Chaperones in crisp white uniforms. A man in an Authority uniform sat on a bench. The gold trim of his jacket gleamed. A woman sat next to him. They raised glasses full of red liquid to each other, and then each took a small sip.

Colorful plants blossomed all along the front of the house. Pink, purple, yellow, and red mounds of flowers contrasted sharply against the whiteness of the building. A worker was picking some of them and putting them into a container of sorts. Citizens weren't allowed to pick flowers. Why was this person able to? I waited for the Authority to scold him, but no one seemed to care.

In the distance, off to one side, was another large fenced area where cows and horses were grazing on the grass.

Men in Gatekeeper uniforms, with guns on their shoulders, paced around the perimeter. Each had a large black dog on a leash walking alongside him.

Two women in Nourishment Team uniforms carried trays of food and placed them on a table near the man and woman. I watched as they began to eat. Not nourishment cubes, but real, fresh food. My mouth watered at the sight.

One of the dogs started barking. Then more dogs barked. I knew I was well hidden, but I recoiled in fear.

I had seen enough. It was time to go.

I retraced my steps, moving from tree to tree. It was growing darker.

Suddenly bright lights lit up the landscape, beaming from the corners and roof of the building. What kind of powerful lights do these people have on their homes? They were unlike anything I had ever seen. Lights powerful enough to slice great distances through the darkness and, at the same time, cause the trees to cast long dark shadows. I stayed low in those shadows and kept moving.

The dogs kept barking.

My heart kept pounding.

CHAPTER THIRTEEN

EMMELINE

Days 4–5

Back at the river, I told David about everything I had seen, including the guards and dogs, and that we had to keep moving. I let David take the lead and set the pace, because he felt poorly and I didn't want him to struggle to keep up with me.

Finally, the dreadful farm commune was too distant to see. We were beyond the big white house as well. Anger pulsed through me at the Authorities who dared to live that life, that comfortable, indulgent, and extravagant life, while Citizens like us lived in despair.

David was moving slower and slower, and then he stopped and leaned against a boulder. I moved up beside him.

"I can't go on," he said. "I have to rest."

I glanced around for a place we could hide and rest. Nothing looked promising.

"I'll find something. Sit here for a minute while I look."

He nodded and slid down to the ground.

"Stay with him," I told Micah. "I'll go a little bit ahead, see what I can find."

Micah nodded and sat down next to David. Leaving our bundles with them, I started off with Elsa, following the path of the river that was now wild and rumbling loudly in its bed. It curved around to the right and ahead there was some kind of structure built over the water. Its foundation on either side rested on large rocks. One boulder jutted out from the bank, and the area underneath it was a hollow big enough for us to hide in. It wasn't far from where I'd left Micah and David.

I went back to them and told them what I had found. Micah gave David a hand and helped him to his feet.

Slowly, we made our way back to the space underneath the rock. Knowing we were reaching our limits frightened me. David lay down immediately, and Micah curled up beside him. I fed Elsa the last bottle I had. She fell asleep in my arms and didn't wake when I laid her next to Micah.

I slept, too, wrapped in the darkness of the night.

I woke early when the fingers of sunlight began to stretch over the horizon, pushing away the night sky. The darkness faded reluctantly.

David looked more feverish. I figured that if I wet a clean diaper, I could wipe David's flushed face with it. I needed to fill empty bottles with water anyway. At the edge of the river I worked alone on my chores, glancing over my shoulder at my sleeping family.

I sensed movement out of the corner of my eye on the other side of the structure that spanned the river. I squinted but couldn't make out anything. Was it a person? An animal maybe? A shiver ran across my skin. I gathered my things, watched for further movement, and scurried back to our hiding place. Everyone was still asleep where I'd left them but David was moaning. I squeezed the cool water out of the diaper and laid it on his forehead. He woke and I put my index finger over my mouth to signal him to keep quiet. He frowned but said nothing. He closed his eyes and drifted back to sleep.

I sat up, vigilant, keeping watch. I scanned the area for any sign of life and strained to hear anything above the roar of the rushing water. My body was tense, ready to spring into action if necessary.

Long minutes passed.

CHAPTER FOURTEEN

THE OLD MAN AND WOMAN

Day 5

The old man shooed squawking birds away from brambly bushes, picked red berries, and then sat cross-legged beside the woman by the edge of the forest. Behind them was the steep rise of a wooded hillside; below them, the raging river spanned by the rusty bridge. The road leading to the bridge was long gone, overgrown with weeds and saplings. He watched their surroundings in all directions, his eyes scanning constantly. Watchfulness had become a habit ingrained in him, and his caution was unending.

The woman sat, hunched and shrunken, like a curved gnome. The fabric of her dress was thin, almost transparent, and frayed along the hem and sleeves. The neckline's opening was far too big; it hung in folds across her collarbones. Her shoulder blades were prominent, like wings attached to her knobby spine. Her gray hair hung in a long braid, tied at the end with a piece of string. Below the string was a ball of frizz, like the period at the end of an exclamation point.

Their dirty faces were dappled with early sunlight and shadows. They might have been shrubs growing there instead of human beings.

"Do you see them?" the woman whispered. She chewed on a fingernail.

From where they sat, they looked down on a man and two children sleeping under an overhanging rock on the other side of the river. A woman, looking around nervously, was at the edge of the water filling bottles and rinsing out a cloth.

"Yes, Ingrid, I see them." He had painted their exposed skin with mud, as he did every day, making them one with the Earth, less visible in the shadows, their eyes a startling white contrast.

"They have a boy child. Don't they? I thought I saw a boy child."

"Yes, I saw him." He wondered how there could possibly be people there, under that rock. Hadn't they all been captured and punished by the Earth Protectors? Hadn't he and Ingrid sat huddled, hidden, while listening to the screaming, the gunfire? Eighteen years had passed since then. No more gunfire. No more screaming. No more skeletal refugees hunted down by well-fed, well-armed Earth Protectors. He felt his pulse, suddenly irregular, like moth wings in his chest, and he felt dizzy. He hit his fist against his chest, against that irregular pulse. He felt a pause in the heartbeat, then a regular cadence. The dizziness passed. That worrisome fluttering in his chest was happening more often. He had to stay healthy. It was up to him to take care of Ingrid. She couldn't take care of herself anymore.

She took a berry from his hand and ate it, then shifted her weight forward, her red-stained fingers on her knees.

"A baby, too?"

"Yes, a baby, too. Do you like the berries? Strawberry season will be over in a couple of weeks." He hoped this would be one of the times when the thread of a conversation would unravel in her mind and trail off. He wished she had not seen those people, wished she had looked at the sky and clouds instead. Look up, not down. Always look to the heavens.

But she continued. "Can we go talk to them? It's been a long time since we've seen children."

"Yes, a long time. Do you like the berries?"

"Of course I like the berries." She sounded impatient. "Can we go talk to them?"

"No." He clenched his hands together briefly, his large knuckles white from the pressure. He scratched at a red welt on his arm where a bee had stung him. There must be a wild hive nearby, probably in a hollow oak. He'd find it and would harvest the honey. They only had about a half-cup of honey left. In fact, all their supplies were running very low even though they had carefully rationed them. At least it was springtime. He knew they could they could survive through to early fall by foraging and preserving what they could. But he dreaded the winter. There were always animals to kill and eat, but once it turned cold, not many plants. Pine nuts and acorns, maybe, but not much else.

"Why not?" She wet her finger in her mouth and rubbed it on his welt. "Does that feel better?"

"It's too risky to approach them."

"Now you're being silly. Look at them. A woman, a man, a baby, and a boy. It is a boy, isn't it?" She squinted and peered down at the people huddled under that rock. "Yes, I'm sure it's a boy. Besides, there haven't been Earth Protectors here for a long time." She was breathless, her words tumbling over each other.

He looked up. There was nothing to see but early-morning sky through the branches of the trees. No clouds. There would be a full moon tonight, which meant no foraging. It wouldn't be dark enough to risk venturing out.

"Ingrid, I don't want to talk to them. It's too risky. And that's final." He felt cold, talking to her like she was a child. Who was he to decide what was final? He brushed away a bluebottle fly hovering over her head. When had her hair gotten so gray? It had happened strand by strand, stealthy but constant. Just as time marched forward day by day: stealthy but constant.

He shifted his position to allow a little more of the rising sun on his feet. Some days he desperately wanted to wash all the mud from his body, strip off his clothes, and lie naked in the sunshine. Just lie there, splayed out, chin tilted, neck exposed, eyes closed, and soak it in. Let the golden warmth wash over him, cleanse him.

"Why is it risky?"

He sighed. She wasn't going to let go of this. "Because we would have to cross the bridge to get to them. And then what would we do with them? Bring them back here?"

"Oh," she said. Her shoulders sagged, the neckline of the dress draped lower. The skin of her chest was mottled with purple cobweb veins like small bruises, and brown splotches of age.

Once they had carried the last of their supplies over that bridge and into their hiding place, they had never crossed it again. There was no reason to and it would leave them too vulnerable. Anybody up- or downstream could see them.

"But there's nobody around. There hasn't been anybody around for the longest time." She plucked a piece of grass and used it to clean between her teeth. "And I'm lonely."

"Being lonely is no reason to take risks." He took her hand in his. "We've been careful all this time and we've been safe. Trust me."

"I still want to talk to them." Her voice was low, pouty. "Maybe they need us. Maybe they escaped somehow."

"All the more reason to stay away. If they escaped, Earth Protectors will be looking for them."

"Well, then, we could help them hide." She clapped her hands together, childlike. "That's it! We could hide them. We could save them!"

He looked at her. How happy she was at that moment of discovery, a moment in which she felt like she had a purpose. His eyes watered. This was like his Ingrid of the past.

We could save them.

"You really believe we can save them?" he asked her, his milky blue eyes looking into hers.

"I believe we can try." She gazed back at him, not blinking. "What are we if we don't try? Not to act *is* to act. You know that."

He held out his hand, helping her stand. Together they walked over the bridge they hadn't crossed in nearly two decades, toward a group of strangers on the other side.

Strangers they might be able to save.

CHAPTER FIFTEEN

EMMELINE

Day 5

There it was again: movement. I leaned forward and squinted. Oh, dear sweet Jesus, what was that? Who was that walking across the structure that spanned the river? I glanced at David, Elsa, and Micah. They were all still sleeping; they looked so thin and pale. Elsa's legs would soon lose their chubbiness. Micah's arms would soon look like twigs. We simply were not getting enough calories with the few edible things we found. Would I be strong enough to deal with these people if they posed a threat? I'd have to be. I had no choice.

I slipped my hand into one of the bundles and felt around for the cold hardness of the knife, and the release button on the side.

Crawling out from the overhanging rock on my hands and knees, I watched as the two people continued walking over the span. They looked old and dirty. Both had long hair. It was a man and a woman, holding hands, close enough now that I could make out their mud-covered faces and thin, frayed clothing.

I moved away from the hiding place, away from my little family and out into the open. I pushed the release button and the knife blade flashed out with a harsh metallic click. No one, absolutely no one, would hurt my family. I would do whatever it took.

They were at the end of the span, walking down toward me with their hands held out in front of them, reaching out to me with their palms up and fingers outstretched. I held the knife in front of me, my arm extended. Sunlight reflected off the blade, flashing sparks of light.

"We mean you no harm," the man said.

"Stay back," I said. "Stay back. Come no closer." I didn't want them to see my family. Surely, they were well hidden by the rock. How foolish I had been to go to the river, exposed and unprotected!

I walked cautiously toward them, trying to measure their intent. Who were they and where did they come from? Finally, I was within a few feet of them, close enough to see their pale blue eyes, and the knotty veins in their thin arms.

"Sit, child. Talk to us," the woman said, a bit out of breath, as she lowered herself onto a log. She folded her legs feebly in front of her. The man, shoulders hunched, remained standing beside her.

"Who are you?" I asked. "And what do you want?"

"I'm Ingrid," the woman said, pointing to herself. "And this is my husband, Paul."

"What do you want?" I asked again.

"Won't you sit and talk?" Ingrid asked. "What is your name, child?"

"No, I will not sit. I want to know what you want. I want to know who you are, what you are doing here."

"We're surviving," Paul said. "That's all. Surviving. Just like you're trying to do."

"How do you know what I'm trying to do? How do you know anything about me?"

Paul sat beside his wife on the log, his thin legs stretched in front of him. He had no shoes; the soles of his feet were thick with calluses, his toenails long yellow horns. "You must have escaped somehow. Lord only knows how. But sooner or later, you'll get caught. They all do eventually. They are nothing if not persistent and ruthless."

"Just where are you from?" I asked, my hand shaking. "What are you doing here?"

"We slipped away a year before the relocations and we've been surviving the best we can ever since," Ingrid said. "Aren't you frightened that they'll find you? They're probably already searching." She turned to her husband. "What are they called? The ones who search? What are they called?"

"Earth Protectors," he answered, patiently. "From the Earth Protection Agency."

I remembered the voices of the men we heard the first day of our escape. They had said, "There will be hell to pay. They'll call in Earth Protectors." And this man and woman claimed to be shadow people, those who had run away. Could I trust them?

"Maybe you're part of them. Maybe you're disguised so you can fool us. Maybe I'm in danger right now, talking to you." My extended arm was getting tired; I switched the knife to my other hand.

"Yes, we're all in danger right now, out here in the open. Let us help hide you. We mean no harm to you," Paul told her. He placed his right hand flat against his chest. "I promise you."

"Why do you want to help me? If they're looking for me and you help me, well, isn't that dangerous for you?"

"We've been safe all these years. We want the same safety for you."

"Why? Why do you care about me? What am I to you?" I heard a twig snap behind me and turned my head. Micah was approaching. No, no, no. "Go back!"

He shook his head and kept coming.

"Go back, now!"

"Elsa needs you," he said. "She's crying really, really hard." The sound of the rushing water was loud; I couldn't hear the baby's cries but I believed Micah.

"We don't just care about *you*," Paul said. "We care about *all of you*. Let us help."

"You saw us? You saw *all* of us?" It would have been easy for them to see me, out in the open by the river, but I had chosen that hiding place, certain we could not be seen. I had failed.

"Yes. And if we could find you, then soon the searchers will, too. You, the man, and most important, the children," Paul said.

"Yes, the children. They're the most important among us." Ingrid said. "Go. Get the crying child. Bring your man. We can see that he is sick. Let us help you. Follow us. We have a safe place where you can all rest." She made a strange motion: she touched a finger to her forehead, then her chest, then her right shoulder, then the left.

I waited, expecting to see the woman make the circle sign or recite the Pledge. But it never came.

Micah tugged on my arm. "Elsa's crying really, really hard," he said again, his small face furrowed with worry.

I stood silently for a moment, thinking. David was indeed sick and we were all weak from hunger. I had no option but to trust these strangers.

The knife was still pointed at Ingrid and Paul. In one quick motion, I snapped it closed and slipped it into my pocket, then nodded at the couple and turned back toward the rock; Micah followed.

David was awake now and trying to comfort Elsa. I took her from him and patted her back. "*Shhh. Shhhh.*" Elsa's sobs subsided to a piti-ful whimper.

"Follow me," I told him. Micah helped David stand; he was un-steady on his feet and put his good hand on the rock for support. I saw how dry his lips were, how sunken his eyes had become. Micah picked up one bundle; I picked up the other with my free hand.

"Where are we going?" David asked. "I can't walk much farther."

My chest tightened. Elsa's crying, David's unsteadiness, and my own hunger and fatigue were combining to make me desperate.

"There's a man and a woman out there. They saw us."

David raised his eyebrows but said nothing.

"I saw them, too," Micah said. "They're dirty and old. I never saw anybody so old." Of course he hadn't. Old people had no value to the Authorities. Old people were recycled to free up resources for the young and productive.

"I think they're shadow people," I said. "I remember when you told me about them, back in the Compound. You said they slipped away before the relocations."

"All these years? And they survived?" David's voice had a croaky quality. He swallowed hard as if to clear his throat. He adjusted the strap of his sling. I could see the raw, red welt where it had rubbed the back of his neck. He was still holding onto the rock, still trying to steady himself.

"They said they want to help us. They said we could trust them."

David looked at me. "Do you?"

"We have no other choice. We'll die under this rock if we don't take a chance."

I carried Elsa and dragged one bundle behind me, feeling it catch on the uneven ground. Micah dragged the other one and let David lean on him for support. Together we left the deceptive security of the rock, stepped into the open, and walked toward the shadow people.

CHAPTER SIXTEEN

The old couple silently led the way and we straggled behind, our feet almost too heavy to lift. Before I awkwardly climbed the slope to walk on the span, I dipped my headscarf in the water. Elsa sucked eagerly on the cold, dirty fabric, her cheeks pulling frantically, her eyes squeezed closed.

"A bridge," David said, sounding surprised.

"A what?" I asked.

"This." He pointed at the span. "A metal bridge. Rusty, but still standing." A broken metal plate fastened to the railing read *Loyalha Bridg Weig Limi*. The right side of the plate was broken off, the edge ragged and rusted.

So, this was a bridge and we were about to walk on it. For the first time on our journey, there was no need to wade through the rough water to get to the other side. What a marvelous idea. Who had thought of it? Who built it? The sounds of our shuffling footsteps echoed around us; the water rushed below us. Micah was wide-eyed, taking it all in.

"Look!" he exclaimed. "We're way up above the water." The novelty of this seemed to give him more energy and he began to hop up and down on two feet. The bridge rocked and screeched with his enthusiasm.

"Quiet," Paul said, turning. "We must be very quiet."

Micah stopped hopping, blushed, and looked down at his feet as though ashamed. I'd seen the same flash of fear in his eyes back at the Children's Village. David stroked his head with a gentle motion; Micah gave him a shy smile. It was a small action, a man reassuring a child with a simple stroke on the head, but I felt a soft warmth spread from my heart through my chest as though a hand was squeezing my heart.

We had an uphill climb on the other side of the bridge. Ferns and vines brushed our feet and ankles. David was breathing heavily, and walking slowly. Once more, I matched my pace to his. Elsa was heavy in my arms; the wet headscarf draped over my arm was clammy and cold.

Paul stopped for a moment, allowing us to catch up to him.

"May I carry your bundles?" he asked. He didn't just reach out and take them, but instead asked permission first. I liked that. I nodded and watched as he took everything that we had, cradled it in his arms, and walked on. There was something reassuring about the way he acted.

The trees grew thicker, bigger, and a rock-strewn hill rose sharply ahead of us. Paul headed straight for it. There was no way we could climb that! Not in the state we were all in. But then Paul pushed through the wall of trees and seemed to disappear, swallowed up in the shadows. Ingrid, too, disappeared into the same area. Frightened, I moved forward, toward that dark space. A cold draft blew over me, making the hair on my arms stand up. Elsa must have felt it too; she stirred, pushing her legs against me. A musty smell of fur and feathers came out of the space, riding on the draft of air.

There was a flickering red glow just inside the entrance. Fire? I could just make out Paul's face, ghostlike, in the light. I edged forward slowly, with David and Micah following.

Cautiously, we stepped into that space. It was an opening into the side of the hill, hidden by trees.

Some daylight dimly lit the inside and I saw that the space we stood in was enormous. I couldn't even see where it ended. Paul and Ingrid moved deeper into the dark coolness. It seemed to go on forever, deep into the earth, under the mountain.

"Welcome to our kingdom," Paul said, his voice echoing. "Our kingdom on Earth. It has kept us safe."

"A cave," David whispered behind me. So that's what this was called. A cave. I had never heard of such a thing. "Is that a fire pit?" he asked.

"Yes, it is. I'll show you how I made it tomorrow. Right now you need to eat and then rest. You look exhausted and ill. Your arm must be injured."

Paul turned to his left. I could dimly make out shelves, rows and rows of shelves with containers of different sizes piled on them. Along one wall were big metal receptacles, some with lids.

"Careful," Paul said, bending over. "Mousetraps." He picked something up and I saw a square wooden thing with metal bands on it. A brown animal hung lifeless, its thin tail dangling. He released the metal, and the animal dropped into his hand.

"What is that called?" Ingrid asked Paul.

"A rat," he answered patiently. He put the rat in a pan near the fire pit.

"A rat has to eat," she said. "But so do we."

Micah murmured: "I pledge allegiance to the Earth and to the animals of the Earth." He started to make the circle sign on his forehead but I took his small hand in mine to stop him. He looked up at me, confusion on his face. It would take time for him to unlearn what the Authorities had been drilling into him almost since the day he was born.

Elsa stirred and whimpered weakly.

"We can offer a little food," Paul said. "Do you have an empty bottle for the baby?"

Micah quickly unrolled a bundle and handed a bottle to Paul. Paul went to one of the containers and scooped something into the bottle. I couldn't see what it was. Then he went to another container and added something else to it. "Powdered milk," he said over his shoulder, "and some sugar for calories. Now I add water to dissolve everything." He dipped the bottle into another container, shook it, and handed it to me. Elsa eagerly took this mixture, sucking, hiccupping, pink fists tight against the bottle.

Paul mixed up more of the powders and handed us the sweet drinks. We took his offering and drank deeply. Gratitude tastes a lot like milk and sugar.

Ingrid gathered up the empty cups while Paul dipped a cloth in a pan of water on the fire pit.

"Let me see your arm," he said to David. David slipped the sling off and the dried moss fell in clumps. Even in that dim light, I could see how red and swollen his arm had become.

Paul wrapped the warm, damp cloth around the wound. "Now, put the sling back on. It will keep this compress in place."

"That feels good," David said. "Thank you."

"You all look like you could use a long, deep sleep." Paul put a thick branch in the fire pit until a small bright orange flame danced on the end of it with a cool blue closer to the wood. It cast dancing shadows in the cave. He cupped his hand around the flame, protecting it.

The branch flickered in front of his face as he led us into yet another chamber. "Just for today, we'll put you here, deep in the cave, where the darkness will help you sleep. And it will be safer in case you've been followed. Here are blankets to lie on and a few extras to keep you warm," he said.

I picked up the bundles. All that we had was in them, and I had to keep them near me. "Where will you be?" I asked him.

"At the entrance, near the fire pit," he answered. "Keeping watch."

"You would do that?" I asked. "For us? Why?"

"Because we can."

He stood with the burning branch until we had arranged ourselves on their bedding. I lay close to David, his good arm brushing my hip, his long legs against mine. Micah and Elsa lay near me, my arm across them just as David's was across mine.

Paul handed me the knotted end of something. "Don't try to walk around in here when we leave. Luckily, this is a dry cave. No stalagmites or stalactites to bump into or bang your head on. But as soon as I leave it will be very dark back here and you'll get lost or hurt if you wander. Hold onto this rope and tug it when you wake up or if you need us for any reason." I felt the coarse lump in my hand, squeezed my fingers around it. A lifeline.

"On second thought," Paul said, "let me wrap a bit of the rope around your wrist so it is sure to stay with you." The rope had the smell of dried brown grass. "When you wake, tug it. I'll have the other end with me and I'll know to come get you."

"My name," I whispered, "is Emmeline." I didn't know if he heard me.

Paul took the light and left us there. His footsteps echoed away, and the slithering shape of the rope trailed behind him.

"David," I whispered. "How do you feel?"

"Tired. Very tired." I felt his lips brush against the back of my neck, hot and dry. A sense of guilt washed over me. Because of me, David was injured. Because of me, the children were cold, dirty, and hungry. I had to make it all up to them. Somehow.

"Now we sleep. Tomorrow we'll be rested." I desperately wanted this to be true.

"Rested." His breath was warm against my neck. "I like the sound of that."

His breathing slowed into the rhythm of sleep. I felt the rise and fall of the children's chests under my arm. I was pained and frightened, but everything I loved was within my reach.

CHAPTER SEVENTEEN

EMMELINE

Day 6

I woke in the inky darkness. I felt David beside me, still curled against me. Reaching across, I felt Micah's arm. I felt frantically in all directions for Elsa but my hand only found the bundles of our few possessions, lumpy and hard against my legs. How long had we slept? It was impossible to say, with no dawn or dusk to measure the passing of time.

I tugged on the rope and felt it being pulled back slightly in return. David and Micah stirred beside me. They woke with little groans; I sensed them stretching out their arms and legs. I continued feeling in the dark for Elsa.

I saw the light before I saw a person. The yellow-white flickering flame moved toward us in a slight bouncing motion with each step. As the light got closer, I made out Paul's face. I looked around for Elsa as the light grew brighter. She wasn't with us. Could she have crawled off and gotten lost in this cave?

"Where's Elsa? Where is she?" I asked him. My voice trembled.

"The baby woke up. We gave her a bottle and she went back to sleep on Ingrid's lap," Paul said. "We kept her with us so you could sleep. She woke up once again and we fed her again."

"I didn't hear Elsa wake up. Was she crying?" I asked. How could I have slept through my baby's crying?

"No," Paul said. "She just whimpered once. Ingrid was ready and eager to feed and hold her. You slept for a day and a night. I'm glad; you needed the rest. Now follow me, bring your blankets," Paul said briskly. "Stay together and hold on to the rope."

We trailed behind him and the faint light, feeling our way with our feet on the uneven, rocky floor.

As we neared the entrance, the opaque darkness began to lighten to a more transparent gray. I could see the outline of Ingrid sitting, and of Elsa on her lap. When Elsa saw me, she reached for me and I gladly picked her up.

Paul took the rope, coiled it, and laid it on top of others, then motioned for us to sit on a smooth log bench inside the entrance. David leaned back against the cold wall and closed his eyes. Micah was so close that I could feel his sharp hipbone against my side. Paul took our blankets and hung them to air out over a rope stretched between two wooden poles.

He walked over and crouched before us, his hair tangled, with stray bits stuck to the dried mud on his face. There, near the bench, was a pail. I could see wet mud in it.

Micah pulled closer to me and whispered in my ear. "Why is he so dirty?"

Paul heard the quiet question and smiled. "We want to blend in with the earth colors around us. Make it hard for anyone to see us. We have to do the same for you!"

Ingrid rose slowly, pushing herself upright with her hands against her knees. I figured that the cold cave had to be hard on her old bones.

"I'll paint your mother's face first so you can see it doesn't hurt. And Ingrid will get you something to eat." He turned to her. She sat in the corner of the cave where she'd been with Elsa, staring at its leafy entrance. She turned toward her husband's voice. "Milk, water, sugar," he said patiently. She looked around for a moment, then seemed to understand what he was saying and began to fill the same mugs we had used before. Milk, water, sugar. I felt my mouth water.

Paul came toward us, carrying the bucket. His face glistened with a fresh layer of mud. He dipped his hands into the pail and began to paint my face with long strokes of his gnarly fingers. It was so cold and his touch was gentle, but I hated the feeling of wet dirt on my face.

"Does it hurt?" Micah asked.

"No, it's just cold." I tried to keep my lips closed, to keep the mud out of my mouth.

"And now your hair. It's so blond, so easy to see." Paul said. "Later, maybe, we'll make you a rabbit-fur hat. But, for now, this will have to do." I felt the mud drying on my face, felt my hair hanging in miserable wet clumps.

Elsa cried when Paul tried to paint her face and turned her head from side to side.

"Well, I better stop." Paul pushed the bucket of mud against the wall. "Someone might hear her crying and we can't have that."

"I don't want mud on my face," Micah whispered to me.

"Please, Paul, no more mud painting for us." I put my hands in front of Micah.

"But, Emmeline, we do it to remain hidden and safe. Maybe in the end it's as useless as Ingrid sweeping the cave floor with a worn-out broom, but it is part of our routine."

"I understand. It's important to you. But it's uncomfortable. Besides, I had to pledge allegiance to the Earth back in the Compound. Smearing mud on my face makes me feel like the Earth still rules over me. I'll leave mine on today but I'm washing it off tonight."

I didn't think he understood, but he just shrugged and set the bucket down. "As you wish."

Ingrid presented us with the morning drinks; the mugs still had rings around the edges from our first night's mixture. I didn't care. I drank the gritty liquid through mud-crusted lips.

"And now, the latrine," Paul said. He saw my puzzled look and explained what the unfamiliar word meant.

Micah stood up as soon as he understood what Paul was talking about.

"Are there rules about when you can use the latrine?" Micah asked.

Paul looked puzzled. "Rules? No. Use it when you need it."

"I need the latrine. Now, please." Micah said, tugging on David's hand. Paul led David and Micah out of the cave. I would have to wait my turn. Ingrid sat beside me on the bench. She smelled of the earth. Shyly, she reached out and touched Elsa's leg with one long finger.

"It's been so long since I've seen a child. So very long. Elsa is such a beautiful name. There aren't any children around here, you know. I wish there were, but there aren't."

She fell silent and I studied her profile. She had a half-moon kind of face, sunken in the middle, chin and forehead prominent, nose sharp. The mud smeared on her face hid whatever wrinkles she may have had, but it couldn't hide the sagging skin of her neck. The fabric of her dress was thin, worn, and frayed around the edges of the sleeves and hem. In this dim light, it looked gray, like the shadows around us. Gray like the Compound we had escaped from.

She gathered up our empty mugs and shuffled to a large metal container. I could hear the swishing sound of the mugs in water. I figured that it must be a washing-up container. She put the mugs in a row on a wooden shelf that housed a stack of plates on that shelf and some cooking pots.

She shuffled back and sat down beside me. "Soon we will forage for more food. Maybe Paul will catch a rabbit or two. Or some fish. You need food. We all need food."

The men came back and it was now our turn at the latrine. I followed Ingrid out of the cave, behind the trees at the entrance, to a small wooden structure tucked in among other trees. Green vines grew up the side of it and across the roof. It was so cleverly hidden and disguised that it would be nearly impossible to see if you didn't know it was there. Paul and Ingrid had clearly planned well for their shadow lives.

If only I had planned as well. If only we hadn't been forced to flee so quickly. If only the Authorities hadn't planned to relocate the children from the Children's Village.

If only.

CHAPTER EIGHTEEN

The day stretched ahead of us, a long ribbon of time. Would we sit all day in this cave? I felt the need to keep moving, to put more distance between us and the evil we were running from. We were still much too close to the Compound and the farm commune. On the other hand, we were well hidden and these people seemed kind and giving. Besides, David was in no condition to start off again.

Paul seemed to sense my impatience. "Emmeline," he said, "you all need more rest. Your man is sick. Your children are thin. And you look so tired."

"Yes, you're right. But do we sit in here all day?" I couldn't help but be on edge. I wanted to be doing something, anything.

"We can sit outside, in the shadows of the trees. We can give thanks for the comfort of the sunrise, the promise of another day. And we can visit, get to know each other. That will be the best use of the morning. We welcome the company after all these years alone. The rest of the day we'll spend searching for food." He gathered up some cloths from a shelf. "Elsa can sit on these. Let's go."

"Emmy," David whispered, "I need to lie down. I don't feel good."

Paul heard him and grabbed another piece of cloth. "You can lie under the trees. The trees are God's gift to us."

What a strange thing to say. *The trees are God's gift to us.* Earlier, he had talked about sunlight dancing. Something about this man made me think that he found goodness in everything.

Ingrid stayed inside the cave. I could hear her moving around, so I glanced over my shoulder; she was pushing a broom and humming to herself.

"She's sweeping the floor," Paul said. "It's part of her routine. Having a routine is a good thing for her." His sentence lay flat in the air, without explanation, but he didn't elaborate. "After she's done sweeping, I'll braid her hair. That's part of the routine, too. Braid it in the morning, unbraid it at night. It's a ritual, and there's comfort in that. It's nice to be able to control something given that there's so much we can't."

Everyone settled outside the entrance of the cave under large trees that cast cool shade. In front of us were pine trees, their branches hanging down like skirts, brushing against the ground. They stood like guardians around us, keeping us hidden. I still kept my bundles near me with all the things Mother had saved and all the things we had taken from the tents at the farm commune.

Paul spread the cloths out. David lay on one and fell asleep almost immediately, his dark hair falling over his forehead, and Elsa settled beside him. I watched them for a moment, and then suddenly she rolled over and pushed herself up on her hands and knees. With her round bottom held high, she clumsily crawled toward Micah.

"She's crawling," I exclaimed. "Look! She's crawling!" At that moment, she collapsed onto her belly, but quickly pushed herself up again and continued scooting toward Micah. Again she collapsed. Again she pushed herself up. I watched with my hands over my mouth. I wanted to wake David up so he could see this, but he looked so peaceful, his wounded arm stretched out at his side.

Ingrid watched from the cave entrance. "What a smart baby," she said.

I felt a swelling inside—pride and love combined. I smiled thinking of how I could now hold her anytime I wanted, not just on the dusk-to-dawn shift in that horrible Children's Village. We had managed our own relocation in spite of the Authorities. I felt a surge of energy that I hadn't felt in days.

Ingrid came out and sat near Paul. He began the ritual of her morning braid. A breeze rustled through the leaves and I could see the sunshine shifting on the ground around me.

"Peaceful, isn't it?" Paul murmured, his fingers separating her long hair into three sections, twisting them one over the other and tying the braid at the end with the string. He was so gentle with her.

I nodded. It *was* peaceful. I could see the sky, blue like Elsa's eyes, through the leafy branches. Down the hill, the river sparkled as it passed under the bridge. Farther away, on the other side of the stream, was the large rock we had hidden under. From here, I could see that we would have been easy to spot. We were so fortunate that it was Paul and Ingrid who had found us first.

David woke and sat up, moaning in pain.

"Let me look at your arm," I said. I untied the shirt from his arm; the cloth Paul had wrapped on it fell from the raw, red wound.

"It's time to take care of that," Paul said. "Please get another warm compress, Ingrid. I put a pan of water on the fire pit this morning."

Ingrid shuffled into the cave and came back with the cloths. She laid them gently on David's arm. It must have felt good, because he gave her a grateful smile.

"We'll leave those on until the sun reaches right below the treetops," Paul said. "Ingrid will change them out when they cool."

"Show me how to do it and I'll change them," I said. "I need to learn."

He nodded. "Yes, that's a good idea." He paused, and then went on. "Emmeline, you know they will be searching for you, don't you?"

I nodded.

"They need to find you, to punish you as an example. If they don't, then they know that others might try to escape. They can't lose control. If they lose control, they lose power. And power and control are all they have." His eyes were piercing, as though he wanted to see into my thoughts. "I just want you to be aware of the danger."

Aware? Of course I was aware. They took my mother. They were going to take my baby. Aware? No one could be any more aware of the danger than I was! But I didn't say that to him.

"I just don't want to think about it or talk about it," I told him.

"I know what you're saying. Believe me, I know. But later, we must talk. We must plan. Planning and preparation, that's the key."

"I have no plan." The only plan I ever had was for the four of us to escape. And that wasn't really a plan. It was desperation. Paul had never lived in a Compound. How could he understand?

"You have that bundle of things. That must have been part of a plan."

"Not really. They're things my mother saved for me. I don't know why or how but she did. I wanted to save what she thought was important."

Ingrid inspected David's arm. "It looks a little better already," she announced proudly. Micah and I moved closer to watch. His arm did look somewhat better, not quite as red. But it was still far from healed.

"Ingrid, why don't you make him some tea of wild thyme. It will bring his fever down. When you pick the leaves, show them to Emmeline before you make the tea so she knows what they look like." She nodded and set off in search for the leaves.

"How long do you think it will take for his arm to heal?" I asked Paul.

"A good week, probably. The compresses and thyme tea will help."

"A week! That long?" I wanted to be far from here with the Compound well behind us in a week.

"A week's rest will do you all good. Let's use the time wisely and share what we know, teach each other. May I see what's in your bundle?" Paul asked.

I nodded.

"Wait," Paul said. "Before we do that, I want to put some of nature's healing product on his arm while the skin is still warm." He disappeared into the cave and came back with something thick and golden in a small container. He put a dab of it on a spoon for me to taste. Oh, so sweet, so good! "It's honey. Made by bees. And the bees were made by God."

I promised myself to find out more about this God thing. Father would get angry with Mother when she said that word. I always figured that it was because it was bad. There were plenty of bad words that we weren't allowed to say.

Paul took another spoon and began to apply the honey all along the open wound.

"Let me do that." I took the spoon from him and spread the thick honey on David's arm.

"The earth is filled with precious things like this," Paul said. "You know, honey is a food that never spoils. But if you're using it as medicine, you don't want to put your fingers in it. Might take on some germs."

By the time I was done, Ingrid had returned, and Paul was helping me wrap a dry cloth around David's forearm once more. "There. Now we can look at your treasures."

I opened the bundle from the farm commune first. The basin, sanitizing solution, a small sheet of rubber, and linens lay in a jumble. I felt no attachment to these things but Micah spoke up with pride.

"I helped her get those things," Micah announced. "We had to run through the water."

I pulled at the knot of the other bundle, slowly releasing the tension of it. The cloth fell aside in gentle folds and there they were: the things Mother had saved—the only possessions I cared about. I picked the items up, one at a time, and handed them to Paul. First, the gold coin. He turned it over and over, then handed it to Ingrid.

"That's a valuable thing, that gold coin. Worth a lot. Gold was confiscated, you know."

"Confiscated?"

"Taken from the people. The Authorities got the gold. All of it. That's what Authorities do. Take from the people and make themselves rich."

I wondered how Mother had managed to keep the coin from being confiscated. I'd never know the answer to that. *Why didn't you teach me more, Mother?*

"That coin might save your life someday," Paul said. "You can exchange it for something more important. Many things are more important than gold."

"Who would I exchange it with and why?"

"There might still be others out there. They might be like us or not like us. Who knows? And they might still value something like this," Paul said, handing the coin to Ingrid.

Ingrid studied the coin briefly, then handed it back to me.

The matches were unearthed next.

"Ah! Matches! We have a large supply of those. Fire is a necessary thing. Especially in winter. It can be a lifesaver. It can also be dangerous. Lots of things are like that, either good or dangerous, depending on how you use them." Paul handed the matches back to me. He was right. After all, the fire back at the Social Update Stage had helped us escape. It had been good for us, but dangerous for the Authorities.

The knife. "That's a very good thing to have." He snapped it open and closed and offered it to Ingrid, but she shook her head no. She had her own knives in the cave. This was not a novelty to her.

The recipe cards. Ingrid took special interest in them, reading each one. "Pumpkin pie. I used to make that. Except I put a splash of vinegar in the crust."

The New Testament. Paul dipped his hands in a pan of water and dried them vigorously before picking it up. Ingrid reached for it but Paul didn't hand it over. "Your hands are dirty," he said. "This is very precious." He held it up for her to see from a distance, then raised it near his lips as if to kiss it. I again promised myself that someday, when we were done hiding, I would read this book.

The Little Prince. They weren't interested in that. It got a casual glance and then came right back to me.

The map. They were *very* interested in that. Paul opened it carefully and spread it out on the ground in front of us. The fold lines were weak, tearing apart. Words that had been printed on it had faded. Most were illegible. "We're here." Paul said, pointing with authority to the upper-right corner. "It used to be called Pennsylvania. Don't know what they renamed it. It'll always be Pennsylvania to me. See that skinny, wavy line?"

He pointed and yes, I could see that line. "That's our river." He pointed to the water below us and to our left. "Now follow that line." He traced it, his finger hovering above the map. "See how it gets a little wider and then joins up with this line? This bigger line, darker-colored?" Again, I nodded. "Well, keep following that line. It's another river."

"And look here." He moved his hand, still hovering, not wanting to touch the fragile paper. "Another river. See how the two rivers meet, here." He pointed to a V shape. "They join and form an even larger, mightier river. It flows across the nation, growing larger, joined by other streams along the way." He moved his finger back in the direction of our stream. "There used to be a dam not far from here. It created a lake of water that people could go boating, fishing, and swimming on. The government tore it down. Tore down a lot of dams from what I heard way back when. Said it was so the water and fish would be free." He sighed. "Water and fish would be free but people would not."

I wondered where the river would lead us if we followed it.

He leaned back on his heels and looked at me, directly and with intensity, but said nothing for a long moment. Then: "What part of the map is important to you?"

His question was as sharp as a knife. My chest hurt thinking of the distance to that place. I pointed to the spot, far away on this map, where I was born, and where I lived with my parents before the relocations.

"Kansas. I was born there."

He sighed deeply. "That's an impossible distance, Emmeline. Impossible."

"Does the river go there?" I studied the map, trying to follow the path of the river. The frayed fold lines made it difficult.

"Maybe not that river. But I'm sure there are rivers in Kansas. Even so, it's an impossible distance, even if you had a boat. And it gets cold in Kansas in winter. Very cold. At least here, we have the shelter of the cave and the fire pit."

I ignored him and carefully refolded the map, putting it aside with my other treasures. Escape from the Compound was supposed to be impossible, but we had done it. Paul and Ingrid had escaped, too, and found their cave. Anything was possible if you wanted it enough.

Finally, I held up the picture of Mother and me standing in the grass in front of a large house, smiling into the camera. My small hand was on her cheek and my little white socks had ruffles. The picture was bent from being in the bundle. I smoothed it out as best I could. My fingers touched her cheek in the photo. Then I bundled everything back up.

"Time to get busy and find something for lunch," Paul said to me. "We'll find something different to eat. You need some protein. Come with me. Ingrid can watch the children. She'll wake David if she needs to."

I followed him into a grove of trees, looking over my shoulder several times. Elsa had been within eyesight almost constantly since our escape. I was uneasy leaving her behind but was curious about what Paul was talking about. "What exactly is lunch?" I asked him as we walked.

"Our middle-of-the day meal," he answered, sounding surprised that I didn't know that.

"Oh! We only got nourishment cubes twice a day in the Compound. Morning and evening."

"Nourishment cubes? What are they?"

Now it was my turn to be surprised. "You don't know what a nourishment cube is? That's what the Authorities gave us to eat in the Compounds."

"Emmy, we never lived in a Compound. We have no idea what it was like. We slipped away long before the government got complete control. You'll have to tell us about it."

Tell him about it? About the energy boards, the cramped living spaces, the fences, the Gatekeepers? The Children's Village? The pledges? *I pledge allegiance to the Earth and the animals of the Earth.* Just thinking about it all made my head spin. Where would I even start?

"I'd rather hear how you and Ingrid slipped away. How did you know to do that?"

"We can all talk it over later. But now, let's see if we caught anything." He took a few more steps and pointed. "Those are traps. And those are rabbits. Two of them! God was good to us today." He released the trap and held the two small brown animals up by their back legs, their heads and long ears dangling. "We'll take them back, skin them, and cook them. We'll save their fur. We might already have enough to make some hats, or shoes. Hold them while I reset the traps."

They were still warm. Their bony legs felt strange in my hands. I couldn't believe I was touching and holding real animals. I had seen pictures of rabbits in some children's books before the Authorities took the books away but I never imagined I'd ever hold one. Now, here I was, holding two. *The animals of the Earth.* I blew on their fur and it ruffled, showing a lighter fur underneath. I ran my finger over them. How soft they were. The inside of their ears were a soft pinkish color, and their heads seemed too small for such big ears. Their eyes were open but dull. I had never seen eyes like that before; just looking at them made me feel sick.

Back at the cave, Paul set about to skin the animals. David was awake and smiled when he saw what we were carrying. "Rabbits! I used to hunt them with my dad." His smile faded. I knew he was thinking of his parents and worrying about where they might be.

Elsa was curled up in a little tight pink ball with her thumb in her mouth, napping. Micah ran to join us. "What do we do with them?" he asked. His face was eager with excitement over this new adventure.

"They're food for us, to keep us alive." Paul spoke directly to Micah, patiently and softly. "Today I will teach you some things you need to know. Are you ready to learn?" Micah nodded. "Good. I'll talk while I work. You must listen and watch carefully. And you can ask questions. Emmeline, you must watch, also. You have much to learn." He was right about that. I knew nothing of this world. Learning could save us.

"Don't rabbits' feet mean good luck?" David asked.

"Luck?" Paul said. "There is no such thing as luck anymore. Not out here. There's awareness. There's preparation. There's hard work. Survival cannot be trusted to luck." Even though his voice was soft, when he said the word *luck*, it sounded like he was spitting. David fell silent.

Paul showed us how to clean the meat and preserve the fur. "Food for today, warmth for later," he said. "Take care of today, plan for tomorrow." Micah leaned forward, his forehead furrowed in rapt concentration, watching as Paul worked and listening intently to his every word.

I watched and listened also. Not just to Paul as he worked, but to the area around us, mindful that, just like these rabbits, we were also being hunted.

CHAPTER NINETEEN

I went with Ingrid to find wild onions for the stew. Paul said he would keep an eye on the children. Ingrid had a little spade to dig up the onions she found and she showed me how to identify them. I watched carefully and soon I, too, was finding some tucked in among the ferns. With a sense of triumph, I dug them up and gently shook the dirt from their roots. I was now what she and Paul called a hunter-gatherer, and my reward was a pungent smell that promised good food.

Back at the cave, Ingrid set about to make the stew. She bustled around gathering up a pot, fresh water, a handful of peas, and the onions. I was surprised to see the peas. Had she gotten them from the long rows at the agricultural Compound?

"Let me help," I said.

"Oh, dearie, I do the cooking. But you can watch and learn."

I sat on the log near the warmth of the fire pit. I watched her rinse the onions and chop them.

"I'm curious. Why did you and Paul know you needed to escape and find a hiding place?"

"Well, let me tell you." She made a little harrumph sound to clear her throat. "I used to be a cleaning lady at a big government building. Like I said, I've been cooking and cleaning all my life." She put the glistening cubes of rabbit into the pot. "You want to know what's going on? Just ask a cleaning lady. They empty the wastebaskets. They see the crumpled memos and notes and meeting minutes."

She lowered the suspension arm on the pit, moving the pot closer to the fire.

"And what did you find?"

She took a pinch of salt from a bowl and sprinkled it into the pot. "Lots of things. Brought them home, showed them to Paul. He thought I was crazy until I put together a shredded one. Can't rightly remember now what it said. Paul would remember. Then he didn't think I was crazy anymore. That's about the time the mandatory meetings started. That's when we knew."

"Then what?"

"Enough talking for now. You want to give this a stir?"

She handed me a spoon as though it was a precious object.

The pot bubbled away above the heat. Curls of sweet-smelling steam wafted from it.

Teaching and learning filled the morning. It went beyond catching and cleaning rabbits or finding wild onions and wild thyme plants. While the stew cooked, Paul showed us how to make a fire pit, and how to dehydrate food. I tucked the nuggets of information into my memory to be pulled out and used in the future. Don't use shale rock for a fire pit, it can explode. Don't use damp wood to build a fire, it will create dark smoke that can be seen from a distance. When dehydrating meat or fruit over a hot fire, shake the container often so the food doesn't burn.

Micah was staring wide-eyed at the fire pit. "Want to be my partner fire-keeper?" Paul asked him. "You and I can make sure we always have enough wood."

Micah's big grin was his way of saying yes. Paul was making this child feel special, important. That was something he had never felt at the Children's Village, that horrid place where the Authorities thought they could do a better job of raising children than their parents.

"Thank you for showing us all of this," I said to Paul.

"I just used the tools God put on earth for man. You have to learn how to safely use what you've been given. God doesn't always give us what we want, but he always gives us what we handle—even if we don't know it yet. And, right now, I think all of us could handle some food. So let's eat."

Ingrid and Paul bowed their heads before they took a single bite. I didn't know why. I started right in on the food.

"Peas? How did you get these?" David asked between bites.

"We forage at night sometimes. We picked those a few days before you came. We'll have to go back when conditions are right. Pea season is almost over. The commune isn't that far away as the crow flies. And the plants are never picked clean. It's amazing they leave so much."

Elsa gurgled happily as she sipped broth from a mug. I noticed two little white tooth buds along the edge of her gums. Soon I wouldn't have to chew her food for her. Micah was busy helping Ingrid scrape the skin of the rabbit fur smooth with sharp-edged stones. Ingrid hummed as she worked. David sat near me, his long legs stretched out in front of him. Insects buzzed in the filtered sunlight and great puffy white clouds floated high above the treetops.

"How did you manage all of this?" David motioned to the cave with his hand. "All the supplies, all the things you have here?" Did he have more color in his face today? Or was I only imagining it because I so desperately wanted him to be better?

"It's a bit of a long story," Paul said. "Ingrid can help me tell it. Sometimes she can't remember the day before yesterday, but she remembers things from the distant past. For now, I think it's time for dessert."

"What's dessert?" Micah asked.

"Something sweet at the end of a meal," Paul said. "Leave the rabbit skins, follow me."

We followed him some distance to a cluster of plants among the trees. Birds scattered as we approached.

"Hope the birds left us some." He motioned with his hands. "These are strawberries. See the red fruit? They are mighty good eating." He plucked a berry and handed it to me. It was cool and sweet. I picked one and gave it to Elsa; it was soft enough for her to gum.

Soon we were all eating berries and smiling at each other with red stained lips. I quit smiling when I saw something dark move in the woods beyond the clearing. I tapped David on the shoulder and pointed.

"Bear," he whispered.

"Back up slowly. No sudden movements," Paul said. "Keep your eyes averted."

The bear shook its massive head, and growled with its huge mouth open. It lumbered toward us. I couldn't keep my eyes averted as Paul had said, though—they were fixed on the massive animal.

The bear stopped at the base of a thick tree and, standing tall on hind legs, reached high up on the tree with its powerful paws. Still growling, it raked long claws down the trunk, leaving deep scars in the bark.

It felt like hours passed as we shuffled slowly backward toward our cave. Finally we made it back inside, but I still didn't feel safe. The rabbit skins that had been on the ground earlier were gone. The mugs we'd stacked neatly before we went for the berries were strewn helter-skelter.

"Since the beginning of time, wildlife has competed with mankind for food," Paul said, settling on a log bench. "Best we stay inside until the bear is done marking its territory. We can sit around the fire and use the time to talk."

They began telling their tale, talking back and forth, remembering, and sharing.

"About twenty-four years ago, Ingrid started to worry about things she found at work. I didn't believe her at first," Paul said. "I had my own problems. I used to be a history teacher."

"Oh, so was my mother!" I interrupted him.

"Really? What did she tell you about that?" Paul asked.

"She didn't talk about it. But Father told me she wasn't allowed to teach real history anymore." I tried to remember his exact words. "She couldn't teach *accurate* history. History was being changed, rewritten by the Authorities."

"Exactly right. I couldn't bring myself to teach their lies, so I quit." He gave a little shake of his head.

Ingrid and Paul talked on and on, often interrupting each other, in their desire to share their story. They used phrases I wasn't familiar with: mandatory meetings, loss of private property, and regulations on air and water use.

As I listened, I watched the area outside of the cave. The bear was out there somewhere.

"We knew we had to find a safe place. And by the grace of God, I found this." He looked around the cave. "Perfect. A dry cave. Shelter. Near water. At the time, we didn't know we'd be near the farm commune. That was a bonus. We made lists of things we would need."

They both talked, tossing words at us rapid-fire: Food that wouldn't spoil; containers; clothing; candles; tools; knives; matches. The list seemed endless.

"Took us four years to stock up. Don't know how many times we drove the truck up here and unloaded it," Paul said. "Had to do a little bit at a time so nobody got suspicious."

"Didn't know who we could trust," Ingrid added.

Paul sounded angry when he described a database that was being built on every individual in a way that had never been done before.

"We knew then that the time for hoarding was over and the time for hiding had begun. Loaded up our truck one last time. Drove it here, and unloaded everything. At that time there was still a road leading to the bridge. I drove the truck into a gully and left it there. It's probably rusted away and covered in vines by now.

"We stayed in the cave for the longest time. When we'd hear people shouting, we'd move even deeper into it so we were hidden from view. Sometimes we heard screaming. Those were terrifying sounds. We heard men shouting commands: 'Stop! Stop or I'll shoot.' Then we heard the sound of gunfire. This went on for several days, maybe weeks. We lost track of time. After a while, it grew silent."

"Then what?" I asked.

"We painted our faces with mud and came out of the cave," Paul said.

"Then what?"

Ingrid took over. "The sun hurt our eyes when we came outside of the cave after so many weeks. We couldn't look up for the longest time. We had to look down at the grass until we got used to the light."

"It's been a while since you've seen anyone?" I asked.

Paul nodded. "Yes, quite a while."

"But you still paint your skin. Why?"

"Because they will never stop hunting us. We aren't important, but catching us is."

I listened, trying to picture all they had been describing, but the only thing I could see in my mind was that large bear standing on its hind legs, growling, and using its massive claws to mark its territory.

CHAPTER TWENTY

"Okay, Emmeline and David. We've told our story, now you need to tell us yours. How did it all start for you and your families and what was it like living in what you call a Compound?" Paul leaned forward, his bony legs folded in front of him, the skin stretched across his knobby ankles, a large dark mole on his shin. He had no fat anywhere on his body.

"Let David start," I said. "He knows more about the beginning than I do."

David took a deep breath, and was quiet for a while. Finally, he started talking. Micah sat near him, his eyes on David's face.

"I was just a kid, myself. Emmy was a baby. Our farms were right next door to each other. No fences between us, except around animal pastures. Those were good days."

"You had animals!" Micah exclaimed. "Real animals?" His mouth was a little round circle of surprise.

"Yes, we did. Cows, horses, pigs. Even chickens."

"Wish I could have seen them!" Micah said.

David went on, looking at Paul. "You already know about the meetings. You said you went to some of them."

"Had to. It was required," Paul said.

"Well, I didn't have to go to them, but my parents did. They didn't talk to me about what went on there. And then, for some reason, we lost the farm. I'm not sure why, other than that the federal government said they owned all the land. They told us that we would be relocated and everyone would be taken care of and they would take us to our new homes on a train."

"You rode on a train?" Micah asked, every detail fascinating to him.

"Yes, my first time riding a train. I thought it was the most exciting thing ever. But it turned out to not be as much fun as I thought it would be. The windows were painted black. Couldn't see where we were going or anything."

"Oh, dear me," Ingrid said. "That's very strange."

"The whole thing was strange. There were lots of trains and lots of people herded in groups under the watchful eyes of guards. The guards called the groups by Compound number. 'Northeast Region Compound Ten over here. Northeast Region Compound Eight, this way.' The guards pushed and shoved at this group or that group and pointed to the train they were to get on." David made a pushing motion with his arms. "Everybody was going to a Compound, somewhere. I heard my dad tell my mother he figured the whole nation had been divided into regions. That was the system."

Micah leaned against me and kept his eyes on David's face.

"I watched them shuffle the other groups onto their assigned trains. Then it was our turn," David said.

"What else do you remember?" Paul's voice had a sad tone.

"People on the train were all so quiet. Strangely quiet. I remember the silence more than anything else about that ride."

"Where did the train take you?" Paul urged him to go on.

"To our Compound. Northeast Region Compound Fourteen. We weren't sure exactly where that was located."

Talking about the Compound made it seem like it was right there, behind me, around me, sucking me back in. In fact, I didn't want to hear any more. I was tired of all the talking, tired of waiting to move on. I moved to the entrance of the cave and sat, looking out, watching for an Earth Protector, an Enforcer, or other predator.

Snippets of conversation drifted my way. I tried to ignore them but sometimes I wanted to scream.

"What are living spaces?" I heard Paul ask David.

Tell them they were gray, cold cement. Tell them about the energy boards we had to walk on every day! Tell them about the bicycle paths, the Transport Teams, the Human Recycling, the Social Update Stage, the Enforcers!

"I was a Gatekeeper," David said.

"Gatekeeper?" Paul said the word like it was in a foreign language.

"Yes, every area had a Gatekeeper. I was basically a monitor, tracking when Citizens left their specific area and why. The Authorities mandated that. Every movement was monitored. That's just the way it was. It was my job."

"You were a Gatekeeper?" Paul asked. "One who monitored others? *You did that?*" I could hear the judgmental tone in his voice.

Of course he did, Paul, I wanted to shout at him. *We all did as we were told. That's just the way it was. Citizens have no power. No voice. You could say no and die, or say yes and live—those were the only choices we got to make.*

"I lived in the Children's Village." Micah wanted to be part of the conversation. "I slept in the boys' room and I had to follow the rules. We all did."

"What kind of rules?" Paul asked him.

"Like this." He made the circle sign and recited: " 'I pledge allegiance to the Earth and to the animals—' "

"Stop!" I left the cave entrance and went back to Micah. "Never, ever say that again!"

His face puckered into a tight little frown. "I was only telling them . . . I'm sorry."

Then shame washed over me. I had spoken too harshly. I knew how ingrained the teachings of the Authorities were in his thinking. No child could escape the indoctrination. Could I change that? They'd had him for eight years! I'd had him for six days.

"I'm sorry, Micah," I said. "You can talk."

He squirmed, not sure what he should say, not sure if I would get angry again.

"You can tell them about the classroom," I prompted him. "I won't yell again. In fact, I'll just go and keep watch for the bear." I went back to the entrance and stared into the woods surrounding us. I tried to listen as intently as I could. I needed to hear what Micah said so I could understand him better and know what demons he might be struggling with.

"It was just a room," he continued. "I was in the boys' classroom. I slept in the boys' sleeping area. The girls had their own rooms. The babies were in the nursery, at the end of the hall. That's all." I think he was afraid he might say the wrong thing.

"Where were your parents? Did they have their own room?"

Micah answered in that honest way that only a child can. "I didn't know my parents. I wish I could have seen them, at least one time. But I never did."

So *that* was Micah's demon.

They continued talking but I quit listening. My thoughts were of Micah, the sad little boy who wished he could have seen his parents just one time.

After a while, I heard David call me. "Emmy, they want to hear what you can tell them." I returned to the group.

It was time for me to speak up.

I knew exactly what to say.

"David has told you the facts. I'll tell you the feelings. It was the everyday, constant darkness of being fenced in with no place to go. It was the feeling of living a meaningless life, and knowing your body, mind, and soul are owned by others. It was the feeling of being helpless and hopeless."

That was the end of our history lessons. And, while I didn't know it at the time, the beginning of the longest week of my life.

CHAPTER TWENTY-ONE

EARTH PROTECTION AGENTS

Day 7

Steven always woke the men well before dawn, and Julia watched, observing how they reacted to him. Each morning, Nigel and Adam were already awake, their backpacks in place, as if they had anticipated an early start. Winston would wake quickly and shoulder his pack. Guy would fumble clumsily with his, the straps twisting on his shoulders.

This morning was different. Guy was still asleep, slack-jawed and snoring, even after Steven roughly shook his shoulders.

Julia watched as Steven reached into Guy's backpack, took out a water bottle, and poured the water over Guy's head. Guy stumbled to his feet and shook his head. Drops sprayed off his hair and more ran down his face.

"You'll learn to sleep lightly, and wake easily!" Steven said. "And that's an order I don't want to repeat again." He handed the empty water bottle to Julia. "Take this to the stream. Fill it and bring it back."

Julia left her pack propped against a tree and walked the short distance to the stream. Looking around as the water flowed into the bottle, she noticed that most of the rocks had moss on them but a few were bone-dry and bare. She also noticed some shriveled brown fern leaves lying a good distance away from the plants on which they had grown. Something didn't seem right to her. She tightened the lid of the water bottle and looked around for anything else that seemed odd. Nothing stood out but she still felt uneasy.

She returned to the group and handed Guy his water bottle. He mumbled a thank-you, slipped it into his pack, and stood waiting with the others for more orders from Steven. Julia looked over at her backpack, and noticed that someone had moved it, if ever so slightly.

"No nourishment cubes until we've walked for an hour. And we'll be walking fast, so keep up with me."

"Excuse me, sir," Julia started to say, ready to tell Steven about the rocks and the ferns.

"I said no nourishment cubes for an hour, so don't bother telling me that you're hungry. I don't care if you're hungry."

"Yes, sir," Julia replied. That ended that. She would not tell him what she saw. She would not tell him anything.

They started walking, in single file, just as they had before. Julia was last, behind Winston. When they got to the edge of the stream, she reached forward and tapped Winston's shoulder and pointed to the bare rocks and brown ferns. He looked where she pointed and nodded. Julia could tell from his reaction that he understood. She wondered if Steven had noticed those things.

She looked at the backs of the five men ahead of her. All of them had broad shoulders, much broader than hers. They were taller, too, with long legs capable of long strides. They could easily outpace her on any terrain. Their uniforms fit better than hers. She had to roll up the legs of her pants to keep them from dragging on the ground; the waist of her slacks was too big. Frustrated, she struggled to maintain their grueling pace.

She was sweating by the time Steven said they could stop and eat their morning cube. Gratefully, she sat down on a smooth rock. For a few minutes, she just sat, exhausted, catching her breath. The others had already eaten their cubes and drunk some water before she even reached into her pack.

"All right, men," Steven said. "Time to move on. Remember, they have a three-day lead on us, so let's get going."

Julia had no choice. She had to move on as ordered. Winston must have seen that she had neither drunk any water nor eaten. Quickly he handed her his water bottle and inclined his head, encouraging her to drink. She took a few quick swallows and handed it back. Steven, apparently busy with his own pack, had not noticed Winston sharing his water with her. Julia knew that Steven would have been angry if he had. She smiled at Winston and he smiled back. It was the first time she had seen anybody in this group smiling at all.

They walked on and on. Julia guessed they'd covered over ten miles, maybe more. Would the day ever end? She noticed broken branches along the way, but this time, Steven did, too. Without saying a word, he would point to every broken branch he saw. She noticed bits of paper in the grass. Steven saw some of those and pointed to them, but missed others. She started keeping score in her head, comparing the number of clues she saw with the number Steven pointed to. She felt proud that her score was much higher than his. In her mind, she imagined what it would be like to say *"But, sir, you missed some. Sir."*

The game would have been more fun if she wasn't so hungry.

They took a water break mid-afternoon and Julia wasted no time digging out her bottle. She had learned her lesson well. Steven allowed them to refill their bottles in the stream, which grew smaller and shallower the farther they walked. It was getting harder to completely fill a bottle.

Julia scooped water into her hands and drank it. It was so cold that it hurt her teeth, but it tasted clean and refreshing. She splashed water on her face, and that, too, rejuvenated her. Then she sat back on her heels and looked around. The clouds were beautiful, great flawless puffs of white scattered across the blue sky. She wished she could sit there forever. She was startled when Winston touched her shoulder.

He pulled his hand away quickly when Steven approached them.

"We're ready to move." Winston took a step back and Julia stood quickly. She knew there would be no more gazing at the sky, no more daydreaming.

They walked on.

Finally, when Julia thought she could not take another step, when night had fallen around them, Steven announced that it was time to set up camp.

"Same partners as last night. Same schedule. Same rules."

They arranged themselves for the night. Julia ate her evening cube quickly, drank a little water, and leaned against a tree, ready and anxious for sleep.

She felt around in her pack one last time.

Her ammonia bottle was missing.

CHAPTER TWENTY-TWO

EARTH PROTECTION AGENTS

Day 8

Julia didn't want to spend another night with Steven, wondering what he was going to do. She didn't want to be in Earth Protection in the first place. She had spent most of her life being where she didn't want to be.

She fought sleep. Her mind wandered. She thought of Robert, her Authority-mandated partner. They had been getting along all right.

Mostly.

They shared their living space in Compound 14 and did their assigned duties. Julia walked her board; he did his job at Recycle. Robert hated Re-Cy. Who wouldn't? It was a messy business, recycling. It must have been foul in there. The acrid smell clung to his clothes. Julia had to hang them out the back window slit of their living space to air them out.

They had lived a dull life of coexistence.

Steven shifted his weight slightly against the tree and she tensed, waiting for what he might do next. She heard him snore and she relaxed. But she had to stay awake, stay alert.

One of the sleeping men coughed, which brought back the memory of Robert's cough. Julia had made him go to Human and Health Services to be checked. Robert said you couldn't judge a department by its name—*Services*—because they all had nice-sounding names to cover up what really went on there. But she insisted, so he went.

And he never came back.

Maybe she was wrong to make him get checked. Maybe she wouldn't be here with Steven if she hadn't insisted.

The Authorities had their regular Social Update meeting the evening that Robert had disappeared. She had to go by herself, wrapped in a loneliness she'd never felt before.

But now, sitting with Steven in the woods, that same feeling of loneliness returned.

The meeting that night hadn't been very long. Only one announcement: the Authorities said it was time for women to be part of the military. That caused a buzz among the Citizens. You could hear it, a ripple of whispers, a shuffling of feet. Julia heard someone mumble: "Not enough men?" She knew there were not enough men. At least, there weren't enough strong, healthy men. Just looking around at the meeting, all she could see were thin, hungry-looking people: men with hunched shoulders, gaunt faces, and women in headscarves, their faces pale in the coming dusk.

The next morning, she was put into the Earth Protection Agency. Two Enforcers gave her a new uniform and escorted her to the Social Update Stage, where an Authority stood with the five men.

"That's Steven. You're now a trainee under his command. Do as he says." Then they left her.

She would not do as Steven commanded.

Adam and Guy shuffled over to wake Julia and Steven. She was awake, aware of every sound. She heard the slitherings and rustlings in the grass, tree branches rubbing together in the breeze, wood on wood, and the mournful hooting of an owl.

Steven and Julia took their watch positions. He didn't lean against her at first. She heard Adam and Guy settle down to sleep, heard them sliding their backpacks across the grass. She had her own pack on her lap, her arms wrapped tightly around it. She could feel the hard handle of the ax and the smooth shape of the knife through the cloth.

Long minutes passed before the breathing of the other men became slow and regular. Long minutes of her holding her body tense, her knees pulled up, pushing her pack against her chest, making her body as small as possible.

She felt Steven shift his position, turning toward her.

She smelled his breath. Foul. Felt his breath on her cheek. Warm.

He was reaching for her, touching her.

"Stop it," she hissed through her teeth.

One of the other men called out softly. "Everything okay?" It was Winston.

"Yes," Steven responded. "Thought we heard something. But everything's fine. Go back to sleep." Then he leaned close to her, his mouth by her ear. "This isn't over."

She reached into her pack and pulled out the first thing she felt. The ax. She held it in front of her, making sure he could see it.

"Yes, it is over. *Sir.*"

CHAPTER TWENTY-THREE

Steven backed off when he saw the ax in Julia's hand, but he pulled his mouth tight into a snarl, teeth exposed. His large hand, curled into a ball of hard white knuckles, was just inches from her face. "I'm in charge of this team and you report to me. You'll do as I say," he hissed.

"Really, sir," Julia said as softly as she could, even though she was quivering inside. "I will report you to an Enforcer when we return. *Sir.*" The ax hung heavily at her side, the wrist strap cutting into her skin.

"Big problem there. First, they won't believe you, they'll believe me. Second, there isn't an Enforcer or Authority who wouldn't do the same with you, given the opportunity."

"There are rules, sir, about pairing. The Authorities make the rules. You know that as well as I do."

"The rules are for the little people. Like you. The rules are not for people with titles. Like me."

He turned away to wake the other men. His back was straight, stiff, his shoulders squared and rigid.

They were walking again, single file. Julia thought it would make more sense to spread out, side by side, to explore the ground beside the stream and in the woods beside it. But she wouldn't make any suggestions to Steven. Besides, she wasn't seeing any more clues or signs that this area had been disturbed.

A band of salty sweat formed under the brim of her hat. It ran down her face, into her eyes, burning them. Her right heel hurt. She thought maybe she was getting a blister. Nourishment cubes would come later, when they took a break. Julia wondered if they would ever feel fully rested.

Winston was in front of her. She watched his back as he walked. She saw the way his arms and legs moved in opposition, right leg swinging forward with left arm and left leg forward with his right arm. Everything about him was strong and balanced. His backpack was centered squarely between his shoulder blades. His neck was straight and his hairline clean, smooth.

He turned his head once toward Julia and whispered. "Are you all right?"

"Okay for now," she answered.

"If you ever need help . . ." He stopped. Steven had turned around, and was walking backward, looking at them.

Her skin felt as cold as snow, but inside there was a soft pink warmth in her chest.

They walked on.

A snake, dull stone-colored, lay strewn like a curved rope across a rock by the stream, motionless, waiting for prey.

Mosquitoes swarmed her arms and face, buzzed by her ears, landed on the back of her neck. She was glad then for her long sleeves and pants. Winston swatted the back of his neck. Ahead of him, Julia could see Nigel and Adam doing the same. They were all being bitten.

Steven held his arm up for them to stop and pointed into the woods. They followed him, slipping their packs off their shoulders with relief. Julia sat on an uneven log, feeling the rough bark through her clothes. Hundreds of ants crawled in and out of cracks in the wood.

Steven sat facing Julia, staring at her as she ate, his face flat, cold, void of all emotion.

There were no mosquitoes in the shade, just cool, damp air, smelling of leaves. They ate their cubes without talking. The only sounds were the crunching of them chewing, the gulping sound as they drank water from their bottles, birdsong, and the rustle of animals in the shadows. There were no fences here in the Human Free Zone, but Julia still felt trapped.

Steven stood but signaled with his hands for the rest of the group to remain seated. He was quiet for a moment, his eyes moving from one face to another, as though measuring them. No one moved; his gaze had the power to turn them into statues.

"We'll continue the rest of the day in the same direction. But if I see no further clues or signs, I'll rethink my plan. They're out there, somewhere, without supplies. They cannot survive and they cannot outthink me. I will find them, mark my words."

He made it all about him, Julia thought. *Me, my, I.* The man had no humility. Julia saw a small smirk on Winston's face. Was he thinking the same thing she was thinking? Steven turned, and started walking. They followed.

Walking, walking, walking. Julia's heel was a burning hot blister. She longed to take her shoe off, pour some water on it. But she couldn't. She followed, limping a bit, pulling her uniform up, feeling the sweat under her arms. Why pursue these escapees if they had no chance of survival anyway? Was punishment really all that important?

Finally, dusk fell. The sun slipped away slowly, reluctantly, trailing the last bit of daylight behind it like a backward glance. It was time to bivouac.

"Same teams as before. Same time slots."

Shouldn't we switch time frames, Julia wondered, so the middle team could have uninterrupted sleep for once? Shouldn't a good team leader have considered that? But she knew that Steven wouldn't.

They settled in, one team on watch, the rest leaning against trees. Julia dreaded the night that wrapped around them, making the world murky, full of dark shapes and sounds. She didn't sleep, couldn't sleep. Steven slept. She heard his breathing, and could picture the way his mouth hung open with an occasional puff of air moving his lower lip. She pulled her pack closer, between her legs, and waited.

And then it was their turn to keep watch.

Steven surprised her and didn't try to touch her for the longest time. Not until shortly before dawn, right before the edge of the sky turned a rosy red, and the stars one by one tiptoed away. Then it began. She was ready. She knew what she was going to do.

She would scream and run to Winston. He had said he would help her. At least he had started to say that, until Steven turned and stared. Julia knew where Winston was, off to her left, past some small rocks, leaning against the middle tree of three large trees and just several footsteps away.

Steven started to move and Julia instantly stood up. With lightning speed he put his hand over her mouth before she could scream. Then he grabbed her arm, trying to pull her down. She resisted, pulling her arm away, trying to push him back, but he was bigger, stronger than her, and she felt herself slipping backward. In desperation she buried her teeth in the fleshy part of his hand. It tasted of dirt.

Furious, he shoved her. She lost her balance and fell, her ankle twisted under her. That's when she screamed.

The others woke immediately. Winston ran to her; Steven stood, looking down at her, his arms folded tight across his chest. Winston bent down to help her up. She tried to stand, to bear weight, but pain like lightning shot up her leg from her ankle. She crumpled back to the ground. Winston took her shoe off and felt her ankle with his fingertips.

"Probably just sprained," he said. "You'll need to elevate it and rest it."

"Just like that? *You* decide what she should do?" Steven stared at Winston.

Julia tried again to stand but couldn't.

"That's it, she's worthless. She's a weak link. A weak link puts us all in danger," Steven said to the men standing around her. "We'll move on without her. That's the way it works. She's not worth a bullet." He smirked.

Winston's mouth dropped open. "Leave her behind? Alone?"

"That's what I said."

Dawn had pushed itself higher on the horizon; the pale light reflected off dewdrops on the leaves and shimmered on the stream.

"I'll stay with her," Winston said, standing and facing Steven, his arms across his chest, mimicking Steven.

"I think not." Steven reached for his waistband.

"We can't leave her alone here."

"I say we can and we will. We are no better than our weakest member. My job is to rid the team of any weak member for the sake of the rest of the team. I have an assignment. I do it. If things go wrong, if the team is weakened, or worse, attacked and killed, no Authority will send help or come to our rescue. You hear me? *No one*. The Authorities will never come to our aid, acknowledge our destruction, or take responsibility for it. We're on our own." That was the most Steven had spoken since the beginning of the mission. His face was flushed an angry red. And he wasn't finished. "I've seen other teams disappear. No one ever finds out what happened to them. I won't let that happen to my team." He pulled the gun out and pointed it at Winston. "She'll be just as alone if you're lying dead on the ground beside her. Now move out."

Guy jumped back a step when he saw the gun. His left eye twitched more than usual and he put his hand over it. Nigel and Adam showed no reaction. After all, they had been on missions with Steven in the past—they knew how it worked.

Winston didn't flinch at all but kept his arms folded across his chest and stood firmly facing Steven. "I'm going to refill her water," he said. He didn't ask permission. Julia admired him for that.

"Do it fast."

Winston sprinted to the stream, filled all her bottles, and ran back. He laid them, wet and cold, against her ankle.

Then they were gone. Julia thought she heard Winston whisper that he'd be back. Or did she want to hear that so badly that she had imagined it?

She knew one thing with certainty. At least for now, she was completely alone.

CHAPTER TWENTY-FOUR

JULIA

Days 9–10

She couldn't believe they'd left her like this in the wilderness. Surely they could have found a way to help her bear weight and walk. She knew it wasn't *they* who made the decision to leave her. It was *he*. Steven. Julia believed the others would have helped her, somehow. Winston would have. She had seen the look on his face. Nigel, Adam, and Guy would have, also, *if* Steven had given the command. But they wouldn't say anything. Steven had a gun. They didn't. It was that simple.

Command and control was what it was all about. And the only ones who have the power to command and control are the ones with the power to kill.

Julia took her hat off and let her hair fall down over her shoulders. She pushed it back, tucking it behind her ears. Robert had liked it when she did that. Sometimes he would reach out and do it for her. She hoped he was in a safer place than she was. The woods, the stream, the day stretched before her and she sat there, helpless. She pushed her fingers against the side of her swollen ankle. Two dents, like fat dimples, were left when she took her fingers away. Pushing on it didn't really hurt. That was a good sign, she guessed. Maybe it would heal quickly. But she didn't like the bruised blueness of it. The water bottles Winston had left were no longer cold. At first they felt good. Now they just felt heavy.

She tried to stand. She rolled onto her knees and gripped a small, low branch on a nearby tree. It bent, but didn't break, when she used it to pull herself up. She stood on her good foot unsteadily. The branch creaked an objection to her weight. She swayed a little with it, like a one-legged dancer.

Slowly, ever so slowly, she put her right foot down, testing it. Again lightning-white pain streaked from her ankle up her leg. Not quite as bad as when she first fell, but still painful. She raised her foot, rested a moment, then tried again, but the pain was intense. Unbearable. Maybe, she thought, if I can get down to the stream and put my foot in the cold water, that would help. Sitting back down, she grabbed her backpack and slid, using her good foot to pull herself forward. The fallen leaves were damp and slippery. That made it a little easier. Her uniform bunched up around her hips; she didn't care. There was no one here to see her. No one here to help her.

The stream was shallow. She rolled her pant leg up to her knee. The only way to get her ankle into the cold water was to turn it sideways and lean it on a smooth, mossy stone underwater. Not bad. The moss was soft. The cold water felt good, washing over her ankle, rippling between her toes. Rummaging through her pack, she counted her nourishment cubes. She still had the ax, the change of clothes, and the water bottles. Everything she was issued, except the ammonia spray, but nothing that would help her walk. Only the cold water could help her with that.

Maybe when it didn't hurt so much to move around she could make some sort of a crutch from a tree limb.

The sun changed slowly from pink dawn to full golden daylight and moved from peering shyly over the horizon to its lofty position overhead. No clouds today. A small brown deer came to the creek, splayed its spindly front legs and dipped its head to drink, but spun around and raced off when she moved, the white patch on its raised tail visible before disappearing into the shadows of the woods. She pictured herself leaping onto its back and riding away somewhere. Anywhere but here.

Her head hurt, both temples throbbed. She cupped some water in her hands and splashed her face. Water was such a simple thing, but so important. If the people in the Compounds only knew how much there was, they would be outraged. Instead, they accepted their humble rations of water without a murmur. Julia promised herself that if she ever got back there she'd tell them. *I'll whisper it to one or two people,* she thought, *they'll whisper it to others, and it will ripple out. Ripple out like water itself.*

But someone might report her.

Risky business, whispering the truth.

A dark green bullfrog croaked, its throat puffed out, making it look bigger. It reminded her of the Enforcer who gave the orders to go into this Human Free Zone. All puffed up and loud with its own importance.

Dragonflies with silver-blue bodies and black wings skimmed above the surface of the water. Other frogs, smaller than the bullfrog, their faces green, bodies brown, floated in a still section where the water wasn't moving. On the edge, great reeds and other plants grew. A bird, black with splashes of red on its wings, kept some kind of vigil, flying from tree to tree, crying out shrill warnings. It must be protecting a nest from her. Little did it know that Julia was more helpless than it was.

Her mind wandered, her thoughts random. Looking at dragonflies, listening to frogs, she was doing what Robert said she always did. Daydreaming. What good was that? She had to focus, had to think.

Could she crawl back alongside the stream to where they had

started three days ago? How long would it take to crawl all the way back to the Compound? And if she did make it, what would the Enforcers or Authorities do to her for not being part of the team, for not being productive?

She knew sitting here was not a solution. She had to try *something*.

She pulled her foot out of the water, forced her shoe on over her wet, swollen foot. She slipped her backpack onto her shoulders, got onto her hands and knees, and tried to crawl.

Immediately, the backpack slipped off her back and dangled by her side, the weight of it pulling her off-balance. One canvas strap pulled tightly against the side of her neck. She took it off her shoulders.

Dragging the pack beside her, she tried again to crawl. The pack bounced beside her. She could hear the ax banging against the water bottles inside and against the ground. Rocks and pebbles dug into her knees, ripping her trousers. She kept trying to go a few more feet, then a few more feet.

Soon her knees were bleeding.

She couldn't go on. It was too painful. Reality swept over her, trailing cold fingers up and down her spine: she was going to die here. Alone.

The sun made its predictable journey across the sky while she passed a long day sitting with her foot in the cold water. Then the sun sank below the horizon and she spent a long night in restless sleep.

Finally, dawn erupted all around her again, waking her with the sounds of the forest.

As the day passed, she tried several times to stand, but the pain was too great. There was no sign of Winston or the team. She felt helpless and, more than that, hopeless.

A wail rose in her throat, a burning rush of air that poured out of her.

She screamed.

CHAPTER TWENTY-FIVE

JOHN AND JOAN

Days 8–10

They had walked upstream for eight days. John decided they should walk two more days in the same direction, dropping clues, then cross over to the other side and follow the water back downstream. He was hoping they had thrown off any search teams and that he and Joan would eventually catch up with David, Emmeline, and the children. In Joan's opinion, he was hoping for a miracle. If they each walked for ten days in opposite directions then, by her math, it would take them nearly a month—assuming they walked much faster than the children—for her and John to catch up. And she honestly didn't know how much longer she could do this.

How far had they walked that day? The terrain was so rough. Rocks and logs and little black bugs, hard to see, nipped at their faces and arms.

They had scavenged for food as they walked, things like berries and even grass. They left clues, scattered along the trail like flotsam. Their shoes were wearing thin. Their nerves were wearing thin. The stream was growing thin. And so were they.

They only talked when they took a break or stopped for the night.

But they had lots of time to think between dawn and dusk. Joan pulled her memories out and looked at them, thought about them. Some were like precious stones, pretty to look at, the kind of memories that made her smile. She thought of their farm back then, in the before-times, with long, straight rows of corn, standing still as sentries in the field, and bushy green tomato plants that hid their bright red fruit under the leaves. Standing in the field, picking one of those perfect, sun-warmed gifts of food, the juice running down your chin, made you feel child-like and carefree. They'd had picnics with neighbors and the children caught fireflies and put them in canning jars with holes punched in the lids. Sometimes they'd take the children to the zoo. She thought of her rose garden, and the little stone bench in the middle. John had laid a stepping-stone path so she could walk among the roses and tend to them. Her roses won prizes at the county fair. That was long ago, back when she thought roses were important.

Other memories were dark. The way their lives changed, slowly at first. A little regulation here and another one there. Nuisances, but they tolerated them. Then came bigger rules and regulations rolled out at what later became known as "reeducation meetings." They weren't called that at first, of course—they were called "sustainable development meetings." Sustain this, sustain that. Protect this, protect that.

Protect the Earth. Protect the water. Back then, they had to pay taxes for rainwater runoff on the farm. How ridiculous that was, a rainwater-runoff tax. The corn, the tomatoes, all the crops shriveled one hot summer when they couldn't irrigate. Joan's roses died, too, that same summer. All that potential food lost, food that people needed, just to protect water. The people weren't protected. Ah, but the government was there to help, they said. Yes, indeed, they were there.

Before the government took over their farm, they promised Joan and John positions in charge of the farm commune. That made sense since they were, after all, farmers. And David was promised a job as a

Gatekeeper. They would be provided with housing, clothing, and food. It all sounded good.

At first, Joan didn't see a big problem with any of it. She had no idea, no suspicions, at the time, because, by nature, she was hopeful and trusting.

John didn't like the idea of not owning his own property, but private property ownership was outlawed under new regulations, regulations passed by their duly elected representatives, so he had no choice but to accept what they said.

Joan thought she could still grow roses in their new job. She couldn't. No roses at the farm commune. No flowers at all. Flora and fauna were to be protected from humans. But Citizens were not protected. They were worked until they no longer had any value. Citizens had to give more than they took.

She quickly lost her naïve and trusting nature. But by then it was too late.

Later, long after the relocation, the Authorities decided the farm commune didn't need managers anymore. They said that armed guards would be enough to keep the workers doing their jobs. Joan and John were reassigned. John was put on the Transport Team; Joan was to manage the Children's Village.

John was signaling now that she needed a break, pointing to a little grove of trees. Was John as tired as Joan was? Probably not. His job on the Transport Team was physical and gave him endurance. Her job as manager of the Children's Village was mental, not physical. Even still, she had failed miserably at it. The children under her supervision hadn't thrived. They were going to be relocated, and that's why Emmeline had escaped with Elsa. It was all her fault.

Joan sat beside John, grateful for the chance to rest.

"What do you think?" he asked. "Should we continue?"

Joan shrugged. "Whatever you think best. I trust your judgment."

"I've changed my mind about going upstream for two more days.

I think it's time to cross over. Walk on the other side and start down-stream. Start going in the direction David would have chosen."

"I like the sound of that," Joan said, eager to reunite with her family. "Let's do it."

"If we're lucky and the Protectors have been following our clues, they will be walking upstream while we are on the opposite side. They could easily spot us if we're not careful. We'll have to move away from the stream, deeper into the woods, where we can't be seen. But we'll still keep the stream in sight and follow it as best we can. We must be very vigilant at all times. Keep our eyes and ears open."

Joan nodded that she heard him. "Can we sit for a while longer?"

Squirrels skittered around them and chased each other, spiraling up and around tree trunks, like playful children. When had they last seen playful children? Playfulness had been programmed out of them in the Children's Village. Walking on toy energy boards was not play, it was training at the most basic level.

"We can't waste time," John told her. "The longer we sit, the greater distance we'll have to cover to reach David." He was right. But then he rubbed her arm and added, "Two more minutes can't hurt."

"I thought there were wolves in the Human Free Zone," Joan said. "That's what the Authorities told us."

"The Authorities told us a lot of things that turned out not to be true. Wolves probably aren't native to this area," John said. "Farther west is where they'll be. Probably coyote and fox around here, but they won't attack us."

A hawk swooped in, its great wings beating the air, and hooked its talons into one of the squirrels on a distant branch. The other squir-rels played on, oblivious, while the bird soared away, its prey dangling helpless.

They crossed the shallow stream, stepping from stone to stone to keep their shoes as dry as possible. John spotted some edible mush-rooms and they ate them as they walked. The stream curved this way and that, following the path of least resistance. That's what they had done when it came to the relocation. They too had chosen the path of least resistance and look where it had taken them.

They moved away from the stream, into the edge of meadows and woods. A furry red animal ran in front of them, its tail full, feathery almost, with a white tip. It turned, and headed into some underbrush. Joan could see its pointed nose, small ears like triangles standing up on the side of its head. She stopped walking.

"Only a fox," John said. "They're shy, unless they have rabies. That one looked healthy enough."

Joan hoped he was right about that. And she hoped he was right about the wolves not being native to this area. She had to trust him. He was all she had. Everything else was gone.

They walked for two days, careful now not to leave any trace or clue they had been there. Insects buzzed in the grass and in the air with whirring sounds and chirps. Leaves rustled. As silent as John and Joan were, they were always surrounded by one sound or another. Even the breeze made noise as it moved past their ears, across their faces. The earth was abuzz with the music of living things.

And then there was another sound, a distant, faint but desperate sound. It was the sound of a woman. Was she crying or shouting? Joan couldn't be sure what it was. She leaned forward, listened harder.

Maybe it was Emmeline.

CHAPTER TWENTY-SIX

EMMELINE

Day 10

We were all outside, in front of the cave's black opening. The cool morning air coming from the cave felt like the river water washing over my clean skin.

"Tonight we forage." Paul looked up through the tree branches. "Lots of clouds today. And the moon will be low."

"Forage?" I asked Paul. "Tonight *we* forage?"

"We," he answered. "You and me. The night walk is getting harder for Ingrid, and David still needs to rest. I know he's getting better but I don't want him to have any setbacks."

I looked at David as he cuddled Elsa. Paul was right. I could tell from the way he moved his arm that it still bothered him a little.

"How do we gather food? How dangerous is it?" The thought of venturing back in the direction of the commune and the Compound made me uneasy. But I couldn't deny it; we needed fresh food.

Micah, done gathering twigs for the fire pit, moved closer to us. He was always curious. I loved that about him.

"The commune is an accessible distance from here. But we have to plan to get there when it's dark and the workers are asleep."

"Don't you worry about leaving a path in the woods? A path that would lead guards back here?"

"The forest destroys any path with plants that grow quickly. Ferns, for example. And falling leaves quickly cover footprints. And, when we go to the river for water, we walk on the stones I scattered so no trail is created."

He had thought of everything.

"What time of day will we leave?"

"Afternoon. We'll walk through the woods. We get there around dusk."

"I think it took us longer than that to get from the commune to here," I said.

"You followed the water and it meanders. It's not far as the crow flies," Paul said.

Meanders. That sounded so casual, so carefree. Our painful, rushed escape was anything but casual and carefree.

Micah looked at me. "Where are you going?" His voice was frail, thin, worried.

"It's all right," Paul said. "We're not going away for long." He must have heard the worry in Micah's voice.

"But where are you going?" Micah persisted.

"The more important question is 'Why are you going? Always ask why. Where doesn't matter as much as why."

Micah gave an impatient shrug of his shoulders. "All right. *Why* are you going?" Paul had the wisdom that comes with age, while Micah had the curiosity of youth, and I loved seeing them interact.

"We're going for food. Our rations are low and we now have more people to feed."

I knew he was talking about us. My shoulders slumped with the weight of that responsibility.

"But if we have more people to feed, that means we have more people to help us forage," Paul said in his even, soft voice. "Does that make sense? Does that balance out everything?"

I knew he was directing that at me, making sure I saw the positive part of the situation. I raised my eyes and looked at him. He was smiling. The mud he still wore on his face cracked along the smile lines.

"We take empty sacks with us. We wait till dark. The guards ring a bell. That's the signal for the workers to go into their tents. Then the night sounds start."

"What are the night sounds?" I asked.

"Owls hoot. Raccoons screech. The workers snore. The night is full of noises. Eventually the dusk-to-dawn guards will also sleep. They always do. That's when we slip in, along the edge of the rows. We'll pick as much as we can, and fill our sacks with all we can carry. We'll slip away before dawn and start the long walk back."

"I'm going with you," Micah said. "Three people can carry more than two." It wasn't a question. It was a statement.

"No, Micah, you can't. It's too dangerous," I said.

Paul turned to me intently. "Emmeline, what is more dangerous? Foraging? Or not knowing why and how to forage? It's not just about picking crops that don't belong to you, it's about knowing how to cautiously enter an unsafe area without being detected, gather food left on the plants, and return safely. It's a skill you will all need to survive."

Indeed, what was more dangerous? I knew that Paul was right.

I looked at Micah. He returned my gaze without blinking. This child trusted me. What was more important? That I keep him safe, confined, and protected? Or that I let him explore and learn? Mother had always kept me protected. But did her shielding me ever really help?

I took a deep breath. David came over, sat beside me, and put Elsa in my lap. The soles of her feet had dirt on them. I brushed it off and saw the healthy pinkness of her skin.

I took a deep breath and squeezed Micah's hand.

"Yes, Micah, yes. You can come."

CHAPTER TWENTY-SEVEN

Micah was so excited, he barely slept. But then, I hadn't either. The best we could do was lie quietly, and even that was hard for eight-year-old Micah.

"Is it time to leave yet?" He asked the same question over and over again. "Is it time to leave yet? Is it time to leave yet?" Every time he asked, he shook my shoulder. The answer was always the same: "When Paul says so." But he would ask again. "Is it time to leave yet?"

"You ask that question one more time," I finally told him, "You're not coming along!"

He was silent immediately. I wished I had thought of that sooner! He still tossed and turned, but at least he was quiet.

Finally Paul came to us. "It's time," he said.

Ingrid gave us sacks made of rough cloth that smelled like old brown grass. Inside were bits of dried meat. Jerky, Paul called it. I had never seen anything like those hard, shriveled brown bits. Paul said it was dried squirrel. He had a strange thing slung over his shoulder.

"Bow and arrows," he said. "I don't have many arrows left. Hope I don't have to use any on this trip. Emmy, bring along your knife.

When we get back, I'll make Micah some kind of weapon. Every boy should have a weapon. Maybe a spear. Should have thought of that sooner."

Bows and arrows, spears, and jerky were all new to me. I had as much to learn as Micah. I slipped my knife into the sack. Then I made David promise three times to take good care of Elsa. Paul waited patiently for a while but then said, "It's time to go, Emmy. Now."

He said *now* quietly but firmly. I gave Elsa and David one last kiss on their foreheads and touched my hand to my heart.

We stepped away from the cave and started into the woods, away from the river. Flowing water had marked our path ever since we escaped the Compound. Now we were leaving it behind.

Every few steps I looked over my shoulder at Elsa, David, and Ingrid. But soon we were in the thick woods and I could only see trees behind me, in front of me, all around me.

The woods were dim. Sunlight filtered through and shadows danced as the leaves moved with the breeze. Micah followed behind Paul; I followed behind Micah. Single file, step by step, we went uphill and downhill. This land was a continuous rolling of ups and downs.

Paul stepped around logs instead of over them. "Avoiding snakes," he said over his shoulder. "Snakes live under logs and on stones."

"Boa constrictors?" Micah asked.

"No. Copperheads," Paul said.

"Copperheads?" I walked a wide berth around logs.

"A poisonous snake with uneven bands of light brown and dark brown. Looks like a pile of fallen leaves."

Now every pile of leaves was suspect. Every log. Every stone. Every step.

We kept walking.

Paul stopped often to point out something.

"That's poison ivy. Leaves of three, let them be."

We rested once. Just once.

"These are morels. Mushrooms. Very good eating." He plucked the oddly shaped brown things and put them in his sack.

We walked on.

"Ramps." He pulled the plants from the soft soil. They had green leaves and white stalks. "The whole plant is edible." The green smell was strong, inviting. He put them into his sack. Micah watched, then pulled more ramps from the dirt, shook them off, and put them in his sack. He was already getting into his role as a young hunter-gatherer. I found some ramps, too.

"Over there," Paul pointed. "A buck." I saw a large animal, brown, with a thick body and wide chest. It had two large curved horns, one on either side of its head, with smaller spikes off the main horns. "An eight-pointer. Good one. If we were closer to home, I'd shoot him for the meat and the fur. Too far to haul him back, though." The animal gave a snort, perked its ears, and with a flick of its white, pointed tail, ran into the shadows. I don't know why, but I felt sad watching it run from us. I didn't want to be feared.

Dusk began to creep in on its dirty little feet. Slowly, the light faded. Birds twittered, settling into resting places in the branches.

Then, there it was, in the distance ahead of us: the flat brown fields of the farm commune. The workers were just dots moving along the rows. Little dots, so small that it was easy to forget that they were people.

"We'll move a little closer. Then we'll wait for darkness," Paul said.

Clouds with dark underbellies lay low on the horizon. As the sun slipped away, the gray-white moon appeared, a narrow sliver, like a torn fingernail.

Micah curled up, a warm little boy, and leaned against me. Soon his eyes were closed, his breathing slow and even. In the distance, there was a low rumble of thunder, and a faraway white flash of lightning. The air grew cooler, the thunder closer.

"Rain," Paul said. "That's a good thing."

"A good thing? Why?"

"When it storms, few workers will leave their tents for any reason. The guards will seek shelter, too, and keep the flaps closed to stay dry."

The first drops of rain pinged against the leaves, my arms, and my legs. Micah sat up, awake now.

The rain came harder, the thunder louder. "Move away from the trees," Paul said. He stood and walked toward the field of food.

A field of food.

The words were like music. Lightning flashed cloud to cloud in jagged lines. Micah clung to my hand. They were wet and slippery together. Our sacks were damp, the smell of wet cloth even more pungent.

The workers were gone from the field. The tents, a straight row of triangles along the end of the field, were being pummeled by the rain. It sounded like a thousand drumbeats. Thunder growled along the horizon.

We stood at the edge of the field. At our feet were plants and food, ours for the taking. "We will spread out. Emmeline, stay where you are. I'll go to the far end of the row; Micah will be halfway between us." Paul and Micah moved away from me, and I was alone. I could barely see them in the dark.

I began picking. The peas were firm in their pods, little bulges beneath the hull. It was easy to snap them from the vine. Hold the plant with one hand, pick with the other. Twist, pull, twist, pull. My sack was an open mouth, waiting to be filled. I did not see the man come out of his tent. I did not hear him walking toward me.

Twist, pull, twist, pull. I allowed myself to eat one or two of them as I worked.

Twist, pull. Fill the sack.

Then I saw bare feet next to me, wet and muddy, toes splayed against the dirt. A heavy metal ball and chain was attached to a leather collar around his ankle. The rain shimmered on the metal and ran down the ball in little streams.

I looked up. The man towered over me while I was bent as though praying over the plants. It was too dark to see his face. I felt pressure in my chest, as though it was being squeezed by a giant hand. Micah and Paul were too far away for me to be able to warn them. I tried, but no sound came out of me. The peas in my hand fell to the ground. My fingers had lost their strength; my arms were limp. If this man saw me, maybe a guard would, too. Oh, dear sweet Jesus, I must not be seen by a guard.

"Stand up," he said. His voice was familiar.

My legs had no strength, would not straighten. I could not stand.

"Stand up." Where had I heard that voice before?

I felt a hand on my shoulder. My clothes were wet, clinging to me. How far away were Paul and Micah?

The hand tugged on my arm, pulling me upright. The man and I stood face-to-face. In a flicker of lightning, I saw his hair, his eyes, and his forehead. I knew him.

It was George, the first partner the Authorities had assigned to me. He was Elsa's father.

CHAPTER TWENTY-EIGHT

He wasn't as large as I remembered. His hair had thinned and his shoulders weren't as broad. It was as if all of him had shrunken, been reduced somehow.

"Emmeline?" George's voice was shaking, unsure. "Oh my God, Emmeline. Is that really you? How did you get here?" He took a step closer, his arms reaching for me. The metal ball dragged behind him. I felt and heard his desperation. I took a step back and fought the urge to run. Would the guard hear him? I looked around. I saw no one.

It couldn't be George standing in front of me. It just couldn't be. The Authorities told me he and Father were dead. "We regret to inform you . . ." they had said, but there had been no regret, no sorrow or pity in their voices, and no expressions on their faces. None. Mother had wailed, her cries so shrill I felt like they were cutting my skin. I had asked to see their bodies but the Authorities said that wasn't possible. They said it was a bus-box accident, that the brakes had failed going downhill. But now here he was, in front of me. If he was alive, maybe Father was, too. I looked around, hoping to see the dark shadow of another man, hoping I'd see Father.

"The baby? You had our baby?"

The rain beat down, relentlessly pummeling us. Were those tears on his face mixed with the rain?

"They said you were dead." I heard myself say the words but it was as if someone else was talking, not me. I felt disconnected from my own voice. "They said Father was dead."

He didn't say anything for a long moment. There was a wall of awkward silence between us. I waited for his answer, afraid to breathe.

Finally, he spoke. "Your father died. I didn't."

I let out a huge puff of air as though I had been punched in the stomach. I had never seen Father's body, so a part of me had held out hope he was alive somewhere, somehow. But George said he was dead. That made it final. Grief lay heavy on my shoulders. George had been there. George knew the truth. I trusted him.

I dropped the half-full sack of peas and sank to my knees, the ground wet and cold on my legs. Peas spilled from the open mouth of the sack onto my feet. George knelt in front of me.

"The night we planned to smuggle you out of the Compound before you had the baby. Do you remember?"

Of course I remembered. It had rained that night, too. I didn't go to the Social Update meeting. I slept instead. Pregnancy had privileges. The three of them—Mother, Father, and George—were whispering, planning. I heard them when I woke. Father was nervous, pacing to the window slit, urging everyone to talk quietly.

"I remember," I said. "I remember asking Mother if it was dangerous. She said yes, that most good things are."

"She was such a wise woman. Is she with you?"

Of course, he didn't know she was gone. "They took her away." The words came out of my mouth as flat and hard as stones.

"Dear Lord. They took her away? It never ends, does it?"

We fell silent for a moment, lost in dark memories. The rain began to ease, the thunder becoming less frequent.

"You didn't answer me about the baby? You had the baby?"

"Yes. I had the baby. A girl."

"I have a daughter?"

"Yes."

"Is she in the Children's Village?"

His questions nearly tumbled over themselves, but I understood why—I had questions, too.

"What happened that day?" I asked. "The day they said you died."

"The brakes failed. It wasn't an accident. The wooden brake had been cut through halfway. The Authorities did that. They must have heard us talking and knew our plan."

Someone was always listening, tracking, collecting information, reporting.

"How did you survive that?"

"When the brake snapped, the bus-box rolled over us. I fell first and . . ." He paused, his voice trembling. "And your father fell on top of me. He took the full brunt of the bus-box on him. I know he saved my life that day. But saved me for what? This?" He pointed to his ankle with the collar and ball and chain. "They pulled me out from under your father and the bus-box. They left your father there to rot. Said Re-Cy was too far away and that he was too heavy to drag. Pure evil. That's what the Authorities were. That's what they will always be."

The clouds lay across the top of the moon like a headscarf. I could see his features more clearly now. He looked tired, older than I remembered. His face was crisscrossed with deep lines.

"First they took everything that ever mattered to me," he said. "Then they took me. Put me in leg irons because I was high risk for escaping. We're not allowed to talk to each other here. I have no human contact. They've taken everything from all of us, piece by piece."

I remembered his kindness, his gentleness.

"I'm not the same person anymore. I'm not the same man you knew." He said this in a monotone, his voice hard. He used to call me little teapot. He used to make me laugh. And now, here we were in the dark and rain on the edge of a muddy field of peas. The twists and turns of time that separated us had now rejoined us.

"I changed when they put the metal and leather of this ankle bracelet on me. When they made me walk here, dragging this heavy ball behind me the whole way. They laughed. That's what changed me even more: them laughing. What's done is done. I can't fight it anymore." He paused, took a deep breath. I could hear the breath, the raspiness and harshness of it. "I wish I had died with your father. I felt like part of me did, the part of me that cared about life."

The cloud that looked like a scarf on the moon slipped away.

"How did you get here?" he continued. "Is it really you, or am I imagining this?"

"I'm here," I said.

"How did you escape? No one escapes. The only way to escape is to die."

"I did. I escaped."

"But how? Why?"

"The how isn't important. The why is. I did it to save our child. I took her out of the Children's Village."

"You did that? Oh, Emmeline, how brave of you. Tell me more about our baby."

"Her name is Elsa, and she's perfect."

"Elsa! Your mother's name. I can't believe I have a daughter! Is she with you? Is she here?" His voice was eager, vibrant for the first time. He stood up, looked around, sat back down, and took my hand. "I want to see her. I need to see her." His hand was cold on mine. I pulled my hand away.

"She's not here with me. She's someplace safe."

"Can you bring her here sometime? Can I see her?"

Could I, would I, ever risk bringing Elsa here? I hesitated before I answered him.

"She's somewhere safe, George. I can't bring her here."

"Is there any way you could help me escape? If you can't bring her here, I could go to her."

Could I? Could I help him escape this commune? Even if I gave him my knife, he couldn't slice through the leather-wrapped metal around his ankle. Even if I could help him, should I? I felt ashamed for the question, but so much hung in the balance. It would mean a lot to him to see Elsa. But it meant more to me to keep her safe. What if the guards noticed that George was missing and were able to track us back to the cave? What if our own safety was compromised? What if I put Ingrid and Paul in danger? I said nothing. It was a choice I didn't want to think about right then. I looked at him uncertainly.

He let go of my hand and stood up. "Now I'm glad I didn't die that day. I have a daughter named Elsa. I will find a way to see her. I have to see her, just once, and make sure she's real so that I'll know that I created something of value in this valueless life. I finally have a reason to live."

"George, I'm afraid someone will hear us talking. I don't feel safe here."

"You want me to go back into my tent? Is that what you want?"

I nodded and sat silent while sadness washed over me.

"You know they will find you, don't you? They won't rest until they do. And I won't rest until I see my child." He walked away, the ball and chain dragging behind him, and disappeared into his tent, the first one in a long line of small, dark tents that served as living spaces.

Living spaces. How ironic. As if these people actually had anything worth living for.

CHAPTER TWENTY-NINE

EMMELINE

Day 11

Paul made no comment about my half-full sack. Instead, he quickly began adding more peas from the ground to it, and Micah joined him. Four hands were frantically stuffing food into my sack. But my hands were shaking so much that I couldn't pick up a single pea. I felt my pulse drumming in my neck and my ears, so loud I wondered if Paul could hear it. Even breathing hurt, as if there were knives between my ribs. I kept searching the flat field ahead of me, looking for George, or worse, a guard, in the moonlight.

The rain had stopped. Stars emerged, one by one, venturing into the sky on sparkling white tiptoes. Some pale light rippled along the horizon, making the stars fade from the competition. Paul stopped picking and tied my sack closed. "Come," he said, in his simple style. Just "come," but it meant *move, move quickly, and follow me*.

We started back toward the cave, our sacks slung over our backs, our clothes wet and clammy, clinging to us. Micah's enthusiasm had evaporated, replaced by fatigue. He struggled to keep up. Paul slowed his pace a little and walked beside Micah, his hand on his shoulder as if he could transfer energy to the child. I followed behind them, looking over my shoulder, watching for any shadow that could conceal a guard following us. All shadows were suspicious. All trees hid danger behind them. Every sound was the sound of stalking.

Finally, after what seemed like an eternity, I could see the cave ahead of us, the entrance darker than the dawn. A few more steps and I saw the vague silhouette of Ingrid, and next to her, David. Should I tell him that I had seen George, that I had spoken with him? No, not yet. I'd have to do it at the right time and in the right way.

We laid our sacks at their feet and collapsed beside them. David reached out and hugged me with two arms. Two arms! He must be feeling better. He picked up some blankets and draped them over my wet shoulders. Elsa crawled over to me and pulled herself onto my lap.

Ingrid dumped the sacks onto the grass and began freeing the peas from the vines and leaves. "In the old days," she said, "we'd throw away the pods. That was wasteful. Now we eat the peas with pods and all."

"Today we'll have a banquet of peas. A celebration!" Paul said. "The three of us gathered so much, far too much for just one feast. After we eat, I'll dehydrate the rest of them for the winter. But for now, we're all exhausted, so it's time to take a little nap." He motioned for Micah and me to follow him inside the cave. Micah yawned.

"I'll rest right here, Paul," I said. David squeezed my shoulder. I leaned against David, his arm around me. Ingrid's fingers flew in a blur, working on the peas. I felt my eyelids slip down, heavy, weighted, but, startled by my own thoughts, I opened them.

Was George as desperate to see Elsa as I was to save her? He was a good man, a kind man. I did not have the right to deny him the chance to see his daughter. Nor did I have the heart to deny him. I would just have to be aware of the risks my decision would create.

Birdsong was all around us with soothing chirps and twitters.

The smell of grass and leaves filled my nose.

The warmth of David's arm was a comfort to me.

Ingrid hummed a tune Mother used to hum. *The itsy, bitsy*

spider . . . I could almost see Mother climbing off her energy board to read to me, before they took the books away.

The sound of peas dropping into a container. Ping . . . ping . . . ping.

I had to get up and walk around. Handing Elsa to David, I went to the latrine just to be alone. There was a burning behind my eyes, and a tightness in my throat. I cried silently, and a stream of hot tears ran down my face. I cried until I was empty of emotion. Or so I thought.

I went back to David. He stared at me and I know he must have seen the streaks on my face. He reached out a finger and traced my cheeks. "Are you all right?" he asked.

"Just tired." I answered. Partly true, I told myself, so it wasn't really a lie.

"Then sleep," he said.

I lay down with my head on his lap and slipped into slumber.

Too soon, David shook my shoulder. I didn't want to wake up. He shook it harder. "Emmy," he said, "You're having a nightmare. Wake up."

I sat up and smoothed my clothes around me. They were still damp.

"You were shouting in your sleep. What were you dreaming?"

"I don't know. What was I shouting?" I had to know what I said, what he heard.

"You were beating your hands on my legs and shouting 'No! No! No!' What were you shouting about?"

"We need to talk," I said. "I have to tell you something." The word *something* didn't seem big enough for what I had to tell him.

"Follow me," I said to him. "Ingrid, will you keep an eye on Elsa?" Elsa was still asleep. Ingrid smiled, her teeth white against the mud on her face. She nodded and kept working on the peas, pinging them into the pot.

We went down the hill to the river. "Splash some water on your face. It will feel good," David said.

I bent toward the cold, rushing water, cupped my hands, and

splashed great handfuls of water on my face and arms, over and over again. The water ran down my chin, my chest, my forearms.

"There she is. My beautiful Emmy." David helped me stand, looked at my damp face, touched my cheek with a single finger, and then kissed me. Standing by the flowing water, I felt his power and love. I felt safe.

"We're alone here. No one can see us." His voice was strangely thick, deep.

He kissed me again, this time with urgency, pressing against me.

"Be with me," he whispered into my ear.

I was suddenly filled with overwhelming desire for him. It burned in me, hot, consuming.

With the stream roaring beside us, our passion was as powerful as the force driving the water, as free as the wind blowing in the trees, as joyful as the birdsong around us. During that time, nothing else mattered.

He never asked me what I meant when I said we needed to talk. And I didn't want to ruin this precious time together.

CHAPTER THIRTY

Ingrid made a meal of peas and some kind of salted fish she had soaked in water all day. I forced myself to eat even though my stomach was queasy. A cold, clammy dread washed over me, chilling my skin. I had to tell David about George even though I knew David would think that doing anything to help George would increase the danger for us. I also knew that David would be right to think that.

Micah was exhausted after the foraging, but grumpily agreed to an early bedtime when Paul promised to take him fishing in the stream soon.

Both children were asleep inside the cave, near the entrance. I could hear the rhythm of their slow, even, deep-sleep breathing. We were sitting in front of the cave as evening veiled us in transparent grayness.

"Tea, anyone?" Ingrid asked in the chirpy voice she had when she talked about cooking.

"Ingrid makes the best dandelion tea! Watch how she does it." Ingrid beamed at Paul's compliment.

She had a pile of plants heaped in front of her. They were the same yellow flowers I had seen on our first day outside the Compound. Ingrid rinsed the plants, roots and all, in a pail of water, then set about crushing the roots between two stones. I moved closer and watched.

"May I try?" I asked. She moved aside and I crushed some roots while she picked the smallest leaves off other plants. The smell of the roots was like wet wood; the sound of stone against stone was grating, like grinding your teeth. When we'd finished with all the plants, Ingrid scooped everything up and dumped it all into a pot of hot water on the fire pit.

"A watched pot doesn't boil," she announced, like she was giving a cooking lesson, then sat next to Paul. "It'll be ready in a bit."

We sat quietly, waiting for the tea, watching the stars appear, one by one, like shy children tiptoeing across the sky. The trees were dark silhouettes around us. Most birds had roosted for the night; an owl let out a lonely call from one of the nearby trees. Far away, a fox yip-yip-yipped.

Ingrid served the tea proudly, breathing in the steam and giving a satisfied nod of approval to each mug, before handing them to us. The mug was warm in my hands; I wrapped my fingers around it. I thought I saw movement in the trees, something, I didn't know what. George? It couldn't be, not with that ball and chain. Maybe a guard from the commune had seen me? Even worse, could it be one of the Earth Protectors? Startled, I spilled some hot tea on my leg. Paul quickly got a dipper of cold water and poured it on the burn.

"You jumped." He bent down and looking into my eyes. "Why?"

"I thought I saw something."

He stood, gazed into the woods, then turned back to me. "I don't see anything." He stared at me for a long moment; I had to look away. I felt like he could read my mind.

"Something is bothering you, Emmy," Paul said with quiet conviction.

David looked at me, his face concerned. "Are you okay?" I nodded yes, I was okay.

Liar. I was a liar.

"What makes you say something's bothering her?" he asked Paul.

Paul hesitated. He gazed into the woods again.

"Well?" David said.

"Just a feeling." Paul sat back down by Ingrid and picked up his mug of tea.

"What kind of feeling?" David rested his hand on my knee.

"Yes," I said. "What kind of feeling?" Had he seen George? Or was it just his uncanny ability to know what someone was thinking? I hoped it was neither.

"Last night, at the commune, we were spread out. I was down field; Micah was in between us, and Emmy was at the start of the row, near the tents."

"Why did you let her near the tents alone?" David asked. "That doesn't seem very safe."

It bothered me how they were talking about me as if I wasn't even there.

"I should have known better. But nobody was around. The guard must have been asleep somewhere. They do that, you know. Sleep on duty. When it was time to start back, I gathered up my sack. It was full. Got Micah and his sack was full, too." He took a long drink of the tea and looked up at the sky.

"When we got to Emmy, she was shaking like a leaf, and her bag was only half full and there were spilled peas on the ground around her. She tried to help us pick them up and put them back in the sack, but for every one she picked up, she dropped two. It was as if she had seen a ghost."

Oh, how I wanted him to let go of this! But Paul continued.

"On the way back from the commune, she kept looking over her shoulder. She was practically walking backwards. I was afraid she would trip. And today, she's been jumpy, and even cried out in her sleep. I heard her saying 'No, no, no.' What did that mean?"

"She was just tired," David said.

"Really?" Paul said. "Tonight she thought she saw something in the woods and jumped so bad she spilled tea on herself. Something's on her mind."

"She's been through a lot. That's why she's jumpy tonight. That's all."

Oh, David, if only you knew, I thought. If only you knew. A knot of indecision tightened in my chest. Then I remembered: No secrets. That was our promise. The knot loosened.

I set my mug down and reached for David's hand.

"Paul, you said I looked as if I had seen a ghost."

Paul leaned back, a knowing look on his thin, old face. David peered at me, his brow wrinkled in puzzlement.

"That's because I did."

CHAPTER THIRTY-ONE

"George? That's impossible. George is dead!" David said after I'd told him the whole story.

I heard Micah stirring inside the cave, the rustle of his bed linens, a small cough.

"I saw him. He was standing right in front of me."

"He died in the bus-box accident," David said. "You couldn't have seen . . ."

Paul raised his hand and interrupted David. "Who is this George?"

"He was my partner, before David. He is Elsa's father."

"Emmy, you're tired. You haven't slept. You walked through the woods at night, probably frightened every step of the way, and completely exhausted. Maybe you fell asleep and dreamt it," David said.

"Let her talk. She was there; you weren't. Emmeline, what did you see, what did you hear? Go through it again, tell us everything." Paul was trying to make me relive that night and I didn't want to. My mouth and throat felt dry as paper. I remained silent.

"Well, Emmeline, only you can tell us. Could you have been hallucinating, perhaps?" Paul, with his patient voice and gentle presence, invited me to speak as only he could.

I took my last sip of tea. It had grown cold and bitter, but it still soothed my parched throat. I set the mug down on the ground beside me and looked up at the sky. Should I say, yes, I was just hallucinating? That would be the end of it as far as David and Paul were concerned. Maybe then they would quit talking about it. That would be the easy way out.

Easy, yes, but it would still be in my head, a tarnished memory that would haunt me, a black secret. *No secrets between us, ever.* That was a promise David and I had made to each other, and I had to keep that promise.

"It wasn't a dream, David. He was real and alive." I leaned against him, wanting to be as near to him as possible as I talked.

"What did he look like? What did he say?" Paul urged me forward.

"He's thin now. He said Father saved his life by falling on top of him, taking the full weight and force of the bus-box."

Micah coughed again, and small echoes of that cough bounced off the walls of the cave.

"He has a ball and chain on his ankle."

"A ball and chain?" Ingrid exclaimed. She was following this conversation with unusual interest. "It sounds like he's a slave."

"From what I've learned about the conditions in the Compound, the whole thing sounds like slavery, or worse," Paul said with a grim look on his face.

"What did he say?" David asked.

"It was sad. He said he stopped caring, and that he wished he had died that night along with my father." A feeling of mourning washed over me, the same feeling I had when the Enforcers told Mother and me about the accident.

"What else?" Paul was still pushing for more.

"He didn't know they had taken Mother away. He had no way of knowing about that." I paused. "When I told him, he said, 'It never ends, does it?'"

The weight of those words settled on my shoulders. Would it ever end for me and my family, either?

"Then he would have had no way of knowing about Elsa being with you, either," David said, with some hesitation.

Bats swirled over the stream, dipping and turning, making occasional high-pitched clicking sounds that sounded like tsk-tsk-tsk. It was funny what I could focus on when my whole world was turning upside-down.

"I told him. I told him about Elsa."

"Why? Why would you do that?" I felt the tension in his body.

"What would you want her to do in that situation?" Paul asked David.

"I guess she did the noble thing, but telling him about Elsa was risky. He is her father and he might do something dangerous to try to see her. He might lead danger right to us."

How that hurt me. Clearly he was saying that I had put us all in danger. I had to defend myself against those hurtful words. "I told him because he asked how and why I escaped. The *how* was the hole in the fence and the *why* was Elsa. I escaped because of Elsa and I told him that. I wasn't being noble; I was being honest." I tried not to sound angry. I tried to be calm. But it didn't work. My voice trembled, as fluttery as those bats. "And after I told him, he said he was glad he hadn't died. He was glad he has a daughter. He said he finally had a reason to live."

"There's more, isn't there?" Paul leaned forward. For the first time, I wanted to tell Paul to leave me alone.

"Yes. I had my knife with me. I could have at least tried to cut through the collar on his ankle, to weaken it a little, but I didn't. He almost died for me and I didn't set him free."

"Good," David said. "That was the right decision."

"But did you hear what I said? I could have set him free and I didn't. I walked away from a man who simply wanted to see his daughter one time. I left him as a slave. What kind of a person does that make me? And you think that was *good*?"

"This isn't about good or bad. This is about keeping Elsa safe. Keeping you, all of us, safe."

David stood up, stiff and tall, and walked to the edge of the clearing, his back to me. I went to him. I ran my fingers through the dark hair that curled down over his neck.

"Are you worried that I have feelings for him? Gratitude, that's all I feel. He was kind to me, and gentle. And he and Father risked their lives to get me out of the Compound. But it's you I love. And I love you of my own free will."

His lips brushed my forehead. "Thank you."

Free will. That's the secret. That's the answer. You can tell someone who to pair with, but you can't tell them who to love.

We walked back to the others.

"This is not my business," Paul said. "But I have to ask this question. Isn't freedom what you are looking for, what you're sacrificing everything for? Yet you would deny someone else theirs?"

I felt David shrug, his shoulder moving against mine, but he remained silent.

Micah's cough was a little louder. Was he getting sick?

"What is your decision, Emmy?" Paul asked quietly.

"I don't know. I don't know what the right thing is. I have to keep Elsa safe. I have to! But he is her father and . . ." My voice trailed away.

"It's the danger that I worry about," David said, putting his arm across my shoulders. "That's all."

"Everything is dangerous. Sitting around here and not moving on is dangerous. I just want to do what's right."

"If I could see my father just one time, I would want to." It was Micah! He had been listening, but hesitant to interrupt. His little cough was his way of telling us he wanted to be heard. "So maybe Elsa should, too." He walked over and sat down next to David and me.

I put my finger under his chin and tilted his face up toward mine. "Elsa is too little to remember if she sees her father," I explained to him.

"But you could tell her about it when she got older. You could give her the memory." Micah spoke with the sincerity of a child. He had grown around my heart like a vine.

Give her the memory. Father gave me the memory of my learning to walk just by describing it to me. Telling me how I would fall, laugh, and pull up clumps of grass with joy. Things I would never have known about if he hadn't told me when I was older.

I sat there, quietly thinking. What was the right thing to do? Was there any way to keep Elsa safe and at the same time honor George's request? What would Mother have done? Or better yet, what did I *wish* Mother had done?

I wished she had told me everything, taught me everything.

Had Micah, little Micah, given me the answer?

Give her the memory.

"You and David are the only ones who can decide if that man, George, sees little Elsa. I know you'll make the right decision. I have faith in you." Paul stood up and extended his hand to Ingrid, helping her up. She groaned slightly, and stood slowly.

Paul must have sensed we needed time alone. "It's late. Bedtime for us old people. And little people, too. Come, Micah. Let your mother and father talk alone."

"Come here, Micah. Let me give you a kiss good night." He came to me, smiling his crooked little smile. I kissed his smooth forehead and he kissed mine. What a little mimic.

They went into the dim interior of the cave, leaving David and me alone. Silence settled over us, like a heavy blanket. A ghostly pale barn owl, its heart-shaped white face visible even in the moonlight, settled on a nearby branch.

"Something important did happen when I spoke with George," I said softly.

"What?" David asked warily.

"I saw him change from a man who had no reason to live to a man who had something to live for. That's no small thing. And Elsa is the reason for that change."

A long, heavy silence fell between us. Fireflies flitted, blinking on and off, here, there, little flares of light in the darkness. If Micah were awake, he'd try to catch them. In the distance, from the direction of the field, a small animal screeched. The barn owl must have found dinner.

"Sounds like you already made up your mind."

"No, I haven't."

"What are you waiting on?"

"I'm waiting on you, David. I need your help deciding. It's too big for me to decide alone. We have to do this together. We have to be a team."

"What are our choices?"

"One choice is to do nothing." Doing nothing would mean I didn't have the courage of my convictions, of my belief in freedom. But I didn't say that out loud.

"That sounds the safest. But what other choices do we have?"

"We go back without Elsa and cut off the ball and chain. He'd be free but that wouldn't give him a chance to see his daughter."

"And what would stop him from following us so he could see Elsa? He'd follow us, the guards would follow him, and that would be the end of Paul and Ingrid and our entire family." He began pacing. "There's got to be a way to do this without risking so much."

"How are we going to know what to do; what's right?" I asked him.

"Paul always says look to the heavens."

"Then we should ask Paul for advice."

He smiled and touched my cheek with his hand. "I think we can ask him in the morning. And we can make our decision after that."

Morning, when the sun rises with the promise of a new day, would be the best time to make a decision.

CHAPTER THIRTY-TWO

EMMELINE

Day 12

In the morning I tended to David's arm. Ingrid stood by, watching. As I unwrapped the dressing, she chewed on her lower lip, her teeth pressed so tightly that her lip turned white. When David's wound was visible, she clapped her hands and made a cooing sound. "Oh, that looks good! I'll go make him some more thyme tea."

Indeed, the wound was healing nicely with the edges coming together. This would probably be the last day he'd need to wear dressings. David was well enough that we could move on as soon as the issue with George was settled.

Micah busied himself with his newfound chores, bustling about finding dry wood for the fire pit, checking the traps for rabbits or squirrels. He chased down crickets and other insects for a crunchy breakfast, and presented them to us in a small bowl, smiling proudly, even though we each only got one. We washed them down with the water, milk, sugar drink. Elsa gurgled with baby talk.

I went to the stream, careful to walk on the stones Paul had placed, and rinsed our meager changes of clothing while I watched the fish rise to the top of the water with mouths wide open for insects, and gulp them down. As I splashed the clothing in the cold water, I looked upstream and downstream, watching for anything out of place, any strange movement or sound. No matter how far away I was from the Compound, being watchful was a habit I would never lose.

Paul helped me drape the wet clothing over the vines behind the latrine. If it didn't rain, everything would be dry by afternoon.

Breakfast was over, Ingrid's hair was braided, and all of our chores were done. The day stretched ahead, hours to be filled, decisions to be made. Elsa busied herself with Ingrid's pots and pans, her little fingers picking them up, setting them down, and nesting small things in large things. Sometimes she'd throw one of the smaller cups and then crawl after it. I loved looking at her perfect little feet as she churned forward.

Micah approached Paul with a worried look. "The traps were empty this morning."

"Not to worry, Micah, they often are. Maybe they'll be full later today. And don't forget, there are lots of fish for us to catch. We'll be fine."

Ingrid came out of the cave and propped her broom by the entrance. "Dandelion blooming time is about over," she told Micah. "So let's go find some this morning while they still have their yellow flowers."

David, Paul, and I sat there, wondering who should speak first on the subject of George.

Elsa picked up a small cup, crawled to Paul, and held it up to him.

"Why, thank you, precious." He took the cup, pretended to drink, and handed it back to her.

"She is precious," David said. "Just like her mom." He smiled at me so broadly that his eyes crinkled at the corners.

"So, tell me," Paul said, "what did you both decide to do?"

"We haven't decided." I took the cup Elsa was holding out to me and pretended to drink from it. She gave me a baby grin, the little white tooth buds shining.

"We have some options. But none of them seemed quite right," David said.

"So, tell me what you are thinking."

I listed all the potential plans we had discussed. Paul listened intently as I talked, his eyes never leaving my face.

"May I comment on your ideas and suggest another option?" Paul asked.

"We were hoping you would," David answered him.

"Option one. Do nothing. I don't think Emmy would be happy ignoring that man's need for freedom. She values freedom too much, for herself and for others."

I nodded in quiet agreement.

"The second one. Free him but deny him seeing Elsa, the one thing that apparently is still important to him. Sentencing him to always wonder about her, is she alive, is she well? That would be merely an artificial freedom."

David and I glanced at each other. Paul made sense.

"The last one. Take Elsa to him and free him based on a promise never to lead anyone to her or us. That's too dangerous. Carrying that child through the woods at night to the farm commune? Who knows what could go wrong with that? At the very least, she might cry from being carried for so long and someone would hear her. I say no to that idea. You've risked too much to expose Elsa to that kind of danger."

That left us with no options and I shook my head in bewilderment.

David said what I was thinking. "Then nothing works?"

"I have another idea. I'll go to the farm commune, alone. I will speak with this man and use my judgment on his character. If I judge him trustworthy, I will free him and bring him here to see the child."

"Bring him here? What if you're followed?" David asked.

"David, I've never been followed after I foraged. Never. So I'm not worried about that. Trust me." His voice had a sharp steely tone.

"I'll go with you!" David said.

"No. I'll go alone."

"But why go alone? What if something happens to you?"

"What might happen to me?" Paul asked, serene once more.

"You might get hurt. Or lost."

"David, I'll do my best not to get hurt. And as for getting lost, I've gone there many times and I know the way. I follow the stars. Men have been following the stars since the beginning of time."

"What if he harms you in some way?"

I had to speak up. "David, he would never hurt Paul. He would have no reason to hurt him. It's not in his nature. And besides, if he hurt Paul, Paul wouldn't lead him back here."

We sat quietly for a few minutes. The music of the forest was all around us.

"You need to stay here, and make sure the women and children are safe." Paul was firm on this; I could tell from looking at his face. There would be no further negotiations.

"When would you go?" I asked.

"When conditions are right. When the stars are right but the sky's partially overcast. I'll know. It might be tomorrow night or it might be several nights from now."

"Sooner is better," I said. If it was several nights, that meant travel time lost, never to be recovered.

"A great storm is coming tonight. I can feel it in my bones. When I go depends on the weather."

"Why would you do this, going to the farm commune, risking so much?" I asked.

"Why? Because I can and because it's important to you, Emmeline."

His answer left me speechless. I felt gratitude wash over and through me, warm and soft.

David looked at me and smiled. He liked Paul's idea.

And maybe, just maybe, it would work.

CHAPTER THIRTY-THREE

JOHN AND JOAN

Day 12

"Stop!" Joan called to John. "Listen!"

He turned to her, a puzzled look on his face, and put his finger to his lips, reminding her to be quiet. She touched her ear, then cupped her hand around it, signaling for him to listen. He cocked his head to the side for a moment, then shrugged. She listened, too, but heard nothing more than the noises of nature all around them. Bees, birds, breeze. But there *had* been a sound, a sound of a human being. She was sure of that. As sure as she had ever been of anything. A person was in need, somewhere, within the range of her hearing, and the sound was coming from the other side of the stream.

John walked back to her. "I heard something," she whispered.

"What?"

"A person. I think it was a woman. Crying, I think, or calling out." She pointed across the stream. "From over there, somewhere."

He put his hand above his eyes, shielding them from the sun, and peered intently in the direction she had pointed.

"I don't see anything."

"Neither do I, but I'm telling you, I heard something!" She wanted to search for the source of that noise and she wanted to do it now. "Maybe it was David or Emmeline."

"I don't hear or see anything. Do you think maybe you imagined it? Maybe it was an animal."

She moved closer to him, and touched his shoulder. "Look at me! I didn't imagine it. And it wasn't an animal. We're not alone here. Someone is over there. It sounded like a woman." Her chest tightened with the thought. If it was Emmeline, why was she calling out? Was David with her? If he was with her, why would she scream? The back of Joan's eyelids felt hot, and tears throbbed against them. "Please, John, trust me on this."

She could see his face soften, the frown lines smooth, and his shoulders relax. He gave a little nod of his head, took her hand, and together they headed back toward the stream.

Soon they were at the edge of the shallow water. Joan plunged across, not caring if her shoes got wet. They were pretty much worn out from walking on the rough, stony ground anyway. John was right beside her, his rolled-up Transport uniform hidden under the stolen Enforcer's uniform. Joan's white garments were stained green from moss and grass, and brown from dirt. The Earth's colors had rubbed into the fabric. Her headscarf was draped around her neck and dangled down her chest.

On the other side, they scanned the area but saw nothing. There was no sign of anyone.

Risking all, she called out softly. "Hello? Hello?"

No response.

John surprised Joan. He actually shouted. "Hello! Hello!" That was the loudest sound she had heard since the chaos and gunfire the night they escaped from the Compound. Then silence settled briefly around them. Even the birds were quiet.

Then they heard a response, a faint, faraway plea. "Help."

They headed toward that sound, running, not caring how rocky it was, not caring that their feet hurt. They only cared that someone needed help.

Then they saw her in the distance, lying on the ground. It was a woman with dark hair—not Emmeline. She pushed herself into a sitting position, watched them coming toward her.

When Joan and John were just a few steps away, the woman made the circle sign on her forehead, then put her hands up, as though surrendering. Joan glanced at John. His face was pale, his lips tight.

She was in the Earth Protection uniform.

He was in the Enforcers uniform.

Joan was the only one in clothing that didn't signify power.

Even here, in the Human Free Zone, uniforms had meaning.

CHAPTER THIRTY-FOUR

John wondered who this woman was. What was she doing here? Was she really one of the Earth Protectors? She must be, her uniform had the logo on it. Why was she alone? They always traveled in teams. Always. Then John noticed her ankle. On the outside it was swollen and a painful-looking dark blue. She probably couldn't walk on it, or, if she could bear weight, she'd walk slowly. Either way, she wouldn't be productive. But still, where was the rest of the team? Surely they didn't just leave her here alone. John looked around the area, scanning for any other Earth Protectors. He saw no one. The woman just sat there, staring at John, her hands still raised, her lips trembling. Her face was eggshell-white with fear.

The oddity of the situation settled heavily on John's shoulders, weighing him down as if forcing him into the ground, planting him like a tree in the wilderness.

Joan spoke first, breaking the silence. "Who are you?" she asked the woman. She knelt beside her and tried to make eye contact. The woman turned her face slightly, meeting Joan's gaze briefly.

"My name is Julia." Her voice was low, no louder than a whisper, but the quiver in it was louder than the words themselves. Then she turned back to look at John with that same frightened yet defiant look.

Joan spoke again. "My name is Joan." She reached over and gently touched the swollen ankle.

"Does it hurt?"

Julia nodded and a slow, shining tear slid down her face. She wiped it away with the back of her hand. John could clearly see her red, scraped knees through her ripped trousers and the blood on her hands. There was no way she could harm either of them. No way. Joan must have sensed that Julia was far more vulnerable than them, despite her uniform.

"You can put your hands down." Joan reached up and gently lowered one of Julia's hands and cradled it in her own. "I mean you no harm." Julia put her other hand down, dipped it in the water, and splashed some on her face. Strands of dark hair clung to her cheek; she pushed it behind her ear with a smooth motion.

"How did you hurt your ankle?" Joan's voice was soothing, motherly.

"I fell." Julia reached down and touched her injury with one finger. "I was running and I fell."

"Why were you running?"

Julia shrugged and didn't answer. John looked around again for the Earth Protectors. The team must be nearby, he supposed. But all he saw were trees, squirrels, and helter-skelter piles of fallen, rotting logs. A large turtle, with random brown and dull copper markings on the dome of its shell, lay in the shade on a bed of leaves. John almost didn't see it because the shell was perfect camouflage, protecting it by using the colors of the wilderness. But the movement of its outstretched head and neck caught John's eye. That was the secret to survival out here: blend in. John was grateful for the dark Enforcer's uniform he was wearing, and Julia's camouflage was perfect for this area. Joan's clothing, even though it was dirty, was still far too white.

"Are you really an Earth Protector?" Joan asked.

"Just a trainee."

"A trainee? Really. When did they start using women in the military?"

Julia responded with a shrug. She continued to glance at John frequently, watching to see what he was going to do. He stood erect, feet apart, with his arms folded across his chest as he had seen other men with power standing. The uniform gave him the right to do that.

Joan took her own shoes off and put her feet in the shallow water. "Oh, this feels good! My feet hurt from walking." Julia's face softened a bit and she smiled at Joan. Joan reached into the water, just as Julia had done, and splashed water on her own face.

"So, if you're a trainee, where are your trainers?"

"Last time I saw them, they were headed that way." Julia pointed upstream. John turned and looked but saw no one.

"When did they leave you?"

"Yesterday at dawn."

The sun was high, nearly overhead.

"Why did they leave you?"

Julia didn't answer.

"Because you can't walk? And no one stayed with you?" Joan laid her arm across Julia's back, pulling her closer. Julia didn't resist. She leaned toward Joan, her small frame resting against Joan's side.

"Winston would have stayed. But Steven had a gun and wouldn't let him stay."

"Steven?"

"The team leader."

Bit by bit, Joan was drawing out the information they needed.

"How big was the team? Surely they could have spared someone!" John saw Joan give Julia's shoulder a little squeeze. A squeeze that said *You're important and I'm here to help*. Seeing this, John knew that Joan would have been an outstanding manager at the Children's Village if only she'd been allowed to actually care for the children.

"Six of us, counting me. I don't think I counted very much. Look at me. I'm not much of a team member."

"Who else was on the team?"

"Steven was the team leader. He's the one with the gun. Winston." Her voice softened, then moved briskly on. "Adam, Nigel, and Guy."

So, Winston meant something to her. John, too, was absorbing as much as he could from her short answers.

"And what is the mission of your team?" Joan asked this as though asking what the weather was like, without stressing any importance to the question.

"You probably already know this, him being an Enforcer and all." Julia nodded toward John.

"Oh, he hadn't been briefed on your team, just on his mission." She smiled up at John. "Communications are difficult out here, aren't they?" she asked him.

He nodded in response.

Joan took her headscarf from her neck and dipped it in the water. "Let me wrap this around your ankle. It might help reduce the swelling." With quick, sure motions, she wrapped the ankle. "There. How does that feel?"

"Good. Thank you."

"So, what was your mission?"

The long pause was filled only with a soft breeze, and a white moth fluttering on a small purple flower.

Joan smiled patiently.

"Our mission was to find and return people who escaped the Compound." Her words were flat, her facial features flat, as though she was emotionally detached from her words.

"People? More than one?"

Julia nodded.

"That's impossible. How in the world did that happen? How many?"

"Two men, two women, a boy, and a baby."

"Children? Out here in the Human Free Zone? How will they survive? Have you seen them? Has your team seen them?" For the first time, Joan's voice had urgency.

"No, we haven't seen them. There were clues but no people."

Joan managed to look shocked at this information. Her hands flew to her cheeks, her eyes opened wide. "That is truly unbelievable!"

"I have no reason to lie to you. You asked about our mission. And I told you." She paused and gave John a cold, brave stare. "Now I have a question for you. What are you doing in this wilderness? What is your mission?"

There it was. The question John dreaded. He gave a long pause, then answered it the only way he could.

"My mission is to enforce whatever needs to be enforced." He knew it was not much of an answer, but a citizen would never dare push an Enforcer any farther.

CHAPTER THIRTY-FIVE

JOHN

Day 12

"When is your team returning for you?" John asked Julia, still scanning the area for any movement.

She shrugged. "I don't know. They might never return for me. The mission is more important than any single member. Steven made that clear from the beginning."

"How could a mission be more important than a person?" Joan asked her, sincere concern on her face. *Dear God, Joan,* John thought. *You know people aren't important to them. Who are you trying to convince here? Yourself or her?*

"He had no use for what he called 'weak links.' My ankle made me a weak link. I made myself a weak link by running and falling."

"Let me rewrap that brace. Make it a little tighter and more supportive." Joan removed the dirty headscarf and rewrapped it, starting at Julia's foot, crisscrossing it above the ankle, and finally tucking the loose end neatly into the top. "There. Is that too tight?"

Julia shook her head no.

"Why were you running?" John asked her. "Was there danger? Did an animal try to attack you?"

"In a manner of speaking, yes. An aggressive animal." She lowered her eyes.

John had tested her and she had failed. She wasn't telling the truth. If, indeed, she had been running from an animal and fell, she wouldn't be sitting here talking about it. The animal would have killed her. She fell for a different reason. Joan looked at John with puzzlement, eyebrows furrowed close together, mouth downturned. She must have been thinking the same thing.

"What kind of animal?" Joan asked her.

Julia turned to face Joan. "If I told you, you wouldn't believe me. So what's the point?"

John didn't like standing there, in the open, visible. He didn't like answers that led to more questions. Frankly, he didn't like anything about this situation.

John spoke directly to Julia, his eyes never leaving her face. "Here's the point. I don't believe you were chased by an animal. I want the truth. Then I'll decide if we should help you or leave you. What we do depends on what you say."

"Was it a man?" Joan asked, in a soft, knowing voice.

Julia nodded. "Yes. It was a man. Steven, the team leader. But he said no one would believe me, I had no witnesses, and any other man in a position of power would do the same thing. I would rather die out here than be back on his team. So go." Her face hardened into a fierce scowl. "Leave me. My ankle will get better. I have some supplies. I don't want to be near any man who thinks he's more important than me just because he has power." She stared at John as she talked, her eyes narrowed.

"Go away!" she said again while reaching into her backpack, trying to pull something out. Whatever it was caught on the fabric; she shook her head violently and her dark hair fell forward. With an impatient gesture, she smoothed it behind her ears.

"Can I help you?" Joan asked. "Do you want something out of your pack?"

"Leave me alone!" And then she crumpled forward, her face in her hands, back bent, shoulders shaking. Joan laid her arm across Julia's back and patted her shoulder.

"We're not going to leave you alone. We're going to help you." Joan looked up at John, her eyes begging him to agree. He knew Joan would never leave this woman alone in the wilderness, and he respected her for that. But his wife looked so tired, her face pale and thin, dark shadows under her eyes as though smudged by ashes. He nodded his head at Joan and was heartened to see a faint flicker of a smile play across her lips.

"But he's an Enforcer. Why would he help me? Why is he even helping you?" She said *Enforcer* with a fiercely disdainful tone.

Joan was quiet for a moment, then said with quiet confidence. "It isn't the uniform that makes a man evil. It's the man that makes the uniform evil. They want and get uniforms because they crave recognition, prestige, and, of course, power. But I think this Enforcer may be better than the others."

Well done, Joan, John thought. As long as she thinks I am an Enforcer, she'll never be able to disclose that I'm not. And it might be important in the future that I be seen as an Enforcer to anybody we come in contact with.

Julia looked at John, her eyes swollen from crying, her face streaked with dirt and sweat. "Are you really different?"

John nodded. "Yes, we will help you. The first thing we must do is get away from the stream into some cover. You can lean on us." John saw a faint smile on Julia's face. "Stand in the water," he said. "I'm going to erase any signs that we've been here."

Joan supported Julia and they moved into the stream. John filled their trash bucket with water and poured it over the dirt bank several times. All traces of their footprints melted away into the mud.

With Joan on one side and John on the other, Julia laid her arms across their shoulders. She was fragile between them, and hobbled the best she could without putting weight on her right foot. Together they made it to the other side of the stream, up the bank, and into the darkness of the woods. John was relieved that they were no longer out in the open.

"Wait here," he told them. He went back and, using the bucket again, erased their footprints from the bank.

When he was satisfied that all traces of their presence were gone, he returned to the women and they began walking. Deeper into the woods he saw what must have been a road at one time. There were traces of asphalt, black splotches among the grasses and ferns, a road long neglected, no longer useful. He decided to follow it.

"We'll stay on the asphalt as much as we can. We'll still be able to see the stream, and we'll leave less of a trail on a hard surface."

Julia was breathing hard from the effort of leaning on them and mostly hopping on one foot, but she didn't complain.

They walked because they didn't dare stop. Julia's arms ached from reaching up and across their shoulders. Joan was breathing hard; Julia was a heavy burden for her, even with John to help. They walked until their shadows grew long in front of them, the sun low behind them. Dark clouds were gathering on the horizon. A storm was brewing.

In the distance John saw a familiar shape. As they got closer, he realized it was a rust-colored vehicle of some sort, abandoned.

He pointed it out to Joan; she nodded and they headed toward it.

Finally, they were close enough to see that it was an old, abandoned school bus, with bits of faded yellow paint hanging along the bottom like fringe on a skirt. The tires were flat. The bifold doors were frozen open, and the two steps up to the bus were lying useless on the ground. Joan pulled herself up into the unexpected shelter, then reached down for Julia's hand. She pulled, John pushed, and then Julia was on the bus. John pulled himself up and surveyed the interior.

Most of the seats were torn, probably chewed by animals. A forgotten lunch box lay in the aisle, decorated with cartoon characters from long ago faintly visible through the rust. Incredibly, none of the windows were broken. John walked the length of the aisle, looking for useful items. but there was nothing of value. Vines grew up through holes in the floor, twining their way up the seats toward the light of the windows.

Julia sat in one of the seats, her leg propped beside her, her head against a window. Joan sat across from her and mirrored her position. The fading sunlight that came through illuminated them, Joan's light hair with streaks of gray, and Julia's pale porcelain skin. Both women looked exhausted. John knew they needed to rest.

But first, he had some questions.

He slid the pack off his back and held it out to Julia. "What's in your pack?" he asked her. Surely, they would have supplied her with nourishment cubes, water bottles. Who knew what else? Things they might need, things that might save them. Things that would help them survive.

Slowly and carefully, Julia pulled out the contents.

The sunlight faded, the skies darkened even more.

They each ate one of Julia's nourishment cubes, not even letting the smallest crumbs drop from their lips. Every morsel counted.

"Don't you have packs with supplies?" Julia whispered to Joan.

"We did. But they got ripped apart by foxes or coyotes or something. Stuff like that happens out here."

Joan hoped her explanation satisfied Julia's curiosity. There was no further conversation.

Julia and Joan fell asleep, but John couldn't. David, Emmy, and the children were still out there somewhere, and Earth Protectors were out there, too. John peered through a window, but it was too dark to see anything clearly.

A storm began, slow at first, distant, then closer, and rain and hail raged against the fragile old school bus. John was grateful for the shelter. It was like a gift left there at the side of the road just for them.

Gusts of cold air swirled through the open door, plastering wet leaves on the driver's seat and windshield. Lightning flashed with the fury of nature gone insane.

John could only sit, helpless, weighed down by an overwhelming sense of futility.

CHAPTER THIRTY-SIX

WINSTON

Day 12

Winston had no choice. He had to do as Steven commanded and leave Julia behind. No doubt Steven would shoot him if he disobeyed orders. Steven would destroy any lower person who got in his way or challenged him. But Steven was the right man to be in power, at least by the Authorities' standards, because he would do whatever it took to meet, even exceed, their orders just to retain his position, or better yet, get a promotion. It was all about him. If this low-level man had an ego so big, Winston hated to think how big the ego of the ultimate, all-powerful Central Authority was.

Steven barked out the orders. Nigel would be point man and lead the team farther upstream. Nothing about Nigel impressed Winston. Oh, sure, Winston could see that Nigel was tall and muscular, but his face never showed any emotion. He had a squared-off chin, and blue eyes that pierced you, knifelike, when he looked at you. Though he never *just* looked at anyone. He stared at you without blinking, without smiling. His hair was so blond it was almost a transparent white, his pale pink scalp visible through the thin strands. Winston doubted that there would be any bonding or friendship between Nigel and him.

Next in line was Guy. How he ever made Special Teams was beyond Winston. He was too twitchy for this kind of mission. There must have been a reason he was assigned here; Winston would try to figure out what it was. Maybe the Authorities were just desperate for a healthy male, and Guy was the best they could do.

Next was red-haired Adam. Winston thought Adam had probably been with Steven since the beginning. He had that whole "sleep lightly, wake easily" routine down pat. He wasn't startled by the gun and wasn't bothered by leaving Julia behind. Orders were orders and he followed them.

Winston knew why he was next in line. Steven was sandwiching the new guys, the ones he wasn't sure about, between the experienced ones, the ones he could count on. Despite Steven's cruelty, he was cunning. He had risen to the level of team leader for a reason. It wasn't his people skills. It was his power skills.

Steven would bring up the rear, right behind Winston. Winston couldn't turn around, but he sensed that Steven had his gun out and pointed right at his back.

"We'll walk upstream till noon," Steven said when they were beyond Julia's hearing. "If we don't see any clues, any signs of humans, on the way, we'll turn around and head back downstream. See how the *trainee* is doing." His lips curled on the word *trainee*.

What if Julia still couldn't walk? Surely Steven wouldn't . . . Winston interrupted his own thoughts. Steven would do whatever it took to keep his team strong. He'd made that obvious. Ego had replaced all emotion for him.

They marched at a determined clip, with long-legged Nigel setting the pace at four miles per hour. By noon, they would have traveled almost twenty miles.

That would be twenty miles from Julia. Winston felt red-hot anger pulsing through his veins, directed both at the man behind him and at the situation created because of stupid decisions made by the Authorities. The Authorities had assigned a woman to this Earth Protection team in the first place. But most women didn't have the physical abilities to do the work of an Earth Protection team. To make it worse, there was no pretraining. That guaranteed a disastrous outcome. Winston wondered what it would be like to have a system that allowed people to do what they liked to do, what they were good at, then stand back and watch them succeed.

They walked on and on. They saw no clues, not a single thing. The stream was narrow, shallow, and moving slowly. Mosquitoes swarmed in small dark clouds around them. They were all slapping at their faces, trying to stop the insects from biting.

Finally, it was noon. Some cloud cover kept it from being unbearably hot. The water in their bottles wasn't cold anymore, but it was better than nothing.

"Sit," Steven said. Winston was more than willing to stretch his legs out and lean back on his elbows. Steven sat facing them. Winston wondered why the man never looked tired. Guy's face was blotchy red with mosquito bites, and even Nigel's scalp was pinker than usual, sunburned in spite of the cloud cover. Adam just looked bored. "Five minutes' rest, relieve yourselves in teams, and then we start back downstream."

Nigel and Guy went into the woods first.

Then it was Adam and Winston's turn.

"You must have always been a Protection Team member," Winston said to Adam. "You like it?"

"What's not to like? Bigger nourishment cubes, other perks."

"I was Maintenance," Winston said. "But we never had the right tools. Sometimes no tools at all. Things got broken but not fixed. Then they moved me to Protection. But I still have a lot to learn."

"Learn this: shut up and keep up," Adam snapped at Winston and walked away.

The walk back was just as tedious as the walk up had been. There was no talking, just walking. He was tired of knowing that Steven was behind him with a gun. Winston let his mind go blank and just took one step after another. The sun was starting its downward arc.

They were nearing the area where Julia had been left.

"What the hell?" Steven muttered. His heat and motion detector should be vibrating by now. They all stopped and turned to Steven.

"What the hell?" he said again. "She should be here. But she isn't." He was pointing into the woods. He walked faster and they followed him.

"You're right." Nigel pointed. "That's the rock she tripped over." All the rocks looked the same to Winston. "I stuck a stick in the ground, right there." He pointed at a thin broken branch that was wedged upright between the rocks. "I memorized the exact location. Four rocks close together near three trees, also close together, with a pine sapling to the right. This is it."

"Agreed. I memorized it, too," Steven said. "This is the spot. And she's not here."

Winston could see that these two men obviously had experience and were good at what they did. He didn't have to like them, but he had to admire their skills.

"That bitch! Pretending she couldn't walk." Steven walked around the rocks, bent down to retrieve something, and held it up.

Julia's dark beret.

CHAPTER THIRTY-SEVEN

EARTH PROTECTION AGENTS

Day 12

Steven felt his face flush hot with rage and his jaw clench with anger. That traitor! Damn the Authorities who put a woman in a military operation. In *his* operation! But he knew he had to calm down and stay composed in front of his men. That's what a team leader did.

He could see where Julia had crawled to the stream. Ferns were broken off and turning brown. But he saw nothing near the water itself. No clues. No footprints. Just mud. Somewhere, there had to be a clue, and he would find it.

"All right, then. In addition to our original missions, we now have another one." Steven decided that he would still not tell his team about the gun that one of the escapees allegedly had. "We must find Julia." He shoved her beret into his backpack. A memento.

Nobody questioned him. Nobody said anything. But Winston wouldn't look at him.

"We covered upstream well until there were no more clues. Whoever we were following must have crossed the stream and switched direction. Otherwise, we'd have encountered them." Steven was confident in his reasoning. This mission would be a success because of his skills; he just knew it.

He shouldered his pack; the men did the same. "Same marching order as before. Nigel leads off. I'll be rear guard behind Winston. We have a few hours till dusk. Move out!"

They crossed the shallow stream, stepping from one slippery rock to another without falling. Steven would have enjoyed seeing an Authority or even an Enforcer navigate as well as he and his men did. They'd fall flat on their smug faces. Imagining that scene made Steven smile. How he'd love to see them fall. Right now, he thought, they're probably all lapping up their special supplies, eating fresh food, sipping forbidden beverages. He slapped at a mosquito . . . damn mosquitos!

The stream widened and the banks rose steeply beside it, limiting their visual field. They needed to move to higher ground, where they could see the stream along with more of the surrounding area. Steven gave Nigel a birdcall signal and motioned with his head to climb the bank. Nigel understood and obeyed. Steven appreciated that about him. He decided Nigel had potential. Maybe he could even be promoted someday. Steven liked holding Nigel's future in his hands.

They climbed the bank, single file. Guy, that weakling, slipped back one step for every two forward. He slowed Steven down and Steven didn't like being slowed down. Nigel waited at the top, vigilant, looking around. Steven briefly wished they could go back to the good old days, when there were lots of shadow people, and they could be rounded up—hungry, skinny, dirty—and then marched back for ridicule and punishment. Now, that was power! This business of chasing only a few at a time was, in Steven's opinion, a waste of valuable resources. Just let the fools die out here in the Human Free Zone. Hopefully, this would be the last assignment. If Steven did it right, it would be.

Clouds were gathering low on the horizon, but they still had plenty of daylight left. Nigel set a good pace. Guy was starting to look winded. He'd have to just suck it up.

Still, they found no clues. Nothing was out of place: no broken branches, no dropped paper. For all Steven knew, these escapees might already be dead. But then, if that were true, he'd have located their bodies—or at least what was left of them after the animals had had their way. No, they were out here somewhere—all of them, including Julia. He couldn't wait to find her and shove her stupid beret down her throat.

Steven signaled for a break. It was time for food, water, and a few minutes' rest. The men sat quickly, gulped water, ate their cubes, and were back on their feet. Guy scrambled but managed to stand at the same time as the others. He was learning. Winston still wouldn't look at Steven, but Steven didn't care what he thought of him.

The sun was at their backs, the sky ahead darkening, and the stream to their left had grown wider. To their right was a strange area with little vegetation. Steven signaled for Nigel to lead the team there so they could reconnoiter. They followed patches of black asphalt, crumbled but visible. It was an old road, unused and unnecessary. They might as well follow it and see where it led. An abandoned structure, maybe; the Authorities hadn't been able to pull down every building. Instead, they left them to decay over time. That could offer a hiding place for escapees. This road might lead to a big payday. Nigel sensed it and picked up the pace.

In the distance were rumbles of thunder, and the wind was picking up, tree branches were swaying. Nasty weather was on the way. The sun had almost set. They would keep walking till it started to rain, then they would hunker down for the night. None of them wanted to be near trees if lightning was close.

The thunder got louder. Lightning slashed the sky, cloud to cloud. It was time to stop and find a clearing away from the trees. The rain began, fierce large drops. They stopped walking, put on their torches, and pulled out their waterproof jackets. Their uniforms were already wet as they struggled with the tangled sleeves and pulled the hoods over their heads. The torches cast a weak light a few feet in front of them.

Then the hail started. Pellets of ice bounced when they hit the ground, and beat against their backs.

And then they heard a strange noise: the sound of hail on metal.

CHAPTER THIRTY-EIGHT

JOHN

Day 12

John knew he should sleep. He knew he had to be rested and strong for whatever tomorrow might bring, so he could continue the search for David, Emmy, and the children, and, at the same time, be alert for whatever dangers they might confront. He had to protect Joan and help this weak, injured stranger. How had she ended up in Earth Protectors? What were the Authorities thinking?

He wished they hadn't stumbled upon her. She was going to slow them down, and increase their risk of being captured. But they *had* stumbled on her, and Joan was right, they couldn't just abandon her. John knew he, too, would have trouble living with himself if they had left her behind. He'd be no better than those merciless guards and Enforcers who ruled the Compounds. He'd just have to deal with the additional responsibilities.

Weary with worry, John closed his eyes. The pinging of the rain and hail on the tin roof was discordant and disturbing. He heard Joan groan and opened his eyes. She was shifting her weight on the seat, trying to get comfortable. Tomorrow he would give her Julia's extra camouflage clothing. That would be better than her white shirt and pants.

John closed his eyes again. Maybe everything happened for a reason and maybe the reason was just too big for him to understand. John prayed that sleep would come and wrap itself around him like a blanket, forming a pillow under his head, calming his soul, giving him peace.

The storm continued, gaining in fury. Sleep would not come. Everything John could see through the bus window was illuminated into a stark black-and-white landscape. The trees, dark in contrast to the lightning, swayed and bent. Clouds rolled in great dark waves, ominous with power. How long could nature rage like this?

A sudden crash shook the bus, waking them all and bringing John to his feet. Peering out through the wet window, John could see a large branch leaning against the bus, lodged against the roof. He also saw something else: men moving toward the bus. How many? Another flash of lightning, and he quickly counted five dark figures wearing head torches. He took his gun out of his waistband, felt the cold metal, and released the safety lock. His heart raced. This was it.

He turned to look at Joan and Julia. "Stay here." Cautiously, he started up the aisle, toward the door. The roof had a dent in it, bulging like a tumor. The floor was slippery, covered with wet leaves. A side window had cracked into a large spiderweb shape, stretching from one side to the other.

Reaching the door, John stood as a barrier between whoever was out there and the women inside.

Lightning flashed again.

Then John saw the leader. Though they wore rain jackets, their insignia was clear.

An Earth Protector.

CHAPTER THIRTY-NINE

STEVEN

Day 12

Steven wondered what caused the sound of hail on metal so far out in the Human Free Zone. He figured it must be something that was abandoned long ago, when this remnant of a road was still intact. His men heard it, too, and were watching him for his reaction. They moved closer to him. He could smell the odor of their wet jackets and see the rain dripping from their faces in silvery rivulets. He motioned for Nigel to lead the group toward the pinging sound. Steven ran his thumb over the butt of his pistol, then made sure the safety was off. He was ready for whatever might happen.

They moved forward cautiously, five men stooped to a low profile, no more than shadows moving through the night. The fierce thunder grew louder, closer, and more ominous. The trees on either side of them swayed in the wind, and branches whipped back and forth, groaning. Twigs blew across their path, tumbling end over end. Wet leaves clung to their clothing, their cheeks. The pinging was louder; they were closer to whatever it was. A flash of lightning lit the darkness with a flickering white light.

Nigel began running now, moving toward the sound. Steven could make out a dark shadow, something long, rectangular. Another flash of lightning lit the sky, illuminating the object: an abandoned school bus, a relic from the before-times. Still cautious, but eager for shelter, they crept closer, knees bent, backs bowed, heads up, light from their torches slicing through the night.

They were close enough now that with the next lightning strike Steven thought he could make out the shape of at least one human head in one of the windows. His detector wasn't vibrating, so he might have just imagined it. There was no sound other than the hail, the rain, and the wind. Clouds covered the sky. The moon and stars were obliterated. All he could see was the dark, hostile night.

Steven moved to the front of the line, the men close behind him; close enough that he could hear their breathing in spite of the storm. There was a vague outline of an opening where there must have been a door at one time. Steven signaled for the others to stay where they were. He would scope this out alone and determine the potential risks and benefits of taking shelter inside the bus. Cautiously, gun in hand, he approached that black hole of a doorway.

A hailstone hit his cheek, right below his eye. As he crept closer, the wind plastered his cold, wet hood against the side of his face. Steven moved slowly, but his mind raced ahead. It just didn't feel right. He could sense it. These escapees were more determined, more elusive, than the shadow people he had tracked before. What was driving them? If it was blind panic, he'd have captured them by now. And then there was the whole Julia thing. Was that her he'd seen in there? It couldn't be . . .

A tree branch crashed to the ground beside him. Then another one fell, hitting the top of the bus with force. If anybody was asleep in there, they'd be awake now.

Soon enough, Steven was at the doorway.

Lightning flashed all around him. He stood and stared.

There in the doorway, in the unholy light of the storm, stood an Enforcer in his coal-black uniform, pointing a gun at him.

The metal of the bus must have stopped the detector from working. It had failed to vibrate and warn Steven of danger. What good was all of the Republic's technology if it didn't work when you needed it to? But he knew his gun would work if he had a chance to use it. He slipped it into his waistband. He didn't want this Enforcer to know he was armed.

What the hell was an Enforcer doing out here? Steven made the circle sign against his hood; it had slipped down even lower over his forehead. The Enforcer stood staring at Steven and finally made the circle sign in return.

"May we come in out of the rain, sir?" Steven asked him.

"How many total are there in your group?"

Steven wondered if he should bring all the men in or just a couple of them. He could bring in the new ones, to keep them close, and leave Adam and Nigel outside in case there was trouble. Better not try to fool this Enforcer. Better play it straight.

"Five, sir." The wind was carrying his words away. "Five, sir," Steven shouted again, louder. Steven saw the Enforcer look back into the bus. So there were others in there. Who were they? None of this made any sense.

"Let me see your team," the Enforcer shouted.

Steven motioned for them to come and stand near him. Their torches shone on the Enforcer's face.

"Turn off your torches," the Enforcer said.

One by one the torches were extinguished.

A tree branch crashed to the ground behind them, just missing Guy, who wrapped his arms around his chest. *Man up*, Steven wanted to shout at him.

"Wait here. Don't enter yet."

They had to wait, standing in the rain. He was, after all, an Enforcer. Already Steven hated him.

CHAPTER FORTY

JOHN

Day 12

As John walked down the aisle toward the rear of the bus, Joan and Julia stared at him, their eyes wide with fright, their lips trembling. With each step John took, he thought frantically, searching for an idea that would keep them safe and, at the same time, hide their identity and delay the Earth Protectors' search for David and Emmy. John sat on the edge of a seat in front of Joan and faced them.

Julia leaned forward and whispered, "Is it the Protectors?" She had a line of sweat above her lip that shimmered when lightning lit the inside of the bus.

John nodded. "Yes, five men. They probably have guns."

"Just Steven has one. I saw it. No one else does." Julia seemed eager to share information.

"Tell me their names again."

"Steven, Adam, Nigel, Guy." She paused. "And Winston."

"What else you remember about them? Especially about Steven?"

She thought for a moment. "He likes to make his own rules. He said so himself. And the way he acted was kind of arrogant when the Enforcer deployed us; I got the feeling he either hates Enforcers or is afraid of them. Maybe both." She shrugged.

Another branch crashed against the bus. How long would the Protectors be willing stay outside in this storm? Julia said Steven likes to make his own rules. John wondered if Steven would lash out at an Enforcer. Would he be filled with hate, fear, or a combustible combination of both?

Joan reached forward and put her hand on John's shoulder. Julia noticed and looked puzzled.

"Tell her the truth, John," Joan whispered. "Truth leads to trust."

"The truth?" Julia asked. "What truth?"

Yes, the truth. John knew he had to take that risk. "I'm not really an Enforcer. I'm just a man in an Enforcer's uniform. We"—he pointed to Joan and himself—"are two of the people Steven's team is looking for. The others they're looking for are our son, David, his wife, Emmeline, and two children."

"You can't let him know that!" Julia pounded the seat beside her, with as much fright as vehemence. "He has to think you're an Enforcer. Do whatever you have to do, say whatever you have to say. I'll follow your lead."

"If we let them in here with us, they won't be out there looking for our family," John said. "And maybe we can stop them, God willing."

Joan nodded in agreement. "You lead. We'll follow." Their ashen faces were grim with resolve.

Taking a deep breath, John went back up the aisle to the gaping doorway. The men were still standing there, huddled together. The last branch that had fallen was lying just inches behind them on the ground, a gnarled knobby piece big enough to have killed one or more of the men if it had fallen just right.

"You and your men can shelter with us, provided you follow my rules." John pointed his gun at them.

They inched closer to the door.

"First, give me your gun."

Steven shook his head no.

"Then no shelter will be given."

A blast of wind was forceful enough to push the men a bit sideways as though they were made of straw. It swirled, cold and full of fury, around John in the doorway.

John gave him an icy stare, then continued, "Do you think so little of your team that you would deny them shelter? So be it."

The men murmured to each other.

John turned to walk away.

"Wait!" Steven said. "I'll give you my gun."

"Give it to me handle first, barrel pointing toward yourself."

Steven did as he was told. The gun was wet and cold in John's hand. He held it leveled at the men, and slipped his own gun into his waistband.

"Second, leave your packs and torches in the front of the bus." Julia had an ax in her pack; these men would also.

They all nodded in agreement and slipped their packs off their shoulders, and their torches off their heads.

"Third, you and your men go to the back of the bus. Understand?" John would station himself between these men and the women.

Steven nodded and his hood slipped farther down on his forehead, pouring rain over his face.

"Fourth: There are two women on this bus. You will not speak to them. One is a team member that you abandoned."

There was another vicious flash of lightning, followed by an angry roar of thunder.

"The other is a woman you should have captured but didn't." John spoke loudly enough for Joan and Julia to hear him. They would follow his lead. "I, an Enforcer, was able to do what you couldn't. I assisted one of your own team members and captured a fugitive alone. Something you couldn't do with your entire team. This will be reported to the Authorities. Now bring your men in."

John stepped aside and let them pass by him, one by one, eyes downcast. They dropped their packs in a heap inside the door by the driver's seat. Shuffling their feet, they made their way to the back of the bus and sat in silence, two to a seat.

"Spread out. One to a seat, with empty seats between each of you." John didn't want them grouped together, whispering among themselves, conspiring and planning. Separated, they'd have less power. Individuals always have less power than groups.

John sat behind Joan and Julia and leaned against the side of the bus. He was the only thing between those men and the women. In spite of his guns and his Enforcers uniform, he was filled with fear. Would he be enough to keep them at bay?

Steven was a desperate man.

Desperate men are dangerous men.

CHAPTER FORTY-ONE

EMMELINE

Day 12

Paul's old bones were right. Dusk rolled in with great black clouds churning on the horizon. Distant thunder roared and echoed: boom, boom, boom. Cold air swirled through trees where birds clung to sturdy branches and the wind had a fierce, howling sound.

"The wind is what I always imagine God's voice must sound like. Powerful, and not to be ignored," Paul said.

"What do you mean?" I asked.

"We best move inside," Paul said. He didn't answer my question.

We gathered around the fire pit, sitting on the log benches Paul and David had moved closer to the fire's light and warmth. David's arm no longer caused him pain when he used it. Soon we could set off on our journey to my old home.

"This reminds me of Boy Scout camp," David said. "We'd sit around the fire and tell scary stories, trying to frighten each other."

"Maybe Paul could tell us stories. Would you, Paul?" I said.

"What kind of stories would you like to hear?"

"Stories!" Micah repeated excitedly. He hopped up from the log he was sitting on and fed some more wood into the fire pit. We would use up this small supply quickly.

"True stories, important stories. History. Tell us history," I said.

"I would be honored," Paul said. He settled on one of the benches. "Let me gather my thoughts." He had a long, narrow branch lying across his lap. Using his knife, he started carving a small notch at one end.

Micah watched him, leaning close to the stick and the knife. "What are you making?"

"I'm trying to make a spear for you, young man. Figuring it out as I go. But your head is so close, I can't see what I'm doing. And I don't think this is the best piece of wood for the job."

I remembered the peg that held the edge of the tent at the farm commune. I reached into our second bundle by the wall of the cave and pulled it out. Paul smiled when I handed it to him. "Perfect. One little notch at the end will hold a sharp stone or piece of hard shell." He started carving once more.

The black walls of the cave flickered with our reflections in the rosy-red fire's glow.

Ingrid handed out mugs of tea and settled next to Paul, resting her gray head against his shoulder, her long braid dangling down. He laid aside the peg and began to unbraid her hair, letting it fall free over her shoulder. She smiled at him and patted his hand.

"True stories, stories from history, are more frightening than anything anyone could ever think up. More frightening because they are real. And more frightening because the same story happens over and over again even though people cry out 'Never again!' "

"Never again, never again," Ingrid murmured, twisting her hands together.

"What kind of things are you talking about?" David leaned forward, his elbows on his knees, his chin on his hands. His profile was so handsome in this romantic light, with his dark hair draped in a curve across his forehead.

"Naturally, most people want to be left alone, want to take care of themselves and their families. But events get in the way."

"What kind of events?" I asked.

"It's getting late. Telling all I want to tell you would take too long. So let me summarize, because even though these events happened at different times, in different places, they have a common theme. The facts are these. Some people got power because they desired it more than anything, and would do or say anything to get it. They either had some pathology—a twisted way of thinking, that made them want power—or, when they got power, they wanted even more, until it became pathological. Power leads to pathology or the other way around. Either way, the little people, people like you and me, were controlled and at risk. They couldn't control their own destiny."

"At risk how?" I asked.

"Sometimes it was a civil war, or the genocide of specific groups. That's called ethnic cleansing. Citizens are stripped of their guns and then murdered by their own governments, historically within ten years after the guns are confiscated. Sometimes it's a war between nations. Other times, people died of starvation because of poor management and redistribution of property. In the last century, one hundred and seventy million people died because of events like those."

I gasped. How many is one hundred and seventy million? How many mothers, fathers, children, aunts, uncles, and grandparents?

Outside, the thunder, lightning, and rain continued. I felt cold from my core to my skin listening to the storm outside and to the horrific words of history.

"In the history of the world, only one very special nation was founded on the principal of personal freedom, and personal destiny. That's the history you need to hold dear."

"What nation is it?" I asked. "Where is it?"

"You mean *was*. It's gone. It was called America."

CHAPTER FORTY-TWO

GEORGE

Day 12

George slipped two fingers under his ankle strap and felt the rough area where his skin had broken down.

Human skin is vulnerable to tight shackles.

A callus would form over time to prevent this kind of ulceration, but who knows how long that would take. Sanitizing solution helped prevent infection, but it burned like fury. If George could find any moss alongside the field, it would help, but there wasn't much in this area.

He lay back on his mat, hoping he could sleep, but his heart and mind had been racing since seeing Emmeline in the middle of the night, foraging in the field of peas. She had been right there, beyond his tent. He had touched her shoulder and her hand. She had stood trembling in front of him, so pale in the moonlight, so fragile. But now, when he tried to remember her features and the look on her face, the image took on a translucent quality.

He turned onto his side and pulled open the tent flap so he could see outside. It was dark, with no stars, and no moon . . . and no pale figure of a woman at the edge of the field. The wind was blowing, hard and cold. The guard would be in his own tent on a night like this. Why didn't the other farmworkers, the ones not shackled with a ball and chain, try to escape this desolate life?

Had they no desire to make their own fate? Had that basic human desire been programmed entirely out of them? George watched their faces as he worked alongside them. They were flat, with no emotion. No tears but no smiles, either. No joy, no sorrow. All of them were younger than George, all of them were products of their narrow world—the only one most had ever known.

George had known joy. George had known sorrow. Joy is a fragile, fleeting thing. Sorrow is stronger and lasts longer. It can weigh you down, paralyze you.

Thunder rolled in from the distance. Rain began, large fat drops of it, hitting the sides of the tent, fast and furious. A puddle was already forming outside in front of the open flap. The field would be muddy tomorrow.

George had asked Emmeline if he could see his daughter. A slim thread of hope now wound around his heart. For the first time in his life he felt joy and sorrow at the same time.

Hail was beating against the tent, rapid-fire and harsh.

She had said she couldn't bring the baby here. It would be too dangerous. But she never said he couldn't see Elsa at all. He just couldn't see her *here*. He had felt the pause before she answered and sensed the hesitation in her voice. Somehow, George *would* see his baby. He had faith in Emmeline. She had always cared about people.

White jagged streaks of lightning flashed across the sky.

For one small, dark minute George thought that if he couldn't see his child, he'd crawl out of this tent with the metal ball on the end of his leg, offer it up to the god of storms, and pray for lightning to strike him.

He pushed that thought away.

Instead he vowed to lie down every night with the tent flap open, watching and waiting, hoping to see a woman and a child at the edge of the field.

CHAPTER FORTY-THREE

JOHN

Day 13

Dawn rose with great red fingers of light piercing the gray sky. The storm was over. Through the window, John could see the damage it had done. Evergreens, the most vulnerable of trees with their shallow roots, lay fallen, their majestic limbs sprawled against the ground. Broken branches littered the area.

One by one the sleeping men stirred, stretching their legs, rubbing their eyes. Joan and Julia were already awake. They had communicated through silent gestures that they would take turns keeping watch through the night. By now, it was almost as though they could read each other's minds. They had formed a sense of togetherness in the middle of chaos.

"The women will go out together for a short break," John told the men sitting behind him. They did not respond, but sat slumped in their seats. John noticed one of them had a twitch in his eyelid which he quickly covered with his hand.

Julia limped up the aisle of the bus, holding onto the backs of the seats as she went forward. It looked like she was able to put a little weight on her injured ankle. John watched as Joan helped her off the bus and they disappeared into some thick woods.

"When the women return, you will go out one by one, and I will accompany you."

Steven looked surprised. Any thoughts Steven might have of overpowering the women when John left the bus would soon be dashed.

The women returned in a short time and returned to their seats, watchful, waiting to see what would happen next.

John pointed to the one with the twitchy eye. "You, what's your name?"

"Guy, sir."

"You're next." He stood, but John held up his hand for him to stop. "First I need to give Julia something." Still holding Steven's gun, John pulled his own gun out of his waistband and handed it to Julia. Smiling, she took it with an air of confidence. "She will use it if the situation requires it." John motioned for Guy to exit the bus and followed him. Steven had no way of knowing that Joan also had a gun. Some things were best left secret.

Guy finished quickly and returned to the bus. Another man was standing, anxious to get off. Julia, her arm resting on the back of the seat, was pointing the gun toward the men. Her aim was steady.

"Your name?"

"Nigel, sir."

"Move out. I'm right behind you."

Next came Winston, then Adam. Steven would be last.

As John waited for Adam to finish, he looked at the stream. It was much higher this morning because of the torrential rains, and was flowing fast, carrying debris from trees with it. Above the roar of the water, John heard a man scream and saw Adam running toward him, his face filled with panic. Quickly, John raised his gun.

"I've been bitten. I've been bitten." Adam was holding his right hand in his left. "A snake bit me." He was close enough now that John could see two distinct puncture wounds on his hand.

"What kind of snake?" John asked him.

"Rattler. Big sucker. About five feet long. I was reaching down to retie my shoe. Heard the rattle. Next thing I knew, bam." He was panting with fear. "You've got to help me."

"Get on the bus. I'll look at it."

"Damn, it hurts," he said as he got on the bus. John quickly followed.

John knew from the looks on the other men's faces that they had heard what happened to Adam. Their expressions were a mixture of concern, fear, and uncertainty. Adam stumbled to the back of the bus and fell into his seat. The men clustered around him.

"Back to your seats," John said. He turned back to Adam. "Keep your hand lower than your heart. Slow your breathing. You, Guy, take off your belt. Make a tourniquet on his arm, then sit back down."

Guy fumbled with his belt but managed to do as he had been told.

"Shouldn't you suck the venom out?" Steven asked.

"That's an old-school treatment," John answered. "I was a Boy Scout leader in the before-times. Current recommendations are to apply a tourniquet and immobilize the limb."

Adam was whimpering with pain but there was nothing more John could do.

"Your turn," John said to Steven.

"Where was the snake?" Steven asked.

"Over in that direction." John pointed to the area where Adam had been bitten. Steven took tentative, watchful steps and went the opposite way.

Joan rummaged through the men's backpacks for nourishment cubes and passed them around. Adam refused his cube with a harsh shake of his head as he rocked back and forth in his seat, sweating and whimpering.

When he returned, Steven spoke to John in a tight, polite tone. "Sir, if I may, shouldn't we be moving out and searching for other escapees nearby?"

"You think he can travel?" John scoffed and pointed at Adam.

Steven shrugged. That shrug, along with the fact that he had abandoned Julia in the wilderness, told John all he needed to know about him. The man had no compassion, no empathy. "We're losing valuable time. The escapees are getting farther away with every passing moment."

"It's not a waste of time to take care of your team. I shouldn't have to remind you of that. We are not moving out until I say so."

Steven sat back in his seat with a disgusted look on his face that he made no effort to conceal.

He was right. They were wasting time. And that was exactly what John wanted.

CHAPTER FORTY-FOUR

EMMELINE

Day 13

Paul's tale had left me emotionally exhausted and I struggled to fall asleep. Dark thoughts kept running through my head. David had whispered *Never again, not to us*, as he stretched out beside me, and those words had a haunting, desperate quality.

The next morning, the air smelled sweet and cool. I woke first. Micah and Elsa were curled together like puppies; David was asleep on his stomach near the entrance, his face cradled on his arms, his legs long and straight, the bottoms of his feet dirty, smudged with grime. We didn't wear our shoes here. We had to save them for when we journeyed on.

Paul and Ingrid were propped against the cave wall, seated side by side, gray heads together. They looked so peaceful. I stepped over David's legs and slipped outside to watch the sunrise. The clouds were tinged pink on the bottom edges as if kissed by the dawn and blushing with pleasure.

Paul was right; there was so much contentment to be found in watching the day break every morning. I was learning to take comfort in the dependability, the certainty of a new dawn, and a new day. But how could I be so sure of a comfortable new day after hearing the horror stories of history? Was there another quality of human nature that Paul hadn't listed? Could it be hope?

Yes, hope.

But when these atrocities were happening, what did people think? *It happened to someone else, not me? It happened over there, not here. It happened then, not now?* Thinking like that isn't hope, it's denial.

The truth is, the atrocities Paul had described could happen to anyone, anyplace, anytime, if people did not pay attention. Maybe hope is nothing more than the determination to find freedom. And the belief that you can.

No trees near the cave had fallen, but some that were deeper in the woods leaned against each other at odd angles, with great lumps of root and dirt exposed. The power of nature was always impressive.

I checked the traps. There were two rabbits again today, their fur wet and plastered against their bodies. I left them there so Micah could discover them when he woke. He would be so excited when he ran to us with the news of the catch.

David stepped out of the cave, rubbing his eyes. We spoke little, but sat together, waiting for the others. One by one they emerged. Micah carried Elsa. She reached out for me and I took her into my arms. Ingrid and Paul came out next. Micah headed for the traps and within a few minutes he ran back, carrying the two wet rabbits. Grinning, he held them out as a gift to Paul, who graciously accepted the offering with a slight bow of his head.

"We have the day's work cut out for us," Paul said as he gathered up the tools to prepare the meat. "We'll clean these little beauties, maybe find some more honey, and make a spear for Micah."

Micah followed so closely behind his new friend that he almost stepped on Paul's heel.

"David, is your arm strong enough to bring some water up from the stream? We'll need it for cleaning the rabbits and anything else we find for our meal." Paul pointed to his empty old dented bucket.

David rolled up his sleeve, revealing a long, healed scar. The honey and thyme tea had done their job well.

I went with David to the stream. The morning seemed so normal in contrast to the storm and Paul's horrible stories about history. The water was high, fast, and cold. I scooped up the fresh water with my cupped palms and drank deeply. "Lots of fish in there," David said. "Paul mentioned fishing but I didn't see any poles in the cave. Wonder what he uses." The pail was full in no time and David was ready to return to the group.

"Wait a minute. Sit with me."

He set the pail down and settled beside me. "Look, a dragonfly," he said, pointing to a beautiful insect flashing its silver wings as it flitted above the water. A fish, mouth wide open, a large dark circle, splashed upward, and the dragonfly disappeared, leaving no trace behind.

"What did you think of Paul's story last night?" I asked, still preoccupied with my questions of hope and freedom.

"I don't know what to think. It sounded unbelievable to me. One hundred seventy million people. Gone." He snapped his fingers, but the sound was too small compared to what he was describing.

"Paul wouldn't lie."

"I didn't say he was lying. I said it was unbelievable."

I looked at him in amazement. "Not unbelievable. It was happening all around us. Right there." I pointed in the direction of the Compound, just a few days walk from where we were sitting. "That's too close for comfort. As soon as possible, we have to move on. Get farther away."

"Emmy, we're safe here. We have shelter. We are well hidden. I'm not sure about moving on."

How could I explain to him that it wasn't the *leaving* that was important? What was important was the *finding*. Finding where we began, finding a place where life was good and people were free. Finding ourselves. Before I could explain how I felt, he stood, took a few steps, and moved to look at something by the bank. "A turtle," he said. "I'm sure Paul and Ingrid will know what to do with this." He reached down cautiously and picked the turtle up by its tail. "It's a snapping turtle. Jaw strong enough to take your finger off. Claws are nasty, too. Don't get too close to it."

"Did you hear what I said? As soon as possible, we have to move on."

"Some turtles can pull their heads, feet, and tail into their shell. That's how they protect themselves. Snapping turtles can't do that. So they defend themselves with their mouth and feet."

"I don't care about turtles, David. I want to talk about getting to Kansas."

The turtle was opening and closing its mouth, waving its feet, looking for something to attack. David held it at arm's length.

"I was just explaining that there are different ways to be safe, Emmy. Pull yourself into a shell or use any weapon you have to protect yourself. That's all."

"Fine. I get it. Enough already about turtles. After George sees Elsa, we'll move on. Find a new safe place. We are not turtles."

He picked up the bucket of water with one hand, then set it back down.

"They're old, you know. Paul and Ingrid. She's forgetful sometimes. And he puts his hand on his chest once in a while as if something is bothering him. Can you leave them? We have been protected and safe here. I'm not sure we should move on."

He was right. They needed us. And they had been so good to us.

"We can take them with us! We need Paul to teach us everything he knows about history. Emmy and Micah will have grandparents in their lives." I smiled at the thought.

"What if they won't come with us? Can you leave them behind?" That was the second time he'd asked me that.

"We have to convince them."

"And if they won't? Emmy, whatever decision they make, you'll have to accept. I'm not sure we should keep traveling, but if we do, and they do come with us, you know it will slow us down." Still holding the turtle, he picked up the bucket and started up the hill.

I wanted to pull all of us into a shell just like the turtle, a shell that would protect us and shut out the rest of the world. A shell big enough to protect everyone I loved.

But living in a shell would be no better than living in the Compound or living in a cave. No, a shell was not what I wanted. I wanted blue sky above me, horizons open and safe in all directions.

I wanted to be free from fear.

Ingrid set her broom aside and clapped her hands when we arrived back at the cave and she saw the turtle. "Turtle soup," she said. "Oh, my! I make the best turtle soup! Just you wait till you taste it!" She poured water from the bucket into the pot on the fire pit. "Quick, Micah, the pit needs more wood. Hurry! And then we'll find some greens to go in the soup."

She chattered on as David put the turtle in a basin of water. It tried to scramble up the side but slid back down. Micah looked at the turtle and started to reach for it.

"No, Micah, no!" David said. "He'll bite you! Don't touch him."

Micah pulled his hand back, then scurried off to gather twigs and branches. He returned quickly with his small arms full. "But they're wet," he said, handing the wood to her. "They'll make too much smoke."

"Oh, pshaw. Not to worry. Smoke, schmoke. We're making soup! It's a happy day." She took the wood he was holding and pushed it into the fire pit. It started hissing and gray puffs of smoke curled above the pit. She jumped back, waved her hands in front of her face, and coughed. Paul rushed over and pulled the wet wood out of the pit. The hissing faded but smoke still curled in wavy tendrils above us.

"Ingrid! What are you doing? We don't want all that smoke in here, or drifting outside where it can be seen."

"Just making soup," she said, looking unsure, and twisting the end of her braid in her fingers.

He laid the wood aside, hit his fist against his chest, and sat down on the log bench. "All in good time, Ingrid. All in good time." He hit his chest again, and coughed.

"But we have a turtle!"

"Ingrid, we have rabbits to clean first," he said gently. "Have you finished sweeping?"

"Oh, dear. I didn't finish." She grabbed the broom and began sweeping, her braid swinging back and forth as she moved.

"Why do you do that? Why do you hit your chest?" Micah asked Paul, imitating the motion by thumping his own fist against his chest.

"Oh, it's nothing. Just sometimes I feel like I have butterflies in my heart. Fluttering, kind of. That little punch makes it stop fluttering. That's all. I'm okay now."

As I watched the little scene with Paul, Ingrid, and Micah, I realized how right David was. Paul and Ingrid *were* old. Traveling with them would be very slow and very difficult. It already looked painful for Ingrid as she shuffled in and out of the cave. And Paul had something wrong with his heart. I didn't understand it, but I knew that it couldn't be good.

Still, could I really leave them behind?

CHAPTER FORTY-FIVE

EMMELINE

Day 14

Our morning chores were done.

"It's been two full days since the storm, Paul. Are the woods dry enough for you to go to the commune?"

"That was one of the worst storms I've ever seen, and I've seen plenty in my lifetime. But I suppose there's been some drying out." He poured fresh water into the turtle basin, set the empty bucket upside down, and sat on it. "I'm thinking, when we do kill the turtle, I might be able to use a piece of the shell for an arrowhead or spear tip for Micah."

He was avoiding my question. "Dry enough for you to go tonight?"

"Why are you in such a hurry for me to do this? What difference would another day make?"

"I just am."

Paul pointed a finger at me, the mud under his fingernail caked hard as a rock. " 'I just am' is not an answer, Emmeline."

I had looked at my map earlier, measuring with my fingers the distance from where I thought I was to the place I wanted to be. There was a mileage scale on the side of the map. Using that, it looked like we would have somewhere around an eight-hundred to a thousand-mile trip. I wasn't afraid of the distance. I was afraid of the delay.

"Because," I hesitated, then looked straight into Paul's old blue eyes. "Because we need to move on. Get farther away. We're still too close to the Compound. They're still looking for us. They're looking for all of us. And all of us must move on."

"All of us?" he echoed.

"Yes. All of us. They'll search hard for us because of the children."

He threw his head back and looked up at the sky. "What have you sent us, Lord?"

I matched his upward gaze. Clear blue, the color of Elsa's eyes, with no sign of the dark sky that came with the storm two nights ago. "Who are you talking to?"

"That's another lesson for another time, Emmeline." He waved a fly away from his face and it flew in a circle above his head and landed back on his arm. With a flick of his finger, it was gone. "But let's talk about what you mean when you say 'all of us.' "

"Exactly what I said. All of us: me, David, the children, you, and Ingrid. All of us."

"Emmeline, surely you don't think my old legs could make that journey. Or Ingrid's, for that matter?"

I looked at my legs. They were thinner than they'd been in the Compound, but I still had muscles from walking my energy board. My calves had a roundness to them, while his were stringy and no bigger than my arm.

"We won't walk fast. And we won't walk far every day. We'll take our time, I promise." In truth, I wanted to walk as far and fast as I could. But I had to weigh what I wanted against what was possible for them.

"No, Emmeline. We can't come with you." He paused. "May I tell you something?"

"Of course."

"When Ingrid and I saw all of you huddled under that rock, sick and weak, I thought it was a trap of some sort. I thought maybe you were bait to lure us into the open. I didn't want to help you."

"What changed your mind?"

"Ingrid changed my mind. She said we should help you simply because we *could*."

"And you've helped us tremendously. You took care of David's arm, you've shared your food and your shelter. And you've started to teach us our history."

"I'm ashamed of myself for not wanting to help you at first, and I'm proud of Ingrid for insisting. In such a short time, you and your little family have breathed life and hope into our cold cave."

He brushed the back of his hand across his face, under his eyes. Was he crying?

"There is still so much more to teach you. Things you all need to know, especially young Micah. The future rests on children like him knowing our story. Stay with us. Let me teach you."

"Paul, I want to get as far away as possible. I want to get back to that place where I was a happy child. A safe child."

"We've been safe here all these years. We can keep you safe here, too."

I shook my head no. A strangely familiar wave of nausea rolled over me.

He stood up, walked over to me, and laid his hand on my shoulder. "The truth is, Emmeline, that *we* need *you*. Not the other way around. We're old. We can't forage and hunt like we used to. I shudder to think what would happen to Ingrid if my old heart gives out. We need you, but we can't come with you. We would be so happy if you'd stay with us." He let his hand slide off my shoulder and began to walk away. He turned back and in a quiet, even voice said, "When I think the time is right and the skies are overcast, I'll go to the commune. I'll talk to that man George and use my judgment to see if he can be trusted. Perhaps bring him back to see Elsa. I'm going to rest now."

I put my face in my hands. What was it that Ingrid had said to him about helping us? *We should help them because we can.*

I didn't know what to do. I didn't know what would be right for them, for me, or for my family. I looked up to the sky like Paul had done and tried to mimic his words.

"What should we do, Lord?"

CHAPTER FORTY-SIX

PAUL

Day 16

Paul set off on the journey to the farm commune. He was too ashamed to admit that he was afraid. He had never made the trip alone.

Nineteen years ago, when Paul and Ingrid had moved into the cave before the relocations, there was no farm commune, just a rocky field. A year later they watched from behind the thick shelter of trees as the land was plowed and the first crops were planted. And they had rejoiced at their good fortune. Indeed, they'd felt blessed.

At first the journey to the commune had been easy for Ingrid. She had been nimble and sure-footed, and didn't mind the long walk or the lack of sleep from sneaking around at night. She'd forage quickly, filling her sack with whatever was in season, and carry it back to the cave. They'd preserve what they could. Salt and vinegar worked magic most times. But they had run out of vinegar until more wild apples were available and their enormous stockpile of salt would eventually dwindle.

Lately, the journey had been hard on her. Truth be told, it had been harder for him, too. They had to stop and rest more and more often.

And yet, here he was, alone, risking his own safety and the safety of those back at the cave, to meet a man he didn't know. It was insane, really.

He knew it was for one reason and one reason only: Emmeline. That young woman, so determined to be free and have freedom for her children, had touched his heart in a way that didn't seem possible. It was that determined look on her face, the set of her jaw, which never softened when she talked about the journey ahead, and the glow of her face when she tended to the children. It was her gentle touch on David's arm. She was an amazing young woman and Paul had grown to love and respect her.

Ingrid and Paul had saved themselves when they saw what was coming to the world. But Emmeline, trapped in that totalitarian culture, had managed to free herself and the ones she loved. Against all odds, she defied an evil Authority and risked everything for a better future.

That's why Paul would do this.

There it went again. The fluttering. Best rest for a moment. Just for a moment.

The clouds were clearing and the sun was setting. He was losing the security blanket of overcast skies. He'd just have to wrap himself in the faith that he could do this. But faith can be easily shaken in a world that has lost its moral compass. Faith can be challenged by strange rustlings in the underbrush, by the snorting of an animal that you hear but can't see. He made the sign of the cross and moved on.

Finally, after dusk, he was near the farm commune. He didn't see a guard near the row of pitched tents. The moon hovered bright on the horizon.

It was time to leave the shelter of the woods and walk into the open area, exposed and vulnerable. He held the knife tightly in his hand and patted his pocket to make sure his metal snips were still there.

Emmeline had said that George was in the first tent. Paul paused at the edge of the field, where anybody in the first tent—the first few tents in fact—could see him. And he waited.

Two raccoons screeched in the distance, an unearthly sound.

And he waited.

The first tent was all he cared about. The flap of that tent was open. All the other flaps were closed. There was a reason for that. George, or whoever was in there, hoped to see something. Hope. That person had hope.

Paul saw movement. A man's head emerged from the opening, then his shoulders, and his back. The man moved forward. His ball-and-chain was as Emmy had described it. They stared at each other in the pale light of the moon. He moved toward Paul, dragging the ball chained to his ankle. It left a furrow behind him in the plowed earth.

He was close enough now that Paul could have reached out and touched him.

"Who are you?" he asked Paul, leaning forward, his voice low, his face fearful.

"My name is Paul."

"Why are you here?"

"I was sent here by Emmeline."

He smiled. All of George's fear was gone with just the mention of her name.

"Go on," he said.

"She is safe with my wife and me. She and her husband are with us."

"Husband?"

"Yes. His name is David. He loves her very much. He's worried about her. He wants to keep her safe."

"I only want to see my daughter. That's all." He held his hands out, palms up, in a motion of supplication.

"Emmeline will let you see her daughter, Elsa, just once. Then you must leave. She is afraid they will search for you and put Elsa at risk."

"I understand."

"I told them I would decide how to proceed once I have spoken with you. I must decide if we can trust you before I cut your bonds." Paul pointed with his knife to the bracelet on his ankle.

"You can trust me."

Paul stared at him. Words were too easy. How was Paul to judge this man? He spoke again, hoping to be assured of George's character.

"They have a boy with them, also, a child Emmeline rescued. His name is Micah."

"Ah. And someday everyone will sit under their own vine and under their own fig tree and no one shall make them afraid."

"You know that verse?"

He nodded. "Micah 4:4. I know that verse."

"May it be so."

"God willing."

Paul knelt before him, humbled, his knees on the cold, wet earth, and, with great effort, applied pressure with the metal snips until the metal band of the ankle bracelet broke. It fell away, useless and inert. George picked up the heavy ball and chain and rolled it down the bank into the river.

The cold light of the moon spilled briefly down onto the silvery weight before it disappeared in the dark depths of the water.

George was free.

CHAPTER FORTY-SEVEN

EARTH PROTECTION AGENTS

Days 15–16

Adam's condition had worsened rapidly over the last two days. It was difficult for everyone confined on the bus because of his constant moaning and harsh breathing. The sounds of the dying man grated on their nerves. His hand had swollen like an enormous black rotten mushroom. Too weak to sit up, he'd sprawled across the bench seat in the back, sweat running off his face. They heard him vomit and the bus filled with a fetid smell.

Steven was angry that it was Adam who had been bitten. He was one of his strongest men. If someone was going to die, it should have been useless Guy, or Winston.

The women passed out cubes from the team's packs. Steven resented their using his team's cubes. Why didn't they have their own cubes, their own packs? Something was fishy. That big guy, John, had the Enforcer's uniform and a gun, but no backpack. Steven wondered what the deal was, what was going on. This Enforcer seemed too friendly with the woman he claimed to have captured. Just the way he looked at her didn't fit. Shouldn't he be harsher with her? Instead, he let her go outside with Julia, and didn't guard her at all. She could have taken off in a heartbeat and Julia wouldn't have done a thing to stop her. And Julia behaved strangely, too. She was a team member, for crying out loud, yet she had held a gun on her fellow agents. Steven shook his head, trying to make sense of the situation.

Guy mumbled to himself and shifted uncomfortably in his seat. He hated going out to relieve himself ever since Adam had been bitten.

Steven wondered how long this could go on. How much more time could they waste? Steven had an assignment and his reputation was at risk if he had to spend any more time waiting for Adam to die. Staying here wouldn't help anyone.

Suddenly, the moaning stopped. Adam began to whimper quietly.

Nigel urgently jerked his thumb toward Adam. Steven looked back over the seat. Adam wasn't moaning anymore and his skin had a bluish tinge. His eyes were closed, and his bad hand hung down. His red hair was darkened with sweat, and matted against his head. But he was still breathing. Damn! Nigel rolled his eyes. He was as frustrated as Steven.

Finally, dusk was falling. Surely Adam wouldn't make it through the night. Surely they could move out tomorrow. *Finally.*

* * *

Dawn. The weak early light wove its way through the vines partially covering the windows. Shadows and sunlight played across the seats and the floor of the bus. The Enforcer was awake, watchful, turned sideways in his seat, facing the men, his gun in hand. The women were asleep, their heads bowed low on their necks, their hair falling forward across their faces. Steven felt Julia's beret in his pocket. It still had the lemon smell of her hair. Winston was awake, gazing at the back of Julia's head. Guy was curled up, making him seem smaller than he really was—which was already pretty small. Nigel motioned with his head toward the back of the bus.

Adam was dead. His eyes were open, staring and dull as stagnant water. One leg hung off the edge of the seat. Steven hated losing a good team member like him, but such was life. At least they could now move out. The Enforcer woke the women with a soft touch to their shoulders. They stretched their long delicate arms above their heads.

The Enforcer looked over and saw that Adam was dead. Steven stood, ready to move out, but the Enforcer put his hand up to stop him. Steven sat back down, waiting. *What next*, he wondered. *What the hell next?*

"We'll carry him outside," the Enforcer said. His voice and face were tired, flat. "The women will wait inside." The women kept their faces averted. They must not have wanted to see a dead man.

"Your men will carry him. I'll follow."

Four men: Steven, Nigel, Guy, and Winston. One man for each arm and each leg. The men positioned themselves and lifted his limp body. Steven was glad he didn't get the arm with the swollen hand. Guy got that. They carried him up the aisle of the bus, trying not to bump his head against the seats.

Going through the opening and getting the body to ground level was difficult, since there were no steps. The men were grunting with the effort. The Enforcer pointed to a fallen pine tree lying near the edge of the bank. "Over there," he said. The Enforcer lifted up some branches and pointed. "Put him under these."

They laid Adam where he pointed and then the Enforcer let go of the branches he was holding up, covering most of the body with the greenery of the tree. The only thing showing was the black swollen hand. The Enforcer bent to slide that hand under cover, then he stood up.

That's when Steven made his move.

He ran at him full speed, felt the muscles in his legs pumping him forward, the muscles in his arms stretched out and tight, the muscles in his back taut, his feet moving, toes digging in, propelling him. He collided with the Enforcer at full force, and heard the grunt of air leaving his body, saw his head flail back. Steven saw his feet leave the ground, saw him wave his arms futilely, saw his gun fall from his waistband, watched him sail over the bank like a misshapen bird, saw his head hit a rock, saw him bounce downward, and then saw the splash as he hit the water. Saw him float, facedown.

Steven picked up the gun.

He clicked off the safety and went back into the bus. His men followed.

CHAPTER FORTY-EIGHT

EARTH PROTECTION AGENTS

Day 16

The women stared. Steven was holding the pistol, pointing it at them.

Their hands gripped the backs of the seats in front of them, their knuckles white.

"Give me your gun," he said to Julia. "Now."

She fumbled with her waistband. So she was too stupid to have her gun at the ready. Steven wasn't surprised. She wasn't military material.

"Hurry up. Hand it to me while keeping it pointed at yourself. Now."

The barrel of the gun was shiny from the sweat on her hand. Good. She was afraid.

The older woman half stood, crouched really, leaned out into the aisle, and tried to look past Steven. "Where's John? Where is he?"

So she knew him by name. They were connected somehow. Julia was holding her pack on her lap. The older one didn't have a pack.

Steven handed Julia's gun to Nigel. With a surprised look, Nigel took it. Then he smiled. He knew Steven trusted him.

"Take Julia's pack," Steven said to Guy.

Guy didn't move.

"Do what your leader tells you to do," Nigel said. His voice had a new, authoritative tone Steven hadn't heard before. How quickly power becomes part of a man.

Guy slipped past Steven to reach Julia and took her pack with an almost apologetic nod of his head.

"Where's John?" the older woman asked Steven again.

"What's your name?"

"Joan. My name is Joan."

"Well, Joan, John is gone. Just like that. Poof." Steven held his hand in the air and snapped his fingers. Why did this woman care about an Enforcer? "Tell me something, Joan. Why do you want to know where John is? Why do you care whether an Enforcer lives or dies?"

She didn't answer but slumped forward in her seat, her face in her hands, her shoulders shaking. Steven could hear her muffled sobs and that irritated him. What fool would cry over an Enforcer?

Julia put her arm across Joan's shoulders and murmured something to her. Joan nodded in response to whatever Julia had whispered.

"Spread out, you two. Go to seats on either side of the aisle." That technique had worked for John. He had to hand it to him for that clever command. But now it was *his* command to give.

Ashen-faced, Joan slipped across the aisle and sat two seats away from Julia. There would be no whispering back and forth. No communication between them.

"Let me see you walk," Steven said to Julia. "Get off the bus with Nigel and walk. I want to see how well you do."

She approached the front, holding the back of the seats with each step she took. The lemon smell was gone from her hair. Instead, he could smell the pungent odor of fear, see the half-moon stain of sweat under her armpits.

Nigel got off the bus with her and waved the pistol, indicating she should start walking. She hobbled along, one hand on the side of the bus for support. As she passed by one window after another, Steven could see the pain in her face. Weight bearing was obviously difficult for her and she would slow them down. Guy would slow them down, also. Steven had to decide how best to use the resources he had to complete his assignment.

Julia stumbled and almost fell getting backward on the bus. Winston, standing near the door, tried to reach for her, but Steven stopped him with an outstretched arm. She had betrayed them, held a gun on them. From the moment she obeyed John and pointed that pistol, she became a traitor to their cause. Steven looked forward to turning her over to the Authorities at the end of this mission. All in good time.

Now was the time for action.

Julia made it back to her seat and sat, pale-faced and disheveled. Nigel stood beside Steven, his legs in a wide stance, the posture of a man in charge.

Steven walked down the aisle toward Julia, and stood in the space in front of her. She tried to shrink back in her seat away from him, but he was able to reach her, grab her uniform where the Earth Protectors insignia was sewn, clasp his fingers on it, and rip it off. The sound of the cloth being torn gave him pleasure. Seeing the hole in her shirt, the pale skin of her upper chest exposed, also gave him pleasure. He had removed whatever small measure of status she had. He had reduced her back to a nobody. That's what she really was.

"Thank you," she said. "Thank you for officially discharging me from your evil agency." Her voice was strong, her disdain clear. "I'm glad I'm no longer a part of the so-called Earth Protectors."

Steven ignored her. She was not worthy of a response.

"Nigel, you stay here and guard the women. Never let them out of your sight." Nigel squared his shoulders, narrowed his eyes, and glared at the women.

"You will accompany me," Steven said, pointing at Winston.

"You can't just leave them here," Winston said.

"Who are *you* to question *me*?" Steven pointed the gun at Winston. "I have a job to do and I'm going to do it. Grab your pack and wait outside."

Frowning, Winston picked up a pack from the heap, and before he went outside, glanced at Joan and Julia sitting halfway back in the bus. Steven didn't trust Winston and needed to keep an eye on him. With this arrangement, he could. On the plus side, Winston was in good shape and could keep up with Steven.

"Guy. You're coming with me, too. Grab your pack." Steven knew Guy was afraid of the Human Free Zone. Indeed, he was afraid of his own shadow and he would also slow them down. But if Steven found the four adults and two children together in one group, he would need more than just Winston to help him. Guy had to come along. At least he would try to follow orders.

They were wasting time. Even questioning the women would be beneath his dignity. They had gone far upstream and had nothing to show for it. They'd have to move fast and far.

"We will find the escapees in short order." Steven spoke with confidence because he believed in himself, believed he could do this. "We will bring them back here, pick up the women, and then we'll all return to the Compound."

Steven made the circle sign toward his captives.

The pale-faced women made the circle sign, slowly, reluctantly.

Nigel made the circle sign with a proud flourish.

Winston, standing outside the bus door, slowly brought his hand to his forehead. Guy, standing by Winston, his eye twitching, made the circle sign and fumbled with the straps on his pack.

They recited together: "I pledge allegiance to the Earth."

There is comfort in rituals.

Sometimes.

Through the bus window, Joan watched Steven, Winston, and Guy head downstream. Her breath fogged the window. From the outside they looked just like ghosts.

CHAPTER FORTY-NINE

STEVEN, WINSTON, AND GUY

Days 16–17

"We're moving and moving fast. No more wasting time." Steven made himself clear to Winston and Guy. They simply nodded.

Steven filled his water bottles at the edge of the river. The water was cold on his hands and wrists. He tightened the lids, shoved the bottles into his pack, and shook the water off his hands.

Winston did the same.

Steven slung his pack on his back.

Winston did the same.

Is he imitating me to annoy me? Steven wondered.

Guy seemed to be aware of the tension between the other two men and his eyes darted back and forth.

"We sat around for a couple of days on that damn bus. So we're rested. You guys lead. I follow. Move out."

The river to their left churned forward, little whitecaps curling over on themselves like gymnasts somersaulting on a gray-brown mat.

Bits of black asphalt were still visible through the grass. A metal street sign, pockmarked with rust around the edges, had fallen from its pole and was nestled in a patch of ferns. The words were faded.

Route 30. Below that the words *Lincoln Highway.* Steven wondered what kind of a name was *Lincoln* for a highway? What the hell was a Lincoln? Tenacious vines curled around the useless, empty pole, tilting it sideways, pulling it downward.

Steven kicked the sign and flakes of rust fell onto the ferns.

They made good time. Winston easily kept the pace Steven wanted. His long legs were his best asset. Guy walked as though his life depended on it, keeping up but panting heavily.

The sun was directly overhead. "Time for a break. Head for some shade," Steven said. He could see the sweat stain down the middle of Guy's back, like a stripe.

They sat beneath some large trees. The cool air felt good brushing across the backs of their necks. Winston's face was sunburned, red across his cheeks, nose, and the tops of his ears. The skin on Guy's face was already starting to peel. Steven's skin felt hot and tight. He knew he was probably sunburned, too.

Guy poured some water from his bottle into his hands and splashed his face with it. The silvery droplets dripped from his chin onto his uniform.

Steven looked around the area. Something wasn't quite right. Grass had been pulled up, leaving bare patches. Something or someone had been here eating it. Some ferns were broken at the base, and the fronds were dry and withered.

Exhilarated at finding the first clues he'd seen in days, Steven felt his pulse race.

"Let's go!" he said. He heard the excitement in his own voice, felt the adrenaline pour through him.

They moved out of the shade, back into the sun.

Winston and Guy hadn't said a word all morning. That didn't bother Steven. He didn't bring them along for conversation. He had brought Winston along because he didn't trust him. He had left his strongest man back with the women. He'd catch his prey—that's all they were to him, prey—march them back, gather up the rest of his team and the women, and return to the Compound. His work would be done, and done well. He would be rewarded, and could return to the soft life, the life he deserved, at the Central Authority's mansion.

They walked the rest of the day and saw more signs of disruption: rocks with patches of moss ripped off and more broken cattails. They walked into the wall of dusk and beyond. Each clue Steven saw energized him and fed his fanatical zealotries.

They put on their torches, fastening the bands tightly on their foreheads. The torches hadn't been recharged since they left the Compound, but luckily they hadn't used them very much. The light was still bright enough to show a smoother path.

They were safe using the torches for now. No one was around to see their lights. Steven felt like he could walk all night.

Later, when the torches lost their charge, they'd have to rely on the moon and stars.

When they finally stopped, Steven took a pair of shiny handcuffs out of his pack and dangled them in front of Winston's face. They clanged together with metallic harshness.

"I don't need those. I'm not going anywhere," Winston said firmly.

"You're right. You're *not* going anywhere. Sit over there with your back against that tree." He motioned with his gun to a large silver maple.

The ground under the maple was riddled with large gnarled roots protruding above the surface. Winston found one small, smooth area and sat there with his back against the tree, wondering what Steven was going to do.

"Put your arms back on either side of the tree. I'm going to handcuff your wrists together behind it."

"Are you cuffing him, too?" Winston motioned with his head toward Guy, who sat huddled some distance away with his legs drawn up and his arms wrapped around them.

"Him? No need. He'd pass out if a cricket landed on his foot. He's not about to go off on his own." Steven turned to Guy. "Go fill our water bottles and make it snappy."

"You want me to go out there?" Guy's voice was high-pitched and annoying.

"Don't question me. Don't *ever* question me," Steven said. "This one did and he earned these handcuffs. Do you want the same?"

Guy quickly rooted through the packs, pulled out some empty bottles, and scuttled down to the river to fill them. In the moonlight he looked like a crab going down the steep bank, knees bent and arms akimbo.

Steven managed to get one cuff on Winston but the tree was too big, and the cuffs too short for both wrists to be manacled together behind the tree.

"Damn! Move over there."

Near the maple was a slender birch, its paper-white bark luminous in the moonlight.

Winston spent the night tethered to that birch.

The next day was a repeat of the last one. No conversation, no sense of trust in each other, just three men in the wilderness.

When they stopped for the night, Steven pulled a strange device out of his pocket, a two-inch-square metal box. When Steven pressed a switch, a small red light began to blink. He held it in front of Winston's face.

"Bet you wish you had one of these," Steven taunted. "But you wouldn't even know how to use it."

Winston ignored him.

"It's a heat detector. Set up to detect motion fifty yards away, and only on moving things about the size of a human or larger. Squirrels can't set it off. And people near me can't set it off. There's no point in having to be told my own team is standing right next to me, now, is there? But if it detects a person within its radius, the light stops blinking, and stays a steady red. And it vibrates. I can feel it through my clothes when it vibrates."

Winston continued to ignore him.

"So you're not interested in learning? No skin off my teeth." Steven pointed to a small tree. Another birch. "Get over there."

After he handcuffed Winston's wrists behind the birch tree, Steven continued talking. His voice had a jubilant, almost maniacal tone. "See, I think we're this close, this close!" He held his thumb and forefinger close together and peered into Winston's face. Winston turned his head away from Steven's foul breath. "The clues! They're everywhere. I see them all." He talked rapid-fire, breathing hard, his face flushed. "And I will be triumphant." He raised his fist to the dark sky. Nobody of any consequence could see that small-minded man's fist raised in the darkness of the night.

Steven, caught up in his own theatrics, never took the time to realize that birch trees, like people, could look normal on the outside, but be rotten to the core.

CHAPTER FIFTY

JOAN AND JULIA

Day 16

Joan's first reaction had been denial.

"No! No! He can't be gone. He's out there somewhere. I know he is. You're lying." She had pounded her fists on the seat of the bus.

Steven had just smirked. That little *poof* sound, that snapping of his fingers, dismissed her husband entirely.

And then Steven, Guy, and Winston left the bus.

Time passed. Joan waited for John to return.

But he didn't.

That's when the anger built in her. Not just anger but red, hot rage. If she was bigger, stronger, and faster, she would have ripped that man, Steven, with his smirk, into ribbons of flesh and bone. Emotions pulsed through her faster than she ever thought possible.

The bus was hot, stuffy, and smelled of sour bodies, death, and the green smell of vines growing through the holes in the floorboards. Tiny black insects crawled up and down the stems.

John had promised that he would stay with Joan, that he would never leave her. He had tried to keep his promise. Truth is, he *had* kept his promise—he hadn't left her. He was taken from her, stolen and ripped out of her life. She was left with a huge bleeding hole in her heart and a cramping pain in the pit of her stomach. Nothing she could think of would fill that hole or heal that pain if she couldn't find John.

Julia kept glancing at Joan, soft glances that were a mixture of fear and sympathy.

Nigel stood and stared at the women. *Does he ever blink?* she wondered. His eyes were narrow, with a spray of lines like crow's feet fanning out at the corners. The sun coming in through the windows made his blond hair look almost white, his sunburned scalp shining through. Even his eyebrows and eyelashes were white and looked cold as ice.

Joan saw the trees, the stream, and a few thin clouds drifting by, lazy and formless as smoke, through the dirty windows. She was still crying.

Julia coughed a tiny little cough. Joan glanced at her. With her hands below the level of the seat in front of her so Nigel couldn't see her motions, Julia made a small gesture toward her waistband. Then she pointed at Joan.

Julia did that twice.

Signals. She was sending Joan a signal.

The gun. Joan still had a gun. In her angst, she had forgotten about it. Now she put her hand on it. She gripped the handle, sliding it from her waistband.

Julia watched her, then stood up. "I'll go get water. Our bottles need to be filled."

Nigel looked at Julia for a second, and started to reply.

In that fraction of a second, Joan rested her arm on the seat back in front of her to keep her hand steady.

In that tiny second, she pulled the trigger. The sound rattled around the metal bus like rolling thunder.

In that tiny second, she shot him.

She had never shot a gun before.

She felt no remorse. She felt only victory.

He fell, crumpling down upon himself in stages, like a fan being folded. She watched it in slow motion: knees, chest, arms, head. Finally, there was no movement at all.

Julia picked up the gun Nigel had dropped, and tucked it into her waistband.

Joan and Julia stepped over Nigel, grabbed all the packs, and left the bus. The air outside was cleaner, cooler.

Julia was barely limping anymore.

"Your ankle seems to have gotten better," Joan said.

"Sitting on the bus with it elevated helped a lot."

"But when Nigel took you outside to test your ankle, you were still limping and looked like you were in pain."

She smiled. "My ankle still bothers me, but I made it look worse than it was. It worked, didn't it? We got left behind, and didn't have to march with Steven. I call that a win."

Julia is an impressive woman, Joan thought. They'd make a great team. "Good. We'll head downstream and try to catch up with Steven and Winston. Try to stop them from hurting anybody. If they do find and capture anyone, well, we'll do anything and everything we can."

Joan looked at the wilderness all around them. The overwhelming greenness of it, the absolute beauty of the rolling hills, soft and rounded, the sky a protective blue dome overhead, and yet there was inescapable loneliness in this vast Human Free Zone.

"Pray we find John. My son and his family are out here somewhere, too. We'll search for them. I'm not giving up on anybody. And we *will* survive."

Steven, Guy, and Winston were mere hours ahead of them. Joan knew now that there was no looking back. One way or another, their old way of life in the commune was gone forever.

CHAPTER FIFTY-ONE

WINSTON

Day 16

Winston's shoulders throbbed because of the strained position of his arms; the handcuffs cut into his wrists. Physically, he was miserable. But he was even worse mentally. He believed no good would come of this mission. When all was said and done, everyone involved would be at risk for terrible outcomes. If the escapees were captured, they would face the wrath of the Enforcers. If they weren't captured, they faced an uncertain future in this vast Human Free Zone. Julia and Joan were definitely at risk. Steven would show them no mercy. Winston shuddered to think of Steven with those women. And even if the women survived Steven, an Enforcer would deal with them harshly and order them to be recycled.

Winston was trapped by more than the handcuffs. He was trapped by hopelessness. Sleep was impossible.

The trees were thick and close around him, and made creaking, groaning sounds as the wind rubbed branches against branches, tree against tree. Guy had crawled under a large pine and the branches covered him like a tent.

Steven was snoring, and in spite of his standard order that his men sleep with their backs against a tree, he had slipped sideways. He lay sprawled on the ground with his head resting on his arms. His trouser pocket had gaped open and beside him the motion sensor and the key to the handcuffs laid on the ground, glittering in the moonlight.

Seeing them, Winston thought that maybe, just maybe, he had a chance. He began to make a back-and-forth sawing movement with his hands, rubbing the handcuff chain against the trunk. By leaning forward, he pulled the chain tight against the tree, applying greater pressure.

Back and forth. Back and forth. The pain in his shoulders and wrists was almost unbearable, but the faint sound of bits of bark falling to the ground motivated him. Back and forth went the chain, faster and faster. Sweat rolled down his face. His mouth pulled back in a grimace. He kept working.

Through a small clearing in the branches above him, he could see the moon. It crossed his mind that the stars, the moon, and the sun—indeed, all things in the sky—remained steady, dependable, and predictable over the centuries, even as the mercurial societies below so easily changed.

His hands felt warm and wet. The back of his wrists must be bleeding. He kept working.

He felt a sudden lessening of resistance from the tree trunk that caused him to lurch forward a little. It felt like he had broken through hard wood to a softer center. The tree must have a rotten core. He rested for a short moment. Steven shifted his position on the ground and Winston held his breath, waiting and watching the sleeping man. Steven resumed his snoring and his breathing caused the leaves near his face to flutter slightly.

Winston started the sawing motion again, working to cut through the last part of the trunk nearest him. His shoulders were no longer pulled back as tightly and he could feel the vibration of the chain against the wood in his spine. He didn't know what he would do when he actually broke through and the trunk was severed. It would crash down, and surely that would wake Steven and Guy, but he didn't care. He would do whatever he could, until he could do more.

He looked at the moon again. Winston wished he could measure time by that dependable shift in the heavens. The best he could do was guess. He thought he had been working at this for about four hours. He gave one last push-pull on the cuffs and the chain broke through the last of the trunk.

When a tree falls in the forest . . .

But the tree didn't fall. Its branches were tangled with those of surrounding trees and it hung suspended, swaying above Winston like a pendulum.

He slid closer to Steven, leaned over, and with his hands behind his back, picked up the motion sensor and handcuff key. He knew he couldn't get the heavy gun from Steven's holster without waking him. Clutching them in his wet, sticky hands, he stood slowly. His legs and back were cramped and stiff, but it didn't matter. What mattered was that he could walk away from here, back toward the bus, to save Julia and Joan, and hopefully redeem himself as a man capable of doing the right thing in a world where everything seemed wrong.

CHAPTER FIFTY-TWO

STEVEN

Day 17

Steven was momentarily confused when he woke. The first thing he saw was a tree with a severed trunk, suspended in the air and swaying gently. What the hell? He shook his head, rubbed his eyes, and looked again. He got up and walked closer to it and looked up. Yes, it was a tree. Yes, it was hanging there, its branches tangled with branches of other trees.

In fact, it was the tree he had cuffed Winston to. That was when he realized Winston was gone. What the hell? Gone? How did he get away? Steven turned in a full circle, scanning the area. Nothing, no one. He reached in his pocket for the heat detector. Empty. He pulled the pocket inside out. No detector, no handcuff key. Just like that— gone. He was lucky he still had his gun.

The euphoria he felt the evening before faded, replaced briefly with insecurity. He squirmed in discomfort. How had Winston escaped? Maybe the escapees freed him. But that made no sense. Escapees wouldn't come near an Earth Protector. But who, then? And how?

He examined the part of the tree trunk still in the ground. The core of the tree was visibly rotten, as though the heart of it had died. The rim was jagged and torn as if a crude saw had been used. Could the handcuff chain have done that? And how long would it have taken? All this had been accomplished while he lay nearby, asleep. So much for his sleep lightly, wake easily rule. But, after all, they had covered a lot of ground yesterday, walking way past dark. Any man, no matter how fit, would have slept soundly. The fact that Winston had walked just as far as he had and yet managed to stay awake and slice through the tree trunk didn't enter Steven's rationalization of his failure, and he quickly dismissed any personal responsibility for Winston's escape. Instead, he began to think of what options he had in continuing his assigned mission.

His anger at Winston was now greater than his anger at those who had escaped the Compound. If he made his decision about whom to pursue based on anger, he would go after Winston . . . No, wait. *Focus. Focus. Focus.*

Guy slid out from under the pine tree's shade and sat openmouthed. He stared at the broken tree trunk and then at Steven, but Steven ignored him.

Steven squatted on his heels and reached into his pack for a nourishment cube. Winston's pack was still on the ground, near the lifeless tree trunk. Good. More nourishment cubes for Steven, none for Winston. A small thing, really, but it gave Steven pleasure.

Winston had been so concerned about leaving Julia behind the first time and then about leaving both women on the bus with Nigel. What was it he had said? *You can't just go and leave them.* Stupid words at best, and at worst, a treasonous statement.

Steven figured Winston would head back toward the bus like some ridiculous white knight gallant to rescue the women. But Winston was misguided and foolish. Individuals weren't important. What was important was the larger mission of the Earth Protection Agency. That's what the Authorities valued. Steven would do what the Authorities valued.

He would find the escapees first. He knew he was catching up to them. They couldn't be very far away, and they were his original assignment. If he didn't catch them, he would lose his chance at a position at the mansion, and that was unacceptable.

After he had found the adults and captured the children, he'd head back to the bus. If Winston had made it there, Nigel would have him under guard. Then Steven would get revenge on Winston, and it wouldn't be pretty.

His plan was perfect.

Before setting off with Guy, he reached into Winston's pack and ate one of his cubes, savoring every bite.

CHAPTER FIFTY-THREE

JOAN AND JULIA

Days 16–17

Julia and Joan were driven by emotion.

"What's important to you?" Julia asked once, breathlessly, as they jogged.

"John, my son, and his family," Joan answered, the words firm. "And you?"

"My soul," Julia answered. "But I want to kill Steven, too." Joan didn't question her, because she didn't see the juxtaposition of *soul* and *killing* as a contradiction. Not in this world, anyway.

The sun was slipping below the horizon, the last tendrils of light briefly remaining like fingertips hanging on to the edge of the world.

"I can't go on. I need a break. My ankle is acting up," Julia said, leaning forward with her hands on her knees. Her forehead was shiny with sweat.

"Best then to stop now and rest. It's getting late, anyhow. Not much daylight left," Joan said. They sat side by side. "Were you raised in the Village?" she asked Julia.

"Yes. And I hated it. But I didn't start out there. When I was very small I was allowed to live in a house with my parents. Then, one day when I was eight, a man in a black uniform came into our space and took me. That was the last time I saw my mother. I can still hear what she said to him."

"What?"

" 'Here is her change of clothes.' Then she handed him a bag of my clothes and told me to go with the Enforcer. 'He is going to take you to the Children's Village. They will take good care of you there.' "

"Did they?"

"No. It was hard enough that I had to go in the first place. Most children over the age of four didn't. I still don't understand why. Once I got there, the rules were endless: what you could and couldn't do, when you had to go to bed, when you had to get up—on and on and on. They taught me things that made no sense, like pledging allegiance to animals."

"You don't act like someone raised in the Village."

"I learned to repeat what they wanted me to repeat, but the words were hollow and meaningless. I pretended to be enthusiastic with the pledges and the circle sign like the other children. But I knew I was different."

"Different how?"

"I was an independent thinker, I guess. But I couldn't let anybody know that."

"I'm glad you are who you are," Joan said. "We better sleep now."

"Sleep well, my friend," Julia murmured, stretching out on the hard ground.

The word *friend* was never heard back in the Compound. But here, in this place and under these circumstances, it had great importance.

Friends. People with common values, common goals, and a commitment to each other.

They slept under a blanket of stars, lulled to sleep by the nocturnal chorus of crickets.

They slept so deeply that neither of them saw the blinking red light that became a steady red beacon.

* * *

Winston felt the heat detector vibrating against his fingertips. He stopped walking and carefully scanned the area. He made out the forms of two people sleeping, but he couldn't be sure who they were at this distance. He approached cautiously, staying close to the shelter of large trees, and hoping with every step that they were not dangerous. He wondered if he should slip past these people and continue on to the bus where Julia and Joan had been left under Nigel's guard.

Dawn rippled along the horizon, pushing through the clouds and streaking their edges with rosy light. Birds began their early-morning carefree chorus of chirps and tweets. The sleeping forms were becoming easier to see. One of them sat up and stretched, then pushed back her long dark hair. In the faint early light, her face was visible.

Julia.

Winston was momentarily confused. If that was Julia, was Nigel also here? Why weren't they still on the bus? Hadn't Steven given the order for them to remain on the bus?

Julia reached out and touched the shoulder of the other person. Winston watched as the second person stood up.

Joan.

Winston looked around the area, trying to figure out where Nigel was. But he saw no one. He stepped away from the shelter of the tree and stood exposed in an open area with the morning sun on his face. They stared at him as if at an apparition.

Julia spoke first. "Winston?" she murmured. He nodded.

She looked past him with a fearful look.

"I'm alone," he said, stepping closer.

They were silent for a moment, then Julia smiled. "You're not alone," she said softly. "You're with us."

A sense of relief swept over Winston so powerful that he sank to his knees with his head bowed. The detector and handcuff key fell from his hands.

They gathered around him and knelt with him. That's when they saw his handcuffed wrists and the heat detector.

"How will we get those things off your wrists?" Joan asked. "Who put them on?"

"Steven put them on. I couldn't see the keyhole to free myself, but here's a key. I just dropped it."

Joan began searching in the grass for the key and finally held it up with a triumphant gesture. Quickly she unlocked the cuffs; they fell away with a clang. Winston sighed with relief and ran his fingers over his broken skin. Julia grabbed a water bottle and poured it over the bloody abrasions. Joan offered him water to drink and he swallowed it all in three great gulps.

Then the questions began.

"What is that metal thing?"

"A heat detector."

"Have you found any of the people we're all looking for?"

"No. Not yet."

"Where is Nigel?"

"I shot him."

"You shot him? You have a gun?"

"Yes. So does Julia. Have you seen John? I'm looking for John."

Winston didn't look at Joan as he spoke. "Steven pushed him into the river."

"He can swim," Joan said, her jaw squared in determination.

Hope dies a lingering death.

"Where is Guy?"

"He's with Steven and he is scared to death. He'll do whatever Steven tells him to do."

More questions asked and answered. More grim stories told.

They all fell silent before Joan rose and headed toward the river bank. She was still convinced that her husband could be alive. Desperately, she walked up and down the bank, returning to the area around the bus. Julia watched her, increasingly hopeless. Long minutes passed before her friend returned.

Finally, Julia found words. "Steven no longer has a team. But we do," she said softly.

This new team had to decide together what they would do now, what direction they would go, and what dangers they would face.

"Steven seemed convinced he was closing in on the escapees," Winston said. "He was practically frothing at the mouth with excitement. He was acting like a madman."

"Those escapees are my son and his family. I've got to stop Steven," Joan said, wringing her hands.

"*We*," Julia said. "*We've* got to stop him." She put her hand on Joan's shoulder.

Winston nodded. "Yes, *we've* got to stop him."

They started walking with grim determination.

Through the twists and tangles of fate, the hunters would soon become the hunted.

CHAPTER FIFTY-FOUR

EMMELINE

Day 17

David had been restless all night, tossing and turning, but he slept deeply now, his breathing slow and even. He was nervous about George being followed and our safety being compromised. I understood his concern, but I also knew we were doing the right thing, difficult though it was. The right thing is not always the easiest.

I stood up and walked to the cave's entrance. The sun had not yet risen, but it soon would. The stars had faded ahead of the competition from the coming dawn. I went to the edge of the clearing and peered into the woods. No sign of Paul.

I walked back to the cave entrance but didn't sit down. My legs were restless, and I paced back to the edge of the woods again. My stomach churned with nausea. I went back to the cave again to peer inside. Everyone was still asleep.

Dawn was slowly rising up from the dark side of the earth. It was a pale pink, such a gentle color. The mother deer and her two fawns that I'd come to recognize rustled through the woods nearby. I could make out the white spots scattered on the soft brown fur of the fawns, as though they had been splattered with paint. They slipped deeper into the woods and went down to the bank to drink from the stream. They could have all the water they wanted and it would always be there. Surely, there was enough for all the animals and all the people in all the Compounds.

I was suddenly thirsty. My mouth felt dry, my lips cracked. I wanted to drink from the river's cold, fresh flow. It was light enough now I could walk to the water without tripping over a rock or a tree root. I would fill an empty bucket, and make myself useful. The waiting would go faster if I busied myself.

There was still no sign of Paul. Had he made the trip safely? So many things could have gone wrong. He might have been bitten by a snake, or fallen and struck his head on a rock. His fluttery heart might have stopped altogether. Had he been seen by a guard and captured? My own heart felt fluttery at the thought; my hands were sweating. If anything happened to him, it would be my fault.

Enough, I told myself. I had to let go of my worry. I grabbed the bucket and headed for the river. The mother deer and her fawns were already gone. I looked over my shoulder, back toward the cave. No sign of life stirred. I was truly alone out here surrounded by nothing but nature. At the river, I set the bucket down and had a drink of water from my cupped hands. I splashed water on my face and ran my wet hands through my hair.

Another wave of nausea washed over me. That had been happening recently. I remembered having the same nausea when I was pregnant with Elsa. Could I be pregnant again? That would be wonderful if we were in a safe place, far from here. But we weren't safe. Not by a long shot. We were still too close to the Compound. I resolved again to move on soon. Far, far away.

That's what I wanted.

I couldn't wait to tell David that I might be pregnant. Or should I wait until I was sure? No. This was something I had to tell him now, something he needed to know.

Quiet as a shadow, David came through the trees. He sat near me with his long arm across my shoulders and we watched the sun rise fully, casting golden warmth down on us.

"They'll be here soon," he said reassuringly.

I nodded and laid my head against his shoulder, placed my hand on his leg. "I'm feeling a little queasy," I said.

"I hope you're not getting sick. Maybe it's nerves."

"I think it might be something else."

"What else could it be?"

"I think I might be pregnant."

He tightened his arm on my shoulder. "What? Are you sure?"

"No, I'm not sure. So don't say anything to anyone."

"What makes you think . . . ?" His voice trailed off, as if the word *pregnant* was too big to say. As if it would get stuck in his throat and never come out.

Pregnant. It *is* a big word. It changes everything.

"Some nausea. I didn't think anything of it at first. You know, eating bugs; of course I was nauseated. And that salty fish stew. Other times, like at the farm commune, seeing things that upset me deeply. There was always a reason. But it's more frequent now."

"If you are, you know, it will make moving on more difficult."

"You of all people know how important it is for me to find us a home far from here. So, no matter what, we're moving on. End of discussion."

He put his hand on my abdomen, then quickly took it away, as if my body was too hot to touch.

"I want to start our journey, now more than ever. *If* I am carrying a child, and that's a big *if*, I want to get as far as we can before the baby is born. So far away that no one can take this new life from us."

He ran his hands through his hair and started to say something but I cut him off.

"No more talking about it. We should start back. The children will be awake by now."

He didn't answer but instead picked up the bucket and held his hand out to me, helping me stand. We started up the hill together just as Paul and George emerged from the woods.

CHAPTER FIFTY-FIVE

GEORGE

Day 17

Emmeline and David walked slowly up the slope toward them, holding hands. George noticed how pale she looked.

George was filled with awe, his thoughts free-flowing as he watched David and Emmeline approach. *It's amazing that my leg iron is gone, that I was able to walk away from the farm commune, free. It's amazing that Emmeline escaped and found her way to the commune. It's amazing that I have a daughter.* His heart raced at the thought.

"Hello, George," Emmy said. "I want you to meet my husband. His name is David."

George extended his hand. "Hello, David. I'm glad to meet you. Thank you for agreeing to this."

David extended his hand and took George's hand. His grip was firm. "I did it for Emmy. It was important to her."

"We've walked a long way," Paul said. "We all need to sit and rest."

"I'll see if Elsa's awake." Emmy slipped into the cave. Another wave of anxiety washed over George as he prepared to meet his only child. He could hear a murmur of voices from inside: a child, two women, and the rattle of mugs. The men sat quietly, waiting. Paul cleared his throat, fiddled with his knife and a piece of wood that looked strangely familiar.

Micah came out first. He sat by David and looked at George a long moment before speaking. "I'm Micah," he said at last. "I escaped with Emmy and David. I call them Mommy and Daddy."

George smiled at him. "I am glad to meet you, Micah. Escaping from the Compound must have been scary."

"Oh, it was! I heard guns and there was a fire and a lot of noise and Emmy woke me up and asked me to come with her. And then we ran. We ran a lot and walked a lot. My shoes wore out but David, I mean Daddy, fixed them. At the beginning Daddy hurt his arm and after a while we were hungry and tired of walking. We had to hide in the daytime and walk at night. It was kind of scary walking in the dark, but I did it anyway."

The women were still in the cave. George ached to see Elsa. Paul sat leaning back with his eyes closed. George looked over his shoulder to the entrance of the cave but couldn't see anyone.

"I think they're making something for us to drink," David said. "They should be out soon."

"So, Micah, what did you have to eat when you were walking and running?" George asked him.

"Oh, berries, and grass, and bugs. Stuff like that. Daddy knows about things to eat. And one time, we went to the farm commune. We got some peas there. And things we found in some of the tents. And we saw a lady fall down."

"You did? You were at the farm commune and saw a lady fall down?"

"Just for a minute. Then Mommy covered my eyes. We both wanted to help the lady but we couldn't. So we ran away, ran back to Daddy and Elsa with some peas and other things."

So that explained it. The mystery of why two of the tents had been rummaged through and things had gone missing. The guards were vicious about that, questioning everybody, convinced that one of the workers had been the thief. The missing things were never found. And Micah and Emmy saw the woman who had collapsed. Did they see how she was discarded? Oh, Lord, George hoped not, especially not the boy.

"That piece of wood Paul is working with. Was that a tent peg?" George asked him

"Yes. I pulled it out of the ground." He smiled proudly and made a little muscle with his flexed arm.

"Wow! You are very strong!" George said.

David reached over and stroked Micah's hair. "He's strong and brave and very smart."

"And we are going to keep walking, after we are all rested up. Mommy wants to get all the way to where she lived when she was a little girl. It's far away."

George frowned. Did she really think they could travel that far with two children? It would be dangerous. Impossible, he feared.

Ingrid came out first with two mugs. One was for Paul, the other for David.

"Micah, help me carry out the rest."

He followed her into the cave and they came back out with four more mugs. Ingrid handed George one, and he welcomed its warmth in his hand, his fingers curled around it. Steam rose warm and moist against his face. A warm drink in the Human Free Zone was yet another of today's miracles.

Ingrid sat next to Paul, holding her mug in brown spotted hands, her wrist bones sharply pronounced on her thin arm. She looked at George with open curiosity but said nothing. Even though she was a frail old woman, her eyes were piercing. She was taking her measure of George, deciding if she could trust him.

George didn't know how long they would let him stay. Would he have to leave as soon as he had seen Elsa? George had said he would, but he now realized how hard that would be. What if he promised to help them find food, firewood? Would they let him stay longer?

And then Emmy came out holding Elsa.

George stared at his daughter. Her hair was the color of corn silk, and nearly as fine. A small breeze ruffled through it, lifting it so it was floating like a halo above her head. She had round, smooth cheeks, and rosebud-shaped lips. Her eyes were a startling blue. One soft baby arm rested across Emmy's neck and she was sitting comfortably on Emmy's hip, smiling at her.

George stood, his legs shaking. He put his arms out to hold Elsa. She pulled closer to Emmy and hid her face against Emmy's shoulder.

"Don't rush her," Emmy said to George. Then she sat next to David. David held his arms out for Elsa and she sat on his lap, keeping her face turned away from the stranger.

"Micah said you are planning to go back to where you grew up," George said to Emmy, while looking at his daughter.

"Yes. Kansas," she answered.

"You know there aren't many people out there. All the people were relocated to the East and West Coasts."

"Good," she said. "Then there won't be any Authorities or Enforcers. And you can't know for certain that there are or aren't people out there. No one can know that for sure."

"Before we came here to the cave, the people running the meetings talked about the rights of indigenous people to have their original lands back," Paul said.

"Indigenous people?" David asked.

"People who first occupied the land . . ."

Ingrid interrupted. "Do you know how to clean a snapping turtle?" She asked George.

"Yes," George said. "I do." The question puzzled him.

"Good. Good because it's too much work for Paul. Cutting the shell and all. But I do the cooking. Understand?" she said, rubbing her hands together as if some great concern of hers was resolved.

Paul finished the last of his drink and stood. "I'm very tired and need to lie down. George needs to rest, too. Follow me." He motioned for George to follow him into the cave.

George followed him gladly. His invitation to rest meant he didn't have to leave right away. It meant he might be able to stay long enough to hold Elsa. His arms ached with wanting.

CHAPTER FIFTY-SIX

EMMELINE

Day 17

"I thought he was going to see Elsa and then leave," David said. He stacked our mugs by the entrance with an angry intensity. "But, no. Now he's sleeping in the cave. And the guards at the commune are probably searching for him right now. When they search for him, they will find us. I know it."

"Can I go look at the turtle?" Micah asked.

"No. Stay away from the turtle." David shook his finger at Micah.

"But I won't touch him. I promise."

"I said no," David said, his voice louder. "Don't ask again. Gather some wood."

Micah glanced at David with a puzzled expression. David had never used that sharp tone with him before.

"Go on. Do what I tell you."

With a backward glance, Micah set off to do his chore. Ingrid followed him, her braid swinging back and forth, the importance of gathering wood the only thing on her mind.

"What's wrong with you?" I asked David. "Why are you talking to Micah like that?" Elsa crawled over to the log bench and started pulling herself up. David picked her up and she tugged on his ear with her plump fingers.

"Emmy, I'm so worried. It's chewing me up inside. You might be pregnant, and we're all at risk. My job is to protect you."

"That's no reason to be angry with Micah."

"I'm not angry with Micah." He put Elsa down, and held her hands so she was standing. She bounced up and down, then took tiny, tentative steps, walking on the balls of her feet. It wouldn't be long before she could walk on her own.

"You sounded angry and he sensed it. He was trying to please you and all you did was bark orders at him. Didn't you see the hurt look on his face?"

"All right, already. I was too hard on him. I'll apologize when he comes back." David said. "But can't you see the worried look on mine?" He turned to me, and, indeed, there was a tension around his eyes, the corners of his mouth turned down. He picked Elsa up again.

"Yes, I see it."

He leaned against me, with Elsa sandwiched between us.

"I have to protect you."

"And you are. You have been."

"I can't stop thinking about the guards at the commune."

"Then we should leave this place. I want to live away from all of this, from hiding in a cave, afraid of every shadow, every sound. When can we leave?"

Before David could answer me, George reemerged. David and I stayed close together, Elsa between us.

"I couldn't sleep," George said. "My body feels like I should be doing something. Picking crops or something. I'm not used to being idle and not used to walking without a leg iron." He extended his leg and I could see the red rawness of his skin where the ankle bracelet had rubbed.

"Paul can help that heal," I said. "He healed David's arm with honey."

Before we had to pass any more time in awkward conversation, Ingrid and Micah came back with arms full of twigs.

"Hi, Micah," murmured David. "Sorry I was so grumpy earlier. Give me a hug." Micah ran to David and wrapped his arms around him, smiling and blushing.

"Oh, good, you're still here," Ingrid said to George. "Pretty soon you can get the turtle out of the shell and we'll all have soup."

David snatched up an empty bucket. "I'll get more water," he said. "You'll need it for the soup." He started off alone.

"Wait. Elsa and I will go with you." I scrambled after him. Without speaking, we went to the stream. When we got there, David made no motion to fill the bucket. Instead, he sat, staring at the water for a few minutes.

I watched Elsa pull up some grass and put it in her mouth. I ran my hand over her hair. There had to be an answer to all of this. What seemed so complicated had to be untangled, made simple. And I knew in a flash what the solution was.

"Let him stay."

"What? I can't believe you're saying that."

"Wait. Hear me out, please. He can be here for Paul and Ingrid. That will make it easier for us to leave. We won't feel guilty about leaving them."

I clapped my hands together. Elsa imitated me, clapping her small hands together.

"We'll talk to him about staying here," I said. "They'll keep him well hidden."

David looked at me with the first smile I had seen since George arrived. "You are amazing," he said. "I am so proud of you." He leaned over and gave me a soft, tender kiss.

Then I saw him. A man in an Enforcer's uniform, floating downstream, moving only as the current moved him.

The body bumped into the bank and rolled over. The face was

bloated, bruised, and chewed away by who knows what. He was unrecognizable. His eyes were open, and vacant, but seemed to stare at me.

David gasped, his eyes wide, his mouth open. I snatched up Elsa, held her close to me, both of my arms around her like a shield.

"That's an Enforcer! A dead Enforcer!" David said, his voice gray and gravelly, hoarse with fear.

"David," I looked at him with pleading eyes, "why was an Enforcer here in the Human Free Zone? How close was he to us before he drowned? How did he drown? And are there others?"

David looked around wildly, as though teams of Enforcers could appear from anywhere at any time.

"There must be others. An Enforcer wouldn't be alone out here. We need to get away." I was begging him.

He nodded in agreement, his face grim.

The body rolled over again and floated away, disappearing around a bend in the river.

But the image would never disappear from my memory.

CHAPTER FIFTY-SEVEN

DAVID

Day 17

Paul was awake and outside, sitting in deep shade with George, when Emmeline and David got back to the cave. He was working on the spear for Micah, carefully cutting a slit in the tip of the repurposed peg.

"I'm rested," Paul said, as they approached. "Figured I'd get this spear finished today. George is going to clean the turtle. Bit of hard shell from the belly of the turtle will make a fine point on this. I'll stick the shell in, then soak the whole thing in water so the wood swells up and holds the tip tight and firm."

"Where's Micah?" Emmeline asked, looking around nervously. Her hands were shaking.

"Oh, he and Ingrid finished gathering greens and things for the soup." Paul pointed to a pile of plants near the cave entrance. "Now they're out looking for firewood."

She handed Elsa to David and went to the tree line, looking for Micah.

George was looking at Elsa with a gentle smile on his face. David knew Emmy was right. George was a good man.

"Would you like to hold her before Emmy puts her down for a

nap?" David asked him. He felt a burning desire to be kind to this man who had risked so much for his Emmy.

Gratefully George held his arms out and David handed Elsa to him. He held her gingerly, as if afraid she might break. Elsa studied his face.

Emmy came back from the tree line. "I didn't see Micah," she said.

Elsa squirmed in George's arms and reached out toward Emmy.

"Don't be offended. She's just tired and ready for her nap," Emmy said, taking Elsa into her arms. "I'll put her down now. You can hold her again later. And I hope Micah comes back soon." Her voice was trembling. Paul glanced at her; he must have heard her frightened tone, but he didn't say anything.

Emmy took Elsa into the cave and David heard her singing "I'm a little teapot . . ." There was no joy in her voice; the song trailed away. David waited until she came back out before he told them what they had seen.

George picked a fairly straight piece of wood from the pile. "Going to start on that turtle now. I need a big knife or an ax." The basin with the turtle in it had been pulled out from under the shrub.

Paul laid down the peg, went into the cave, and came back with an ax, which he handed to George. George poked the stick at the turtle's snout, bumping it repeatedly. David jumped back when he saw how quickly and firmly the turtle bit down on the wood, crunching it with its massive jaw.

George pulled on the stick and the turtle hung on, its neck stretched out, long and thick. George pulled some more and still the turtle held on, its neck stretching even farther.

"Give me a hand here," George said to David. "Grab this stick, pull as hard as you can."

David planted his feet firmly in the ground and pulled, lifting the front of the turtle up from the bottom of the basin. George raised his arm and with mighty swings, brought the dull ax down over and over again, slashing at the turtle's elongated neck, each blow cutting deeper through the tough muscle. Blood mixed with the water in the basin, pink tendrils spreading out, and still the turtle hung on.

One last arc of George's arm through the air, one last slice of the knife, and the neck was severed.

"Don't get near the head," George said. "It can still bite like hell. I remember that from my old farm pond." David let go of the stick and stepped back, the bloody, lifeless head, still locked onto the stick, at their feet. Death was an ugly thing. David didn't want to watch any more. Seeing that body floating in the river was enough death for a lifetime.

Emmy came back out and made a gagging sound when she saw what we had done.

"You look upset," Paul said to David. "And so does Emmeline. Something's wrong, isn't it?"

"What is it?" George asked.

"We need to talk." David walked away from the beheaded turtle and sat near Paul. Emmy sat next to him and leaned against him. George stopped working on the turtle and sat cross-legged on the ground in front of them.

Around them was silence, as if the birds and animals were waiting for David to speak.

He crossed his arms over his chest and tucked his hands into his armpits to hide their shakiness. But he couldn't hide the tremor in his voice.

David stared at the ground in front of the cave. A black beetle scrambled over the dirt. He looked at the other men, wet his lips with his tongue, and took a deep breath to release the tightness of his chest.

"We saw a body," David said.

Paul straightened up, leaned forward, attentive. "Where?"

"In the river."

David felt like his senses were shutting down, because he wanted to disassociate from what he had seen.

"This morning?" George asked.

"Yes, this morning."

"A man?" Paul asked.

"Yes, a man. But not just a man, an Enforcer. He had on an Enforcer's uniform."

George stood up and began to pace. He was barefoot and his toes spread apart as he walked. Dust puffed up between his toes.

"We'll gather everybody together and go deep into the cave." Paul said. "We can move some supplies with us, and put out the fire in the pit. The darkness will hide us."

"No," David said.

"What do you mean, no?" Paul asked. "We have to hide. We can't fight them."

"You're right. We can't fight them. And you would be wise to hide deep in the cave. But Emmy and I are going to take the children and go. We'll run until we find a new safe place, a land far from Authorities and Enforcers. We'll build our own new free world. That's what Emmy wants. And I want it for her."

"You can't do that," George said. "It's too risky and too dangerous for Elsa."

Emmy spoke up. "Staying here is too dangerous. If they find us, Elsa and Micah will be returned to the Children's Village. The rest of us will be recycled without a second thought. I can't let that happen. I love them too much. My mind is made up, George. We're leaving."

"But . . ."

"I know you are a good and kind man, George, and for that I am grateful." She put her hand on his arm. "I will always be grateful for that."

"You would leave Ingrid and me?" Paul asked, sounding old and frightened for the first time since David and Emmeline had known him.

"We would never abandon you. We can leave you in good hands, Paul. Kind hands." She looked at George.

George seemed to understand what she was saying.

"Are you asking me to . . . ?" His voice trailed off.

"I'm asking for Elsa's sake."

He looked into the woods, in the direction of the farm commune, then back at Emmeline.

She repeated, "For Elsa's sake. You wanted freedom for her even before she was born. This is a second chance for her to be free."

Paul looked at David, then at Emmy. "You're determined to do this?"

They both nodded.

George rinsed his hands in a basin of fresh water and dried them on his pant legs, leaving wet streaks. He went into the cave and David saw the vague shadow of him leaning protectively over the sleeping Elsa.

Out of respect, they all sat with downcast eyes, waiting for him. They knew he had been hopeful for more time with his daughter and he was treasuring these moments with her.

He returned to the group, walking slowly, shoulders slumped, the posture of a man making a difficult but necessary decision.

He faced Paul. "Emmeline's right. I did want freedom for her and my baby. And that's what I still want." He put his hand on the old man's shoulder. "You cut my ankle bracelet, Paul. You freed me. That is a debt I wish to repay. I will be honored to stay with you and Ingrid and help protect you, if you allow me."

Paul nodded his head, and sighed, a deep, sad sound from the depth of his chest. "Then we need to plan. Get out your map."

Emmy went into the cave and came back out with the map. Paul opened it carefully, spread it on the ground in front of him, and without touching it, followed the lines of the streams and rivers with his index finger.

George turned to David abruptly, "A map! We need to study it carefully. Look for the best route."

"Will you help us?" David asked. "Maybe you can explain some of the geography to us."

"Of course, I'll help. I'll do it for Elsa, and for Emmeline," George said, then added: "And for you and Micah."

They were all quiet for a moment, absorbing the enormity of what lay ahead.

George turned to Emmeline with a sadness in his face. "May I hold her again before you leave?"

She nodded. "Of course, when she wakes. For as long as you want before we have to go."

Emmy and George wiped away tears.

David turned away. He didn't want them to see him crying, too.

CHAPTER FIFTY-EIGHT

EMMELINE

Day 17

Ingrid bustled back from the woods with both hands full of twigs; Micah was close behind her with a jumble of wildflowers. He ran to me and thrust the flowers into my hand.

"For you, Mommy," he said, grinning.

I buried my nose in them and kissed him on his smooth forehead. He puffed up with pride, and smiled, his freckles hidden by his blush.

"I'm ready to cook. Some of those flowers can go right into the pot. Not all, mind you. Your mother can keep the prettiest ones," Ingrid moved about, putting a pan of water on the fire pit, moving the broom out of her way, and gathering up the uneven cubes of turtle. "I don't need any help cooking, Micah. Run off and play. This is my kitchen, my rules."

Micah studied the flowers carefully, gave some to me, and ran over to Ingrid with the rest. Then he joined us and squatted beside the map, curious. "What are you doing?" he asked.

"We're getting ready to start our journey again," David told him gently.

"All of us? Paul and Ingrid and George and all of us?" He grinned, ready for the adventure with his new friends. He must have forgotten his poor tired feet and worn-out shoes.

"Just us, buddy. George will stay here with Paul and Ingrid," David told him.

"We can't leave them! We need each other. Who is going to teach me more history? What about my spear?" Little frown lines creased the space between his eyebrows.

Paul smiled. "George will be here to help us. As for your spear, I think this piece of wood will work just fine without anything added. I've felt it and it's plenty sharp with that little bit of turtle shell in it." He handed it to Micah. "And maybe we can catch up with you later."

Micah looked relieved at Paul's vague promise. "We'll leave a trail for you to follow." He held the spear proudly, my little miniature soldier.

Paul shook his head. "Don't leave a trail."

"Why not?" Micah asked. "How will you find us?"

"People who love you will find you without a trail."

Micah studied his little spear carefully, and then looked up at Paul. "I want you to find us. I want you to teach me more history."

"And I want to teach you more," Paul answered him. "But in the meantime, remember just one thing: freedom. Freedom is more important than anything else. Always."

"Freedom," Micah said. "I'll remember."

"Found some wild garlic," Ingrid called out. "Just you wait till you taste this!"

I squeezed in with the men clustered around the map. Paul showed George the line that was our river and we bent over the map, our heads close together. Micah pushed in beside me, listening intently, with his little spear at his side.

"Looks like it dumps into this river not far from here."

"Down here, look, see how another river meets the first one."

I watched as they moved their fingers above the map, following the curves of the lines that represented our path.

"Comes together, forms a point."

"Bet there was a city there."

"There was a city. The words have faded on this old map but you can make out part of it. Pittsburgh."

"Great spot for a city. River transport and all that."

"It was a big city back then. Probably still has buildings standing."

"They can't have torn down all the buildings."

"Probably not."

"Who knows? We won't know till we get there."

"Might be some boats there. You know, since there are rivers, there's bound to have been boats, too."

"A boat would be wonderful. We'd cover more distance quickly," I said.

"But you'll be easily seen. Anyone along the river—if there is anyone—would see you immediately."

"We'd travel at night. Hide during the day. Same as before."

I heard the excitement in our voices, the back-and-forth of ideas, the possibilities of what might be discovered, recovered, and proven useful. But I also heard the cautionary notes and wariness.

Elsa was awake and fussing. I brought her out and squeezed back in with the others studying the map.

She patted my face and pulled at my hair and I smiled at her. She smiled back, her dimple deep and lovely. She looked the way I looked in that old photograph of Mother and me.

A ladybug crawled along the ground by my foot. I remembered a snatch of rhyme my mother would recite. *Ladybug, ladybug, fly away home. Your house is on fire and your children will burn.*

Ingrid was humming again. I could see her as she bent over the pot, stirring, tasting, stirring some more, adding a little salt, sprinkling the fine white grains onto the liquid with her fingertips.

"Would have to be a boat made of metal or fiberglass. Wood boats would be too rotten by now."

"There might be leftover shoes in the buildings," Micah said. So he hadn't forgotten his aching feet, after all. Shoes would be a wonderful discovery. A boat would be a miracle.

"The big river runs a little bit north but it does go west. Later it dips more south."

"West is what we want but it has to be southwest. Her goal is Kansas."

"Kansas may be impossible. It's too far. Besides, it gets very cold there in the winter."

"There might be other places. Does it have to be Kansas?"

"Maybe not Kansas. But a new world. A safe place."

"Eventually another river will branch off, heading south."

"We'll be safer on water than on land. Not only can we travel faster, but we'll be farther away from wildlife."

"What wildlife?"

"Don't know for sure. Different than here, for sure."

"Do you think there are others out there? Other people?"

"Don't know."

"I heard talk back at the mandatory meetings about the rights of indigenous people."

"What are they? What about them?"

"They are the first people to live in a place. That was supposed to make them have special rights. All part of the agenda. Don't know why."

"What's an agenda?" Micah's little-boy voice, little-boy questions.

The talk went on and on. Ingrid's humming continued.

The sun moved across the sky, predictable, and reliable. A constant force—part of a larger plan I couldn't comprehend but could respect.

Ingrid's soup simmered with plopping sounds, like bubbles bursting. Warm aromas drifted out of the cave toward us.

"When are you all starting off?" George asked.

"Tonight," I said. There was no question in my mind. Tonight might not even be soon enough, but it would have to do. "Tonight, after we eat. We'll walk at night."

I had to get busy, and pack up our bundles. I'd make sure we had everything and tie them securely.

The map was folded, handed back to me.

Paul handed me some packets of sugar, powdered milk, and salt. Ingrid gathered up some jerky and dehydrated apples.

"Can you spare all of this?" I asked them.

They simply nodded. I added everything to my bundle.

Then we ate. And it was good. It would be our last warm meal for some time.

It was time to leave. Somehow, before we walked away, I had to thank Paul and Ingrid.

I reached into a bundle and pulled out the recipe cards.

"A gift for you, Ingrid." I handed them to her.

"Lord, child, thank you." She held the cards tightly, as if afraid I would change my mind. "And I have something for you." She handed me a bed linen she had tied into clumsy knots so it resembled a bag of sorts.

"What is it?" I asked her.

"A sling for Elsa. Let me show you how it works." She slipped it onto me, securely over my shoulders and it rested on my back. "There. This should help." She smiled, proud of her handiwork.

"How clever of you. Thank you so much." I gave her a quick hug.

Then I offered the gold coin to Paul. "For you," I said.

"No, Emmeline. I don't want or need gold. It is enough for me that we could help you. You and your children are more precious than gold. You might need that coin in the future, in an emergency."

I searched through my bundle for something else to give to this gentle, wise man. *The New Testament* with its red cover, gilded title, and onion-thin pages. I looked at what my mother had written inside with her fine curlicue writing. *For my beloved daughter, Emmeline. May she read and understand.*

The first Paul time saw it, he made sure his hands were clean, then held it in a worshipful manner. Surely, this would be the perfect gift for him. I held it out to him, but again he shook his head no.

"No, Emmeline. I know that book quite well. Take it with you. Study it. Teach it to Micah and Elsa. It's an important history book."

"What can I give you? How can I repay you?"

"You repaid me by knowing the value of freedom. That gives me hope for the future of our world. And you should take this little bit of honey with you. Use it wisely."

The jar of honey that he handed me went into my bundle.

"May I hold her one more time?" George asked softly.

I handed Elsa to George and she went without a whimper. He held her in his arms, and kissed her soft cheek. She touched his face with her hand.

He held her for several minutes. We watched silently, not wanting to disturb the beautiful sadness of their special time.

Finally, George handed her back to David, shook David's hand, and hugged me briefly.

"For you, George." I handed him the photograph of Mother and me. "Elsa looks like I did as a child. Take this and remember me. Look at it and see Elsa." It was the least I could do, and yet sadly, the most I could do. The photograph would be his memory keeper.

Then he walked into the cave, carrying the picture. Saying good-bye would be too final for him, one more good-bye in a long list of too many.

There was nothing more to be said. I hugged Ingrid and Paul, feeling their frail, thin bodies in my arms, feeling their tear-streaked faces against my own.

We were all crying.

It felt like the whole world should be crying for so many reasons.

CHAPTER FIFTY-NINE

EMMELINE

Days 17–18

It was bittersweet, walking away from Paul and Ingrid. They had sheltered us, fed us, and helped me tend to David's arm until it was healed. Paul taught us just enough about history that I knew the value of the words *never again, never again*. I regretted that we didn't have time for more lessons. I would miss dear, sweet Ingrid, who took childlike pleasure in rituals and simple things, like sweeping out the cave, finding wild garlic, and cooking with whatever she could find. How hard it was to say good-bye to them. I was grateful that George would be with them, grateful that he was alive and sad that he had endured the farm commune, the ball and chain, all because he had tried to help me and his unborn daughter find freedom.

Leaving friends behind was bitter and, at the same time, escaping from the dark world of the Authorities and fences was so sweet. We expected the journey would be difficult, dangerous, but the reward would be glorious. I wouldn't look back, and I would never go back.

The first night of walking was difficult. We were tired and unaccustomed to the strain. Our bundles were heavy and although the sling helped, I still needed to carry Elsa. David and I switched our burdens back and forth. Micah carried the smallest roll and his little spear but often had to drop them and rest his arms. Elsa napped off and on in her sling but woke frequently to squirm and fuss. Owls' screeches and Elsa's cries made for a strange mixture in the wild dark. When she cried, I offered my finger for her to suck and held her in my arms, but she squirmed and pushed my hand away. She wanted to lie down, not be carried.

"Are we there yet?" Micah whispered.

"Not yet, buddy."

The river bubbled beside us and fish splashed through the water. The stars shone bright tonight, sparkling white dots, with no clouds to cover them. The sky seemed so big, and I felt so small under it.

We walked on.

Paul had added a layer of rabbit skins to our shoes on top of the rubber linings. The soft fur was turned up against the soles of our feet. I wondered how long they would last. Maybe we would find Micah's imaginary building full of shoes.

My calves began to burn. Micah moved slower and slower, until finally he was dragging his roll behind him.

"Are we there yet?"

"Maybe we should stop for the night," David whispered. "We've been up since early morning. And we all need rest."

The river curved around to the right, then ahead rose the shabby skeleton of another bridge. This one was wooden with slats missing, while others dangled down like fingers pointing at the water. At each end of the of the bridge, stood hard, gray beams, upright and stiff like Gatekeepers monitoring the river's flow.

Not us. Never again.

Farther on, David discovered a flat, mossy space, and with barely a word, we settled in there, under the stars, for the remainder of the night.

Dawn woke us as dawn wakes all living things. Pale light seeped silvery gray along the horizon, then spread upward and outward, until the sky was golden and the stars faded. Birds celebrated the light and flew in circles and swirls. From our mossy beds, we looked up and watched their dark shapes dance against what quickly became a pale blue sky.

It was crickets and moss for breakfast. Elsa, on hands and knees, busied herself looking for bugs, popping them into her mouth, and holding the occasional one out to me.

"Can we move forward during the day?" I asked David. "Can we stay hidden but keep the river in sight?"

"I think so. We'll make much better time in daylight."

We spent the day slogging on. Micah whispered a near-constant barrage of questions at David.

"What's this?" He'd point one way. "What's that?" as he pointed elsewhere.

Each time David answered patiently.

"A dragonfly."

"A snail."

"An old piece of barbed wire from long ago."

"Fungus on a tree. Don't eat it."

Elsa wanted to baby-walk between David and me on her tiptoes, holding our hands. That really slowed us down. Finally, David plunked her atop his shoulders and she happily held on, her small pink fingers twined through his dark hair.

For what must have been the thousandth time, I looked over my shoulder and scanned the land around us. We passed through a stand of younger trees in what had been a clearing many years before, now reclaimed by the forest. We noticed patches of a solid gray surface. Then I saw, farther ahead, barely visible above the tree line, a tall silver pole with a drooping tattered flag. On the flag was a faded image of a large dark animal.

"Look," I said. "What in the world is that?"

"I have no idea. Let's check it out."

We walked toward it and found ourselves in an open space, inter-rupted with small trees that had pushed their way up through that hard gray surface. Most of the space was surrounded by a metal fence that seemed to go on forever. Parts of the fence were missing, leaving large gaps.

Everywhere I looked, there were more fences inside the first, larger one. They were cages and they went on as far as I could see.

"A zoo!" David said. "Imagine that, out here in the wilderness." He walked through a gap in the large fence and I followed him. "Before the relocations people used to go to zoos, so their kids could see all the animals, and learn about them. My mom and dad took me to a zoo like this lots of times when I was little."

"Animals?" Micah asked.

"Yes, animals from all over the world."

"Where are they now?" Micah asked, hopping on one foot and his voice filled with childlike excitement.

"You know the pledge: *I pledge allegiance to the Earth and to the animals of the Earth.* They must have released them all after the reloca-tions. They're long gone and scattered all over the place by now," David said.

I was dumbfounded by what he said. First, they relocated people and put them behind fences, and then they gave animals their free-dom. It was such an evil irony.

"Shouldn't we keep moving?" I asked. "There's nothing here but empty cages. I don't want to be near cages. And we're out in the open where we can be seen."

"Let's look around quickly. Maybe we can find something we can use. Tools, maybe, or dehydrated food, or more salt. Stuff that doesn't spoil. There had to have been a concession stand somewhere." His eyes crinkled at their corners, his dark hair dipped over his forehead, and I reached out instinctively to smooth it back.

"Let's make it quick."

"Right. We'll make it quick."

We raced by one cage after another with faded labels: lion, giraffe, elephant, monkey. Inside the cages were different kinds of rock formations. They were littered with broken tree branches, bleached bones, and overturned feed bowls. We passed a building named Reptile House and another named Aquarium.

I saw a jumble of massive bleached white bones under a tree and pointed them out to David. "What are those?" I asked.

"I'm not sure. It almost looks like a human hand but it isn't. It's way too big. These must be the bones of a bear paw." The bones were long and sharp and reminded me of the claws of that black bear that slashed at a tree.

"If they were released, why are there some bones scattered around?"

"Maybe they were old animals and they died. Or maybe another animal attacked and killed them."

"Would the animals survive outside their cages?"

"Some would, if they were from a similar climate as ours."

"And if they weren't?"

David just shrugged. He didn't have an answer.

I thought: *So they released animals just for the symbolic act of releasing them, regardless of the consequences?*

Micah was running ahead of us, peering into each cage, hoping to see an exotic beast.

"Micah, stay close," I said.

He reluctantly returned to my side.

"There." David pointed to an arrow-shaped sign. "Look, it says picnic area."

We ran to it.

The picnic area had some small, dilapidated round tables and some rotted benches. An abandoned bird's nest rested on one of them. Two small white feathers were stuck to the twigs at the bottom.

There were swing sets and faded plastic animals on coiled springs. Micah climbed on one of the horses that had its front legs extended as if it was racing for its life and its tail flared out behind as though blowing in the wind. Micah made the pretend horse rock back and forth.

"This is the best horse," Micah said. "The very best horse in the whole world." He leaned forward and patted its neck. "His name is Micah's Horse."

"Get off the horse, Micah. We can't waste time." David lifted Micah off the horse. "Come on. Let's look for food."

There were some buildings, but most of them were falling apart; bits and pieces of wood were lying helter-skelter. The ones that still stood had the ghosts of words on them. *Lemonade. Cotton Candy. Hot Dogs.*

What, exactly, was a Hot Dog? What were *any* of those things?

We foraged, quickly moving from building to building. Most were empty and dark, with shelves that were broken and strewn on the ground. There were signs that animals had been in the buildings and I could hear the scurrying of smaller creatures in the walls.

David found some unopened bags of things he called pretzels, a box full of little packets of sugar, and another box with several shiny packets of lemonade powder.

He led us to another part of the picnic area, a shelter with a roof but no walls. In it were long tables and benches, uneven on the crumbled, hard surface.

"We'll have a picnic and then get out of here." He spread all his goodies on a table, then, with a sweep of his hand, brushed some dirt off the rusted metal bench for us to sit. The packets of lemonade powder were hard dried lumps. David banged some of them on the decrepit wooden table to break up the clumps, dropped some in our bottles of water, and added a pinch of sugar to make it sweeter. I shoved the rest of the packets into our bundle. When he opened the bag of pretzels, they didn't look like the pictures on the bags. Instead, they were crumbled bits of dry powdery green. He tossed them aside.

"What's a picnic?" Micah asked.

"Eating food outside. That's a picnic," David answered.

"Then we always have picnics. We always eat outside since we ran from the Compound," Micah said, his face flushed with excitement.

"Well, this will be a very, very quick picnic with the lemonade," David said. "Pretend just for a minute there are lots of families here today, having fun. And we're part of that. We're a family that's having fun. We're a family that's growing." He gave me a shy smile.

I tried to picture this place filled with families, before the relocations, but I couldn't. I had never seen any place filled with happy people who were free to be together.

We sat in the deserted picnic area, drinking lemonade, a family out for pretend fun in an abandoned zoo.

It was supposed to be fun pretending, but it wasn't. I couldn't help but continue to look around for danger. I knew they were out there somewhere, searching for us.

CHAPTER SIXTY

EMMELINE

Day 18

We were done with the lemonade in a couple of minutes. As I was retying our bundles, I noticed a raised wooden platform at one end of the picnic area. "What was that for?" I asked David. It reminded me of the platforms the Authorities used to stand on during the social update meetings in the Compound. Surely, there must have been Authorities here. Why else would there be a stage like this?

"It's an entertainment stage," David said, walking over and jumping up on the stage. "I can see almost everything from here."

"Wish we could have entertainment today," Micah said.

"Not today, buddy. It's time to head out."

"Is there a latrine around here?" I asked.

"Over there. It's still standing." He pointed to a square building made of concrete blocks.

"I'll be right back. And then we're out of here." I shoved our bundles under a table, and headed for the latrine.

Beside the doors to the latrine were two little statues, so short they only came to my hips. There was a boy statue by one door and a girl by the other. Their painted, red-striped clothes were faded; their facial features paled, eerie and ghostlike. Something had chewed off the little girl's hand. The end of her arm was a ragged, hollow stump.

I pushed hard on the door, and when it swung open, it hit the wall with a dull, hollow thud. Inside the dark space, I brushed cobwebs from my face, and the filmy strands clung to my arms and hands. The floor was covered with slippery green mold. An old papery wasp nest hung high by a narrow window. Under it, on the floor, was piled a sinister black mound of dead wasps. I finished as quickly as I could. The rust-red hinges on the door creaked loudly when I opened it. I cringed. Anybody nearby would certainly have heard it.

The sun was blinding and a relief after that dark place.

But I wasn't prepared for what I saw.

Micah and Elsa were huddled together on a bench. David, his face as pale as a moth's wing, stood frozen on the stage.

A tall man in a mottled uniform stood near them, holding a gun at his side. An Earth Protector?

"No false moves," the man with the gun said, looking directly at me. His voice was harsh as ice, his face cold as ice. Another smaller man in the same kind of uniform stood beside him; I realized David couldn't see the first man's gun.

I reached for the head of the girl statue to steady myself and she fell forward, her blank, featureless face striking my foot. The stump of her arm pointed up at me. The inside of her arm was black and hollow. Ants scurried over each other where she had stood. Some began to crawl over my foot. I saw each one clearly. I saw the wood grain of the open door beside me, the swirls and cracks in it. I saw everything, every detail, and every color: Micah's freckles, Elsa's round checks, and David's dark hair against his forehead, and round, wet beads of sweat above his eyebrows.

I saw the silvery glint of the gun in the sunlight.

"Walk toward that bench, slowly, then sit." He pointed to a bench away from my family.

I did as he said. I felt each footstep, each bending of my knees. I sat on the bench, and the wood was rough on my legs.

Elsa was crying. The children were still near the stage.

"Micah, hold Elsa," I said. I felt my lips move in my stiff face, heard my voice as though from a distance. He scrambled closer to her, pulled her onto his lap. Elsa's crying didn't stop. It sliced through me like a knife.

"Guy, grab the kids," the tall man said.

"Yes, sir." Guy walked toward my children. Micah, carrying Elsa, ran to me, away from him.

Elsa was still crying. *Don't cry, baby. Mommy's here.* I held her tightly on my lap.

Micah wrapped his arms around my neck. I could feel his warm breath on my ear. *You're my little prince.*

"Hurry up, Guy."

Guy ran toward me. I held Elsa tightly, as tightly as any mother ever held a child, but he wrenched her from my arms and sat her on his hip, her blond hair visible above his shoulder. Her arm was hitting the back of his neck, and her pink foot was hanging down and kicking. Guy grabbed Micah's hand and pulled him away from me.

Micah shouted: *No, no, no!*

Or was that me shouting?

Elsa screamed.

Or was that me screaming?

Micah was wailing, and his face contorted with fear. He used his little spear to hit the man's leg. The bit of pointed turtle shell fell off the end. He threw it down and it bounced on the ground.

The tall man shouted at me. "You'll regret defying the Authorities," he said.

"You can't take my children."

"Your children? What makes you think they're *your* children?"

"They are my children! Don't take them. Please, I'm begging."

"The children belong to the Authorities. Not to you."

"Those are my children!" I shouted. "They're mine!"

A cloud passed over the sun and made a shadow that slithered across the ground.

Before I could warn him about the gun, David jumped off the stage. Dust puffed up where he landed. The particles floated up, then drifted down in lazy spirals to the ground. He ran toward me, his hands reaching out for me. His lips were moving, but I couldn't hear what he was saying. *I love you, David.*

The man with the gun narrowed his eyes and pinched his lips together. He raised the weapon.

David had reached me when a shot rang out with an explosion of sound that silenced the birds.

The tall Protector grabbed at his own arm. I saw blood on his shirt by his right shoulder. It spread out and seeped down over his chest. He raised his arm, whirled around, and pointed his gun at someone I couldn't see. Someone who was beyond the first set of cages. He fired again and again.

From that direction, another shot rang out. And another. Who was shooting?

"Steven, I'm scared," Guy said as he cowered and sank to his knees. Micah bravely snatched Elsa from his arms and, holding her protectively, ran to David and me.

Guy ran toward the picnic table. A stray bullet struck him and he fell, sprawled out and motionless.

"Be careful where you're shooting—the children may be there!" a woman shouted. Her voice was familiar.

Above the trees, the tattered flag with the faded image of a large black animal fluttered gently in the breeze. Black birds flew overhead, little dots against the perfect blue sky.

My heartbeat felt like those bird wings in my chest.

The taste of lemonade rose up from my throat into my mouth. Bitter.

The Protector named Steven tried to shoot again, but the hammer of his gun clicked without results. It was out of ammunition. He fumbled with his left hand through the pack at his feet.

"Rush him!" An unfamiliar man's voice shouted.

I heard the sound of people running.

"Micah, take Elsa into the latrine," David said. "You'll be safe in there. Don't come out until I tell you. And don't listen to anyone's voice but mine." Micah quickly understood, and carried his little sister into the latrine. The door screeched behind him when he closed it.

The sound of running was louder, and closer. Steven, fumbling with his left hand, was trying but failing to put more ammunition into his gun. "Guy, get out here. Help me! That's an order!" he shouted. But Guy didn't answer.

Two women and a man burst into sight. Two of them were in Earth Protectors' uniforms. My heart sank. We wouldn't have a chance against them.

David stared at the one woman in a dirt-smeared white uniform. I stared, too.

Joan!

Steven dropped his ammunition on the ground and pulled an ax out of his pack. With his left hand, he held it above his head.

Standing some distance from Steven, the woman in a torn Protectors' uniform reached into one of the packs they were carrying and pulled out a spray bottle. "You said I could spray animals, *sir*, and so I am, *sir*." I could smell the liquid in the air, and saw the drops on his face.

Steven screamed, dropped the ax, and covered his face with his hands.

Joan looked at Steven with disdain. "You said John was gone, just like that—poof." She snapped her fingers. "Now it's your turn." She nodded at the man next to her. "Winston, do what needs to be done." The man pointed a gun at Steven.

"Wait!" David shouted. "Don't shoot him! Killing him is too good, too easy, too fast. He needs to suffer first." The very words we heard guards say the first day as we hid under a pine tree. The very words that terrified us. And now, full circle, I felt poetic justice.

"Winston, help me put him in one of these cages," David said. Winston put away his gun, and together, he and David forcefully dragged Steven, still covering his face with his hands, to a cage. They shoved him in, and he fell forward on his hands and knees. They slammed the gate and the rusty lock was firmly and securely closed.

David ran to Joan and swept her into his arms. Tears streamed down her face. Winston and the woman in a Protectors' uniform came and sat beside me.

"I'm Julia," she said. "And this is Winston."

"But your uniforms," I asked. "Are you Earth Protectors?"

"No," Winston said. "Don't let the uniforms frighten you. We're here to protect you and your family. That is now our true mission."

David brought Elsa and Micah from the latrine, and they clung to me while staring at the strangers.

They wouldn't be strangers for long. I knew immediately that they would be part of our family—and part of our journey to a new life. To a safe place.

Out of the shadows, and into the light.

You save what you think you are going to lose. You never give up.

I would never give up.

AFTERWORD

"The developmental and environmental objectives of Agenda 21 will require a substantial flow of new and additional financial resources to developing countries in order to cover the incremental costs for the actions they have to undertake to deal with global environmental problems and to accelerate sustainable development."

—Preamble to Agenda 21

UN Conference on Environment & Development Conference, 1992

A few years ago I read a manuscript that a woman named Harriet Parke had submitted to my publishing imprint, Mercury Ink. She had titled it *Agenda 21*, and it told the story of a dystopian future in which citizens' bleak existence inside Compounds was highlighted by their primary responsibility to produce energy for "the Republic." The story resonated with me because it brought a real-life issue, an obscure UN program called "Agenda 21," to life in a compelling and entertaining way.

In deciding to partner with Harriet on the book, and then eventually publish it with Simon & Schuster, I hoped that people would read the novel, do their own homework, and then pass it along. Fortunately, hundreds of thousands of people did just that. Now, two years after the first novel was released, much has changed. A grassroots campaign, which was already under way well before the novel was published, became even more energized. This campaign was influential in educating both politicians and voters on the issue and, in many cases, outright stopping the progress of Agenda 21–related laws and regulations at the local level.

Slowly but surely, minds began to change about these seemingly innocuous "sustainability" schemes. People who had no idea that a UN program could impact their own city laws and regulations realized that everything from "land use" plans to "smart growth" programs to energy efficiency efforts like smart-meter requirements all fit under this massive Agenda 21 umbrella.

Because of these grassroots efforts, many cities and states have formally expressed their opposition to Agenda 21, either by passing laws banning the implementation of its related initiatives, or by dropping out of the International Council of Local Environmental Initiatives (ICLEI), which is the primary group that facilitates the local implementation of Agenda 21.

There is still plenty more to be done, but even educating people on the basics has proven to be successful. The Southern Poverty Law Center, which is about as politically far-left a group as you'll find, has admitted that anti–Agenda 21 activists are making serious inroads into blocking projects. In their report "Agenda of Fear," they wrote, "Supporters of smart-growth and anti-sprawl initiatives should study the Battle of Baldwin County. It was a rout—for the other side." That's great news for those of us who are on that "other side": our efforts are working!

If you are reading this sequel before you have read the first book, you're likely curious about the real Agenda 21 and how much of the story you just read is based on fact. The following offers a brief outline, but a more thorough overview, complete with a resource guide, is included in the afterword to the original novel, which I highly encourage you to read. (Some of the below is excerpted from that afterword.)

As I did in the previous novel, let me first reiterate a few things for the benefit of people who believe that publishing a novel somehow means that I believe that everything in it must be true. This is obviously a work of fiction. The point of a story like this is not to scare people or to somehow get my "real" beliefs out there by calling it fiction, but to get people to start thinking critically about the real issues we are dealing with—both at a national level, and, perhaps more important, at a local one. I think this series of novels does a great job with that because it forces readers to imagine a world where all the nice-sounding things that we think we want come to fruition. It's great to say, for example, that mankind is responsible for a warming climate, or that we are using too much water—but what happens when we try to use government to "fix" those things? *Agenda 21* takes that line of thought to its extreme end, and, in doing so, forces all of us to think about what grand pronouncements regarding the reduction of mankind's environmental footprint really mean.

WHAT IS AGENDA 21?

Agenda 21 is a United Nations program designed to foster "sustainable development," which is the idea that we must decrease humanity's imprint on the environment. Agenda 21's history is tied to the UN and Canadian billionaire Maurice Strong through various Earth-related conferences, originating at the 1972 Stockholm Earth Summit.

In the first book we boiled all of Agenda's 21 various documents and proclamations down to a list of nine basic goals:

1. Move citizens off private land and into high-density urban housing.
2. Create vast wilderness spaces inhabited by large carnivores.

3. Reduce traffic congestion and slash fuel use by eliminating cars and creating "walkable" cities.

4. Support chosen private businesses with public funds to be used for "sustainable development."

5. Make policy decisions that favor the greater good over individuals.

6. Drastically reduce the use of power, water, and anything that creates "carbon pollution."

7. Use bureaucracies to make sweeping decisions outside of democratic processes.

8. Increase taxes, fees, and regulations.

9. Implement policies meant to incentivize a reduced population (i.e., "one-child" type laws).

The 1972 UN Earth Summit resulted in something called the "Stockholm Declaration," which was essentially an action plan consisting of twenty-six principles and seven proclamations, the last of which read:

> [*Achieving our environmental goals*] *will demand the acceptance of responsibility by citizens and communities and by enterprises and institutions at every level, all sharing equitably in common efforts.*

More than forty years later, this has morphed into the UN's official definition of Agenda 21, which is included right on the cover of their program:

> *Agenda 21 is a comprehensive plan of action to be taken globally, nationally and locally by organizations of the United Nations System, Governments, and Major Groups in every area in which human impacts on the environment.*

Both definitions agree that Agenda 21 will need cooperation at every level of government. The UN also makes it clear that that we must address every area where humans have an impact on the environment. The problem, of course, is that that encompasses almost everything we do in life. Try to think of something you do on a daily basis that does not "impact" the environment in some way. It's almost impossible. The simple act of turning on a light switch, taking a shower, or driving to get a coffee has an impact, let alone flying in an airplane or using your air conditioner.

These definitions of Agenda 21 are ridiculously (and intentionally) vague because the overall point of all of this is for us to eventually cede control over nearly every facet of our lives for the sake of the environment.

IMPLEMENTATION

Implementation of Agenda 21 happens via such global "independent" agencies like ICLEI, the International Council for Local Environmental Initiatives. The U.S. version of this (ICLEI USA) uses various means to implement their programs. According to their website (see: icleiusa .org) more than six hundred American land-use bodies have joined and are given training, tools, and programs. Here is how they describe themselves:

> *ICLEI USA was launched in 1995 and has grown from a handful of local governments participating in a pilot project to a solid network of more than 600 cities, towns and counties actively striving to achieve tangible reductions in greenhouse gas emissions and create more sustainable communities. ICLEI USA is the domestic leader on climate protection and adaptation, and sustainable development at the local government level.*

Facing criticism, ICLEI has deleted its publicly available list of member cities. (You can find a cached version of the list from July 2013 here: http://bit.ly/1w5klWr.)

In December 2012, Indiana State Representative Tim Neese introduced a bill to block implementation of UN "Agenda 21" policies. The Bill (HB 1021) stated:

> *An Indiana governmental entity may not adopt or implement: (1) certain policy recommendations relating to the United Nations' 1992 'Agenda 21' conference on the environment and development that deliberately or inadvertently infringe on or restricts private property rights without due process . . . (See: http://bit.ly /1w5l4qO)*

Alabama has also been a leader in this area. On May 6, 2012, the legislature passed Senate Bill 477, titled "Due Process for Property Rights Act." The law was approved unanimously by the House and Senate and later signed by the governor (See: http://bit.ly/1w5lgGr).

In Missouri, State Rep Lyle Rowland submitted a bill to block Agenda 21 in December 2012, remarking, "What I've heard is, they think it's a hidden agenda that being adhered to by some areas. . . . What we're saying is, in this particular bill, that we don't want any of [Agenda 21] coming in to the state of Missouri."

In January 2013, Washington State legislators introduced House Bill 1165, which reads:

> *Since the UN has accredited and enlisted numerous nongovernmental and intergovernmental organizations to assist in the implementation of its policies relative to Agenda 21 around the world, the state of Washington and all political subdivisions may not enter into any agreement, expend any sum of money, or receive funds contracting services or giving financial aid to or from*

the nongovernmental and intergovernmental organizations de-
fined in Agenda 21. (See: http://1.usa.gov/1w5lnBM)

Similar bills have been submitted in Virginia, Maine, Oklahoma, and
Kentucky, where Sen. John Schikel, the bill's sponsor, said, "The people
of Kentucky don't want international groups dictating to us what
environmental policy should be."

Cities and counties are also attempting to stop Agenda 21 by reasoning that parts of it violate local laws. One example is from Oklahoma, where, citing property rights and due process, the Mustang
City Council voted down building codes originating in UN Agenda 21
standards (See: http://bit.ly/1w5lBJg). The residents seemed unusually
well-informed on the subject, undoubtedly the result of activists working to educate people prior to the hearing. The Fairbanks, Alaska, and
Menifee, California, city councils also approved anti–Agenda 21 reso-
lutions in 2013 (See: http://bit.ly/1w5lH3q).

In Cobb County, Georgia, a local board decided it would not accept
Agenda 21–related strings that were attached to federal grants. Among
other things, these grants demanded that the county operate bilingual
services for non–English speakers, create community gardens, and
ensure pedestrian and bicycle access in and around bus stops. Resident
Bill Hudson remarked, "There's nothing that's on the excellence list
that is not Agenda 21 in spades.... The counties, the cities, the state
government, the school boards, they're all just hooked on grant money
like crack cocaine."

In February 2014, the St. Lucie, Florida, Board of County Com-
missioners rejected the Seven50 plan (See: http://bit.ly/1w5lOMD),
an Agenda 21 clone that would've served as a kind of master plan for
seven different Florida counties. According to an article about the
plan's defeat, the mayor had attended a briefing by Seven50 supporters in which they claimed that only "mega regions" were important,
that the Florida counties that would fall under the partnership would

"have someone to control them," and that "Fascism is the best form of government to implement these changes." (See: http://bit.ly/1w5mbXz)

CONCLUSION

What can we learn from Agenda 21 resistance activities over the last few years? A few important lessons stand out. First, most of those touting "sustainability" and "smart growth" plans have no idea as to the source of those concepts. Educating local politicians is not about "indoctrinating" them to a specific ideology, it's about ensuring that they truly understand the origins and long-term goals of the things they are supporting.

The second lesson is that, regardless of education, intelligence, or how well the arguments are presented, those who are willing to stand up will be treated as part of the "tin foil hat" club. The very nature of propaganda campaigns is to demonize foes as ignorant fools—and this one is no different.

Next, it's clear that resistance is not futile. In fact, it's just the opposite—real progress has been made by ordinary people who are willing to educate themselves and their neighbors. The nice part about a plan that requires implementation locally to succeed is that it can also be fought locally. This is not about calling your senator or signing a White House petition, it's about attending committee meetings at your town hall, or having coffee with your mayor.

Finally, remember that, in the minds of the UN and other Agenda 21 supporters, this is a battle for nothing less than control over the future of humanity. They will not give up on that easily—and neither should we.

ACKNOWLEDGMENTS

Harriet

Grateful appreciation goes to:

My family, the most loyal cheerleaders in the world;

Carlow University's supportive fiction writing division of Madwomen in the Attic, mentored by the amazing Evelyn Pierce;

Editors Emily Bestler, Megan Reid, Kevin Balfe, Kate Albers, Hannah Beck, and copyeditor Anne Cherry;

Faithful old friends—you know who you are; and those people who reached out to me after reading *Agenda 21* and became my new friends—you know who *you* are. I am blessed by all of you;

And last, but not least, Glenn Beck, for his inspiration and support.